THE HUNTER
OF PIGEONS

THE HUNTER
OF PIGEONS

Deborshi Barat

PARTRIDGE
A Penguin Random House Company

To order additional copies of this book, contact
Partridge India
000 800 10062 62
orders.india@partridgepublishing.com

www.partridgepublishing.com/india

Contents

To my grandfathers
For all the love and anger
And other important things

"Once upon a midnight dreary, while
I pondered weak and weary,
Over many a quaint and curious volume of forgotten lore,
While I nodded, nearly napping,
suddenly there came a tapping,
As of some one gently rapping, rapping at my chamber door.
'Tis some visitor,' I muttered, 'tapping
at my chamber door –
Only this, and nothing more."

- *The Raven*, Edgar Allen Poe

PART 1

CHHOTOLOK, SMALL PEOPLE

1

Once upon a Redbrick

$\mathcal{S}$hibshankar's spinster aunt, Shelley, kept her comic books hidden in her panties.

The books were shoved under bales of cloth next to the generator. The cloth was smeared with paraffin wax. Some of it fell on the floor, dripping like hot candles. Not much of it was left, the wax having moved somewhere else, but the granny panties were still there.

I knew this because one day at daybreak, I slipped on the stairwell above the generator room.

The railing was a good ride down. It was quick and easy, and once the friction on my arse died away, it was fun. But that day my balance swerved a little. Suddenly I wasn't sliding on the handrail anymore. I toppled off the banister and lost my bearing.

My legs were firmly wedged between two sister bars, leaving me loose enough to wave and look inside the porch, but nothing more. I could see the store-room below, upside down through the spindles of the railing.

Trapped like an insect, I struggled to rescue my left foot. Suddenly I caught a glimpse of the generator. Back then, it was just a machine.

Shibu said it possessed dark, mysterious powers, but he would say anything.

The door creaked. I heard a hiss of slow, seething steam somewhere near the back of my head. It was a sound from the hinges next to the store-room. The door yielded limply at first, but things changed. Someone pushed it hard until the panel swung open.

The wood swung on its flaccid pivot with a twist. All this happened very quickly. The room opened out wide like a dirty woman.

There was no one inside.

Of course there wouldn't be. I wasn't expecting to see anyone. Ghosts and darkness, maybe, sneaking out of the house, the way they do at the end of a rough night. And suddenly it was dawn once more.

Something was wrong. My legs went pop in the air with things between them. Something told me I was being checked out.

From the dingy bowels of the generator room, someone reached for my leg-piece. A few books slipped out of a fold and landed on the floor. I saw them fall but I heard nothing. I saw the fallen covers of heroes and jokers on the ground. The pictures on the comic books pulled faces at me. One of them uncovered itself and ran through its pages.

Meanwhile, I stayed trapped in the banister. I was hostage to a bunch of cartoons. Someone wanted to scream for help. It may have been my voice. A long river of adrenaline dried up and wet its bed in my pants.

Besides, I looked funny. A grown boy hanging from a staircase. His willy stuck between his legs. Butt crack flashing a mile. No thanks.

Eyeing the final step, I grabbed the column of the post. I got a firm grip when I stretched out, more than I should have. Using my torso, I heaved and kicked in fury. My grunts got weaker with every pull. Soon they turned to squeals. What were left of them ricocheted off the silence.

I bit the handrail but it didn't taste right. It was bland and too hard. I put some salt on it. Beads of perspiration trickled down my pout. A smell of food drew very close until it was all over me. My foot went limp, my knuckles buckled, and suddenly, miraculously, I wriggled free.

The smell went with me.

I hobbled down the frontier stairs and ran out of the house. Gasping for air, I turned towards the building, but not before I was safely leaning on a bench. The bench was made of stone.

I was a free man once again. It was good to be free.

I saw Shibshankar on the roof, smugly scraping his teeth. He had mashed a tiny cylinder of beech, squeezing out its antiseptic juice. Then he poured it out like oil on a thin filament of *neem*. The bark disappeared into his clenched teeth and from his wincing I knew it was bitter.

Relaxing his frown, Shibshankar thrust his mandible out. He looked like an ape when he did that, letting the pink of his tongue rove under his lips. He kept his mouth shut. Very slowly, he collected fragments of plaque from his teeth. At last he spat out the herbs, and then he saw me downstairs standing under a great shadow. Someone stood next to my shoulder on the pavement. Shibshankar hurled his toothbrush in the air.

Smiling broadly, he waved as the sun came up behind him. The sunlight bounced off his shoulders in a volley of ping-pong balls.

I remember all this very clearly. It was the day Shibshankar died.

*

2

The Hunter of Pigeons

I grew up behind a top floor window of a faded, three-storeyed behemoth. It was a big ugly building made from a pile of red bricks stacked up together.

The building overlooked a small triangular park that waved tram lines goodbye. Behind the behemoth stood a vast expanse of blue-grey sky and a vast expanse of nothing else. It was one of the many houses that stood on the street, and it looked like any other. But, it wasn't.

The house is now dead. Someone killed it for money. I wasn't around when it happened, but a part of me died with it. So I thought I'd tell you a story from the time that I served there – lest I forget or get dead too.

It was a dirty redbrick building, crumbling and ashen at its edges. A nest of unseen capillaries propped it from up above. The house was big, old and ugly.

Yet, it was there. And we lived in it because it was there.

The lobby was a dimly lit yawn across its face. Smelling powerfully of pungent leather, it bore the memory of a dead animal that once sat on a couch, relishing its hide in a quiet corner. But the lobby had a giant mirror which hid the animal well, housed at the centre where we couldn't miss it.

The mirror was ugly too, but it was shiny. Trapped in a glistening veneer of Bombay blackwood, it reeked of stale drops of turpentine when I tucked my shirt in; and then, its robust float glass whisked me along the vapours of mercury on the wall, from the ugly ballast of fluorescent lamps to the rickety steps winding upwards. They made merry on the staircase for a while, leaving me out of it, until the feeble mercury faded into the mezzanine.

Under the staircase lived a generator room, cluttered with equipment and darkness. Sometimes the door came ajar on its own. When it did, there was an eerie silence inside the room, tense and palpable, and I could've sworn that I felt a sombre breathing each time I slid down the banister.

*

Behind the generator room, there was a separate vestibule sharing one of its walls with the staircase. On the other side of the wall was a medium-sized apartment built as an annex. It lay directly on the road, opening its doors to the concrete patio outside.

Mr. Debangshu Ghosh lived inside the annex, alone, with the legend of his gun. He was a big, bad wolf.

Ghosh was an old tenant. He rented a single unit on the ground floor and fed on grilled squabs, or at least that's what Ganesh told me. Ganesh was the caretaker of the building.

I suspected that he was lying. "It's part of a conspiracy to drive us out," Shibshankar told me. Ganesh had resolved to wait patiently until we moved somewhere else, leaving him alone in his courtyard at the rear of the building.

"Big scoops of bullshit," Shibshankar's father huffed shaking his moustache while his beer drained on the floor. "Nothing but wicked lies," Shibshankar's mother agreed, brushing my head cautiously, since I spent long hours in the courtyard listening to the caretaker's stories. "Ganesh makes them up on the spot," she told me, "don't believe a word."

But my mind was contaminated already.

Ganesh thought I was a pampered child. "It's my job to harden you up," he would say, shaking my shoulders like he enjoyed it. I wasn't pampered in the least, not because my parents couldn't afford it. They didn't have a lot of time to spare.

Besides, I wasn't a child anymore. I had these sudden bouts of migraine that stabbed my head every night, but I didn't tell Ganesh about them. I liked his stories. I sucked up to him like a child.

Maybe he was doing me a big favour. Maybe he was my guardian angel, flapping his wings in the air. "Shibshankar's father is a thief, I tell you, a big thief," he whispered above a dead chicken, laughing, and then he'd say, "His wife, Shibshankar's mother, is a kept woman!" He always slurped when he said that, licking some imaginary drops of blood from the carcass that lay on the floor.

It was Ganesh who first told me about Mr. Debangshu Ghosh.

He said – Mr. Ghosh sat by his window like a sniper and shot down pigeons in the neighbourhood. He had a weakness for doves. The whiter birds were bullied by the males, he claimed.

Mr. Ghosh had lost his wife many years ago, before I was born. He lived alone. He was a very thin man, once when I saw him naked, before he wrapped himself in a towel. He looked thinner when he wore clothes: a sleeveless knitted vest with numerous perforations and a checked *lungi* that fell from his thighs.

Debangshu Ghosh had a squint too. The squint was constant. It stared out of his face, tilting his forehead awkwardly. The hollow of his nose lay above his teeth, which were yellow, set off by thick black spectacles. A sketchy moustache tried to border his upper lip, but it couldn't. It trailed off into his spacious nostrils instead.

I'd heard that his daughter ran away with a slum-boy some years ago. He couldn't keep his women dead or alive.

Nevertheless, every morning, he emerged into the early burst of sunlight, ready to stake his claim before the others. His faint shadow popped out from the annex, showing the outer edges of his thin hair. His moustache resembled a pigeon's cere on the ground. His hair was soft and versatile, growing like tufts of grass.

Very carefully, he fanned out a fistful of wheat seeds on the concrete floor. He loomed over his pigeons when they played with each other, hungrily pecking at his offer. A large bowl of enamel, filled with tap water taken from his small bathroom, was kept ready in a small cleft of the wall. He would mimic their short, sharp thrusts into the bowl. He tilted his neck backwards every time they finished a mouthful.

This went on for a while, until Shibshankar from the first floor crashed the party with a loud whoop. The birds clapped their feathers, rising in a clamour, and then they scattered, seeking out familiar stains of bird poop on the wall. A flurry of white underwings filled the air.

Mr. Ghosh would squint fiercely at Shibshankar (or Shibu, as we called him), quietly putting away the rest of his seeds in a small packet. His granite frame caught the sunlight again, but this time it set his eyes on fire.

"Why do you disturb him every morning?" I couldn't help ask Shibu one day when I found him in a certain good humour. Shibu was older and bigger than I was, and at that age it made a world of difference.

Shibu belonged to a raucous unit helplessly tethered by blood. Trapped under a common name in the letterbox, his family occupied a crooked mezzanine. It was full of dust. The doorbell was small and beady, tucked away in a cobwebbed fold of the door. It seldom got touched.

Shibu's brother Surjosekhar kept chanting gibberish from an armchair. Like him, his sounds were relentless. Sometimes he scared me. In another world, in another time, I'd be like him. That was my biggest worry.

All of a sudden, he would break into a burst of mumbo jumbo. The drone in his baby voice changed to a stuttering invocation. Sometimes he stopped midway to wipe a stream of drool that gathered on his mouth. He wiped it with a swing of his misshapen elbow. A rabid look crept into his pale face each time Shibu and his mother squabbled, which was often. At times, the spinster aunt – Shelley – also got into the fights.

The spinster's entry pissed him off each time. Surjo snatched her comic books and licked the pages one by one. His lips were swollen. He stuck his tongue out. With a fierce concentration, he grazed the surface with his saliva.

Shelley slapped him and retired to her bedroom. She blamed his mother for begetting a monster, "an unfortunate burden," she called him.

"She's like a trained animal," Shibu used to say. Maybe Shelley had a bridle attached to her breasts. "She has a broomstick for sure," we agreed openly, in front of Shibu's mother, "up her arse." That better explained her grumpiness.

A seller of coconut sweets frequented their door. He dressed himself in a white robe stained with blue detergent. A big grey turban sat on top of his head. I saw him standing at Shibu's doorstep or waiting at the mouth of the staircase. Sometimes he stood in the porch below with his ears cocked.

Shibu avoided his house as much as he could. He never spoke about his family.

Shibu was a regular boy. He had two large hands, long legs and two eyes that gave nothing away. He wore his hair untidy and he always needed a shave.

His nose was flat, but it became shiny over the years from sniffing. Shibu sniffed too much. His clothes were cheap, so he got them ironed, not very regularly but often enough. The ravages of an oily adolescence had left their mark on his face. His face stood out like a sheet of blue paper. He was a boy on the streets – in a shop, at the movies, hanging from a bus – but one that you wouldn't remember. Unless he died in a terrible way.

I enjoyed his company but I didn't cross the line. Everything I said was seasoned with tact. "Why do you disturb him?" I repeated softly. "It's so fascinating to watch Mr. Ghosh."

Shibu had a powerful smile. "He's a glutton, that's why. If I don't scare the birds away, he'll eat them."

From across the side street, it was easy to look into Mr. Ghosh's room. A big window with grills remained open all day. The grills were wide and looked like a cage.

Shibu pointed at them. "You see that?"

Shibu leaned into the window one day. There was a small storage room inside the vestibule. Ghosh had an air rifle – the kind used for shooting coloured balloons. He stole it at a fair.

"You mean a toy gun?"

"But with pellets. Sharp pellets." Shibu rubbed his nails together and said – Ghosh stood in a corner, dipping stacks of feather in a bucket. He mixed them with liquid glue. Then he rolled them into balls and hit the ceiling.

"He has a good arm and lots of practice."

Ghosh juggled the strips of feather in his hands before he hurled them. The balls stuck to his roof.

"Then Ghosh picks his rifle up", Shibu continued, "he crouches low on the floor and bangs the feather down." It looked like a massacre when he finished. Bits of quill rained in the little room like locusts in a storm. "And I think I saw him smile. It was terrible."

There was a catch in his voice. I saw the way he rubbed his nails when he lied.

I kept a close watch over Mr. Ghosh's movements. A pattern emerged after a few days.

Every evening, Ghosh came out of his room at half past six. He pottered about the compound, inspecting his uneaten seeds that lay on the floor. Sometimes he walked around the building, all the way to the back. Finally he went inside the lobby. Once he sat down, he saw his reflection in the giant mirror. Precisely at six forty-five, he changed his seat.

I caught him staring at the generator room. He sat slumped on the couch for a few minutes. His legs were dirty. His *lungi* reached his toes. He liked to twiddle them when he got a chance. Once it struck seven, he stood up and walked out of the gate. He disappeared in a bend of the road.

I reported my findings to Shibu. He agreed it was time. Mr. Debangshu Ghosh had to be tailed.

*

Shibshankar and I sucked on an éclair in the *paan* shop opposite our gate. My piece was broken unevenly. We watched Mr. Debangshu Ghosh come out in the open. Daylight was falling fast. The smaller shops were closing for the day.

The streets were grey. It didn't matter. Everything around was grey too. The world needed a coat of paint.

Everyone ambled or stood quietly. They grew roots under their feet. Some of them came to a halt frightened by our speed. Whoosh, we went, and the world stood still.

Mr. Ghosh walked fast but he lacked a sense of direction. He kept turning this way and that way until a wall in a corner slowed him down. In his haste to avoid the wall, he took a wrong turn and wound up in a deserted street.

We straightened our backs, barely able to hold the chocolate in our mouths.

Ghosh didn't have eyes, not on the back of his head. Still we kept a safe distance. It wasn't easy to keep step with him. We could either keep distance or step, not both.

When his pace dropped, we walked along a limestone wall. Its skin flaked off in our palms. We walked in a single file when the alleyway narrowed. The road was littered with garages: dark smelly repairs washed in a pool of engine oil. Greasy mechanics on the ground, entwined lucklessly with the undercarriage, kept fondling their panels.

Shibu stopped to watch a bearded man. He groped the axle of a wheel. Using his grubby fingertips, he touched the rod shamelessly.

Shibu asked me, "Don't you get turned on by cars?"

I gave him a blank stare.

He turned away and sighed, "You're a homo."

Mr. Ghosh walked ahead. Past the meander of the limestone wall, we fell back a fair bit, several steps behind him. The traffic was sparse but the lack of cover prevented us from getting too close.

Mr. Ghosh was completely at ease in the alley. He knew the area well. He walked into tunnelled walkways without thinking. Some of them were hidden under canvas shacks. The shacks had poles covered with bamboo. Finally, moving sideways, he disappeared into a strip of air between two buildings.

The opening was narrower than us.

Shibu drew me away and whispered, "Let him take the shortcut. It's too risky." He pointed at the wall around the crack. "We'll meet him where it opens out."

So we ran along a circuitous turn and reached the other end quickly. We hid behind a tree at the mouth of the tunnel, waiting for him.

We waited there a long time but nothing happened.

Long minutes passed and the man did not appear. The tree above us shed its leaves. Small bits of fruit fell on the ground. Flies started biting our legs. Shibu tied and untied his shoe laces until the knot collapsed. The lace fell on his shoes like pasta. Still Mr. Ghosh did not emerge.

"I wonder if he went the other way."

Keeping me on guard, Shibu checked the surrounding tenements. He looked for interstices in the balcony next to us where Ghosh could've slipped through. We searched for crevices above the sewers with a long stick and pushed on doors to check if he could open them up.

Finally Shibu shook his head. "No, he *has* to come out from here. There's no other way."

We waited some more. Fallen fruits decomposed around us. A few minutes later, I looked at Shibu.

"Maybe he came out *before* we reached the other end?"

He hadn't considered it. "I don't know. Maybe he did? The bugger does walk fast."

"Let's go back and follow his tracks. We'll have an idea how long it takes."

"Good idea."

We went inside the rabbit hole.

Our elbows collided against each other. A long line of window frames emerged through the opening. The path was lit by a narrow strip of blue sky. A fat man would have been stuck inside, clamped by both ends of the wall.

A few steps ahead there was a fork in the road. We looked at each other, barely able to turn our heads, and then we separated.

The path widened up past the fork. I followed the trail until I reached a dead end. There was a hand pump next to a wall. The pump was slightly wet. Its mouth was dripping. Retracing my steps, I went back and met Shibu at the tree post.

"Well?" he said.

"Dead end. He must've gone inside a house."

"That's funny. There's no entry point to the tenements inside the walkway."

"Maybe he went in through a window?"

Shibu thought about it. "I didn't see any windows big enough. Besides they had bars on them. Maybe he climbed a tree?"

"What tree?" There weren't any trees inside. Trees don't grow on concrete walkways, stupid, I said in my head.

We both fell silent. There was nothing else to do.

Trudging back, Shibu suggested: "Let's look around his house."

Mr. Ghosh returned from his evening jaunts under an hour. I knew that. We didn't have much time.

"He's not coming back in a hurry today. Maybe he's gone to meet someone. Come on," Shibu said.

We walked back to our compound. The street lights were shining. We hadn't covered any major distance. The narrow lanes had robbed us of our map.

"Why would he climb a tree?"

"Hunting pigeon nests, who knows?"

I winced at the thought. "You know, Shibu, I think there's more to him than pigeons."

Approaching our building from the other side, we saw Mr. Ghosh's door. We stared at it from the street. The main gate hugged the yellow walls of the compound.

His door was wide open.

✱

His panel had been locked securely earlier that evening. I'd seen him fasten the door. Shibu had caught him pressing the lock with his fingers.

"Maybe the door came undone in the wind?"

Shibu shrugged and pointed me inside. I looked at the frame of the vestibule.

"I hope it isn't a trap."

I checked the window lights above our heads. My parents were back.

"We might need to run."

"Maybe there's a burglar in the house. Let's check."

Just then, Mr. Ghosh emerged. We almost bumped into him at the door.

Ghosh came out with a mug in his hand. He washed his feet on the threshold. Bending slightly, he poured a stream of water on his shins. It trickled down the concrete walkway.

With a series of rapid gestures, he climbed expertly on to himself. He mounted one foot on top of another, back and forth in succession. His heels were callused.

Shibu was stunned. Mr. Ghosh had *returned*. The pedicure we witnessed at the doorstep was done several minutes *after* he returned from his walks. It also meant he had finished his evening prayers. He spent fifteen minutes waving incense at his favourite idol.

I peeped inside his flat. An incense stick was fixed on the stand, smoking a filter with Lord Krishna.

Shibu wrinkled his nose. A heavy fragrance of sandalwood came out of the door. Sandalwood isn't everyone's cup of tea. I prefer jasmine myself.

His routine was clear. After his evening walk, Mr. Ghosh first changed his clothes. He had many *lungis* and vests. There were holes in all of them. Next he combed his hair. He swept the floor thrice a week, using a broom with a short handle. Last, he sang his prayers ringing a little bell. My mother told me later he blew the conch shell that evening, three times, very loudly.

Once he finished all this, he washed his feet at the door.

Mr. Ghosh shook the last water off his feet. He glared at us for a moment, gauging our expressions carefully. Then he slammed the door on our faces.

I wasn't surprised. I knew he spent his politeness sparingly. Like money. Ganesh the caretaker said – "Debangshu Ghosh squeezes a rupee until Gandhi puts down his glasses."

I turned away from the door.

"We have to find out where he went."

I had a bad feeling about the business. The way a dog smells the storm before it comes.

Deep down, I am a coward. I respect fear. I admire its shape and I don't ask questions. At that age it was very strong. Obedience is a good thing. The unknown isn't. I fear what I don't know.

It scares me.

Later I learnt to live with fear. It beats in my heart like a dying pigeon. I hold its throat but it fights back. I can't choke it.

I look at the unknown. I plant a hot kiss on her lips. Or I bite her neck. I feel nothing.

Fear governs my life. It makes me rise and fall.

Mr. Ghosh was an ordinary man. My curiosity was dead. It died when I saw him wash his feet at the door. He did regular things. There was no mystery.

But Shibu wouldn't listen to me. He was a fool.

"I know you are scared," he said. "You are thinking – here's a madman with a gun. What will he do next?"

"Why do you care about him?"

"What if he locks you up in his storage room?"

"Maybe he curled up on a branch. Maybe he has a twin. How does it matter?"

Shibu paid me no attention.

Fools repeat themselves. A week later, we planned another attempt to stalk Mr. Ghosh. This time we walked faster. We sprinted past the corners and avoided the street across the limestone wall. We knew the trail by now – we didn't have to check our bearings.

A month thereafter we did it again. It was a different strategy. We stalked him in single file. He was covered on opposite ends of the pavement. Shibu and I walked separately.

Some months later we tried a guerrilla attack. I walked ahead of Ghosh, checking his movements. Shibu stayed behind him. I guarded the entrance. When Ghosh passed through a tunnel, Shibu went to the other side. Once Ghosh was out of sight, I ran and joined Shibu at the end of the walkway.

But we couldn't trap him.

Ghosh had secret routes in each alley. Was there a passage underground? Maybe he disappeared into a manhole. But the sewerage was sealed. There were dead ends everywhere. Where the fuck did he go?

"It's like black magic."

We tried to predict his route on a given day. Perhaps he walked *this* way on Tuesdays and *that* way every Friday. Those days I had a clear head. But nothing worked.

Ghosh never came out. Once he entered an alley, we couldn't say where he went, how he vanished, or *why* he went inside in the first place. At any given time, he could be anywhere.

"Heisenberg would've kissed him silly."

*

One overcast afternoon in school, Shibu and I convened at the main gates. We seldom saw each other in uniform. But that day we had gone to battle and we'd survived.

A horde of boys from a convent down the diocese had stormed our grounds. They alleged that one of their friends was beaten up. It might've been somebody from our school or anyone else on the streets. Nothing was certain but they bayed for our blood anyway.

I was detained at the Principal's office. I flipped through a men's magazine on the second floor long after the final bell. Suddenly I heard a bloodcurdling cry. I jumped to the corridor to get a look.

The passage was empty. The school field was deserted too. I walked over to the bathroom and met a member of the staff shaking his thing at the urinal.

"What's going on? I heard some shouting."

"Some ruffians broke our back gate." He worked his fly upwards.

I asked him for further details.

"A football match was underway in the common ground." He washed his hands at the row of taps in a long sink. "That's when these thugs came in. They carried hockey sticks and bike chains. They smashed our boundary wall and beat up our students."

I rushed down the staircase and landed in the scene of action.

Our resident soldiers had been alerted. They'd initiated a massive counter-attack from the hostel block. The aliens had blood on their faces. Their ties had been clutched and shaken by he-men from the hostel. Insignias were ripped off their uniforms. There were about fifty of them, huddled in a corner with their shirts tucked out. The home team was roaring wildly, trooping out through the school gate into the road outside for a victory lap.

It looked like a job well done. With nothing left for me to do, I was about to go back upstairs when things took a nasty turn.

Two beaten-up Tata Estates screeched like witches into the tennis court. A narrow strip of the stadium was bounded by chain-link fencing. The station wagons came hurtling through a sheet of galvanized wire on our fence, leaving a big gash in the weave.

People on the road cordoned off our perimeter. Cracks in the wall were guarded by faceless strangers. It happened very quickly. Hatches were unleashed in the wagons; grim-faced hooligans stepped out of their entrails, carrying their wounded brethren back. But they didn't go away.

An ugly group of yo-yo-youths blew into the hostel mess, flashing their fake Sharpfingers and tattoos. A few more trickled out of the Estates and walked towards the main school building. A boy with a frown, looking like an angry Rottweiler, rolled up to me.

That made me secretly happy. "Maybe I can beat him up and become a hero," I thought. He didn't look invincible. He was unarmed too, unless he had a pocket knife handy. His hosiery was well-concealed within his pants in case I pulled his clefts out.

I could take him on, but I wasn't sure what he wanted.

He took up a position quickly and then he held my gaze. We waited for the right moment, sizing each other up like haberdashers. We didn't do anything; he didn't hurl abuses at me; no threat was issued by either of us. He just stood there.

What the hell, I thought. Maybe he wanted me to make the first move.

A noisy bomb erupted in the boys' mess. But the Rottweiler's gaze did not flinch. A ceiling fan came tumbling out into the school field. The blades rotated like a chopper before they crashed to the ground in a cloud of dust. The Rottweiler's gaze did not flinch. I yearned to see the swivel of the fan, but I couldn't. People shouted and stomped their feet in the dust. Still, his gaze did not flinch.

He was a gazer, that one. My eyes watered with the strain of war. I rubbed the tears off my nose and cheeks. Once I was dry I noticed that Shibu was on the field too, flaying his arms wildly. I wondered what he was doing, but the thought quickly passed. My thoughts aren't heavy – they flit weightlessly from one spent moment to the next.

A couple of seconds later Shibu was still waving, only this time he was closer. Heisenberg was spot-on again. My eyes were fixed on the enemy. It looked as if Shibu's hands were on fire. He wanted to unfasten them off their sockets and cool his body.

In a slow pent-up moment, with a force that shook my soul, a punch landed mightily on my left. The Rottweiler charged that instant. Too late, I realized I'd been ambushed. A second mutt had crept up to my flanks while the first kept me hypnotized.

Shibu was trying to break the spell. With a searing pain on my shoulder, I ran headlong like a battering ram into Rottweiler the First. At the last moment, I jumped and kicked his face, cracking it through the middle. The boy collapsed in a heap. I saw delicious drops of blood streaming down his pug-nose.

I swivelled not a moment too soon. My covert assailant, Rottweiler the Second, was poised with a carved willow. I ducked his vicious swing this time. We stood next to the music room, barely balanced on our toes. I held my ground, but only just, while the lag of his swing buggered his balance. He tottered like a prison pie at the instant of collapse.

Resurrecting my spine, I pushed him towards a sub-woofer: it was encased in a dark, rectangular Cyclops with its crusted sides placed in padding. He reeled through the dusty air and tipped over into the room. The music played in my head. I locked the door quickly.

When I raised my head almost deaf with music, two more mutts came running in my direction. They charged in the open. It wasn't an ambush anymore. I felt light-headed; I couldn't hear much. The music was getting sour, rubbing itself relentlessly around me.

I wanted to fight; I wanted to get it over with. Let's have a face-to-face, I wanted to say; I hate being hypnotized. They carried sticks in their paws but I waited. They also serve who only stand and wait.

The boys were about fifteen feet away and gaining ground. Their footsteps lent a beat to my head. Suddenly Shibu came from behind a pillar.

He hit them together like flies, swatting their bodies nicely.

Shibu had a heavy form: the force of collision winded out his victims. The sticks fell lamely from their hands. Sticks and stones can hurt my bones.

Shibu dusted cakes of loose turf from his shirt. He collected their weapons like a hero. The music paused in my head.

The wagons on the field were revved up. The blade-and-tattoo regiment was trapped within the hostel. Stray mobsters roaming the field made a desperate run for their cars. A collective growl came from the road – low and ominous, and suddenly our infantry returned, back where we wanted them.

Two cooks from the mess kitchen hurled massive container drums near the wire fence; the last exit was blocked. The Estates whirled towards the back gate, but the wrath of the mob was upon them. Clouds of terrified dust gathered in the field, and finally, when the police arrived, two pansies had fainted.

Our hostel had no casualties.

Someone bandaged my head in the dispensary. The main quadrangle was situated in the front; a flank of the admin-block separated two halves of the school compound. Shibu and I had averted a potential spree of vandalism, they said. We were heroes in uniform. Anywhere else, they'd have given us a medal each.

We stopped at the school gate and looked back into the field: the greens were lined with blood and red grass. An ambulance was parked in a corner; a police-van drove off with some losers. The entire teaching faculty had arrived, along with some starched missionaries – they gaped at the premises in disbelief.

We had survived well, with some strength to spare. I felt special. It was raw power; it was heady and we were swimming in it, Shibu and I.

High-five, I said. We shook hands like soldiers on the front and we pledged – come evening – we would take Mr. Ghosh down.

*

"Pledges need good preparation," Shibu warned me.

I packed my feet in light badminton shoes with creamy soles. Shibu checked the traction of an old pair of Stan Smiths his father kept inside a shoe-rack opposite their door. We took a test run on the terrace. After a few sprints around the flower pots, we were ready.

"The trick is to be stealthy," he explained.

"Like a cat."

"But don't go meow meow."

We had to follow Mr. Ghosh right into his rabbit hole. We wouldn't let him out of our sight, not for a moment, even if he threatened to explode in gas. If he turned around and caught us, we would pounce on him and crush his bones with our elbows.

I did a few push-ups to strengthen my arms. A brown skull cap hid the bandage on my head.

"It won't help being conspicuous on the road," I said when Shibu looked at my cap with disapproval. He carried his Swiss army knife in a secret pocket.

After a usual round of marking, we were back at the same maze of walkways: it was where Ghosh had disappeared the first time we tailed him. He chose a vaguely common wall coated with lime and went inside. We saw him slither in, and then it was a moment of quick decision.

"We go in after him, of course," Shibu said.

I nodded quietly and made way for him.

"You go first."

I wasn't too sure. "Why?"

"You're quicker and lighter. My shoes squeak."

"What if he changes direction?"

"I saw you tackle that boy in school today. You can handle Ghosh."

I crept into the tunnel without another word. Flattery is a bitch.

"Don't worry, I'm right behind you if you need back-up," Shibu whispered in my ear.

We hopped on the concrete and marched ahead. I couldn't see Ghosh anywhere. "Quick, quick," Shibu spurred me on. "We mustn't lose him."

I quickened my pace and Shibu followed. He struggled to fit his wide frame inside the path; he hopped sideways along sharp turns like a highland dancer. We reached a point where the road tapered to the right. I held my hand up.

"What?" Shibu was breathing hard. His pants were covered in sweat.

"It's a blind curve. He could be round the corner waiting."

I peeped very gradually. The coast was clear. I signalled to Shibu and we started down the turn.

We hadn't taken fifteen steps when I spotted Ghosh.

*

The path was strewn with broken concrete, end to end. Ghosh was swaying as if he'd lost his balance. He searched for something on the ground, lifting his vest a little.

I grabbed Shibu's shoulder and whistled – "Duck! Now!"

We sprinted for cover behind an ornamental lamp post. It had an iron base and a green body. The base was big and wide. We wrapped our limbs around it.

"What's he doing?"

"Shhhh! How do I know? Let's see."

Mr. Ghosh found what he was looking for. He peered at the neighbouring windows to see if anyone was watching him. Shibu's legs were sprawled halfway across the path. I nudged him wildly. With a lot of effort, he locked his knees to his chin.

We watched Mr. Ghosh move. It was a test of our collective concentration. I observed Ghosh in slow motion. When he raised an arm, I saw his elbows twitch. Every detail on his body was visible. His movements assumed a long laborious arc every time I blinked. For a few moments I controlled Time.

His pigeon-head bobbed inwards and outwards. His cere was still pouty. I got absorbed in the black lines on his frame, counting the checks of his *lungi*.

Suddenly Ghosh turned low and crouched on the ground.

He crouched swiftly. In sudden alarm, I looked at Shibu. Ghosh unfurled a few folds of his *lungi* and squatted on the floor. I didn't know what he was up to. Maybe a gun was tied around his waist? What did he have under his loin cloth?

It wasn't long before we realized the truth. The situation was horrific. With a sickening gurgle, Mr. Ghosh's amber urine flowed down the culvert. It came in a steady stream. The urine was unusually dark in colour. Presently he became very still. After a final thrust, he was back on his feet.

*

We remained in our position for a long time. I saw the angle of our bent knees. Our fancy padded soles were balanced on the iron base. My knuckles were white from clutching the post. Suddenly it hit me like nausea. I stood up.

In the distance, Mr. Ghosh had furled up his *lungi*. He stood next to a piston-pump and washed his hands, pressing the handle gently. He wiped his palms and face with the same fold, borrowing heavily from the checks of his man-skirt.

Then he walked straight into a section of the wall that opened out to a temple courtyard. The door was low and painted-in with the wall.

"Camouflage!"

Lord Shiva's well-fed bull sat sedately on a low platform within the temple premises. Ghosh disappeared inside and climbed two or three steps. He stood behind a woman in white. She was offering prayers to a hidden deity in the sanctum.

Someone came and closed the door. The entrance was lost in the cracks of the wall.

I tried the door; it was latched from inside. The door was a solid block of wood without a crack in it. I put my ear to the wall and heard familiar voices. Shibu stood a few feet away.

"Let's go. Nothing here," he said.

I saw an electric pole nearby. Shibu could've given me a push but he didn't. Locking my thighs around the ring, I flitted up the pillar. I shot up like a moth.

I went up slowly in calculated jerks. I climbed a few feet first to check my view. The foliage around the temple was heavy. I couldn't see anything.

"Get higher," Shibu said.

I wasn't sure of my vertigo. Besides I didn't know how to get off the pole.

"How do I come down?"

"The same way you went up. Let your arse go. Don't go caterpillar."

"Should I climb higher?"

"You could, but you might fall."

"There'll be an awful racket if I fall."

"You'll break a few bones. Some very important ones."

I relaxed my grip and slid a few inches down. It was easy. "What's the problem?" I asked Shibu.

"Someone might see us. We look like common thieves."

It was a moment that would go forever. We could do the right thing or regret it all our lives.

I quickly pressed the nearest doorbell.

*

The door was dark. It stood next to a winding staircase that went upstairs. Next to the bell was a tiny stall locked with a chain. Someone had given up on it many years ago.

Behind the stall was a layered building. It was pretty but its upper storeys had begun to sag. An old man wearing cracked eye-glasses sat on a small balcony. The balcony jutted out from three storeys above.

The door opened. A girl with pigtails and bright red ribbons stood in front of me. Clearly she'd been sleeping.

"Who are you?"

Sleep hadn't left her eyes. She rubbed them with her knuckles. Her lids were large and puffy.

I smiled at her and handed a tenner. "Toilet. Emergency."

Shibu clutched my belly.

The girl found it amusing. She let me in.

I tried to rush but the entrance was narrow. A dingy passage stretched before me with a large mat at its centre. It was the girl's bedfellow. The stairs grew suddenly out of a channel and went upwards.

The stairs were two-steps high – each of them. They were carved from a mountain of stone. Its wall was lined with spider webs spun in fine circles. Soot smeared the hand rails.

I was panting when I found myself next to the old man on the balcony. I dusted my hands and breathed out.

The temple was clearly visible from the balcony. The compound was a gigantic square with vast open spaces. A large part of the platform leading to the sanctum showed itself in the decaying sunlight. I saw the shapely bottom of a woman in white offering prayers. Her hands were clenched around her bosom. Her face was hidden by a mass of open hair cascading down her shoulders. Some extra cloth was draped around the neck. Another yard covered her bare arms. Her sari was wound tightly at the hips.

Her waist was slim; her stomach was bare. I imagined the soft hollow of her navel in the front. She wore her sari low. I enjoyed her contours.

But when I looked around, I realized I was the only one watching. There was no one else.

Ghosh was gone.

*

The temple courtyard was empty. The old man turned towards me and nodded through his cracked eye-glasses.

"It's a nice view from here," I said, hiding my gaze quickly. "Any higher than this, the earth would be round."

He smiled. He looked like a tired angel. Only the wings were missing.

"Sit if you want to."

I looked around the balcony. There wasn't any surface to sit on. No furniture, no ledge, nothing. The floor was too low.

The old man kept sitting. He looked beyond the temple. His glasses inspected the details of his kingdom.

The neighbourhood of flat-tiled buildings were burnt in the sun. They absorbed the last throes of twilight. Across the temple courtyard, one could see the redbrick building where I lived. It was propped upwards, but I couldn't see the capillaries above. The giant hoarding on the terrace sat still and gave the house away.

A glint of mercury from Shibu's mezzanine blinded me. Then I realized it was Shibu's brother Surjo at the window with his banging spoon.

Shibu's mother told me – Surjosekhar was afflicted with Rett Syndrome. It was a genetic disorder. All his symptoms were explained by the disease. "He's sick. He'll always be sick."

"There must be a cure?"

"I know what you're thinking."

I put my glass down, full of green mangoes.

"You think he inherited it from me." That's what Shibu's father Mr. Dasgupta said.

I tried to return to my drink. It was more likely *him* that gave it, I told her, or his side of the family. Shelley was Mr. Dasgupta's sister. She wasn't very normal in my mind.

"No, it couldn't have been them. It came from me. My defect, not his."

I sipped the *aam panna* quietly.

"I wonder why Shelley doesn't die!"

She gnashed her teeth. Her face was fierce like a man's. Then she caught me staring at her.

Surjo looked exactly the same when he was angry.

There was a beat. It hung in the air.

"Do you want another glass?"

I'd left it at that.

*

"Have you been here long?" I asked the old man. It didn't mean anything. I just said it.

I was still standing in his balcony. A little conversation wouldn't be a bad thing.

He looked over the world before him. No answer. Maybe he was deaf?

"Have you been to Baghdad?"

His voice was soft. I wasn't sure if I heard him correctly.

Baghdad? No, I replied.

"I was there before the war. Oil complicates things."

He was senile. I could deal with that.

"You should go some time."

He strolled down the west bank of the Tigris. With cracked eyes, he stared at a mosque in the city.

I lost him. There was a big crowd. Bearded men loomed above him. His frame was completely hidden.

I patted his shoulder to bring him back. But he couldn't see me. He kept staring at the mosque. It was built in the centre of a town square. Civilization throbbed around it. People moved back and forth in spirals. The dome was spacious, swallowing a thousand entrants from all sides.

I looked at the roofs and alleys once again. It took me time to understand. There was some meaning to it.

Finally I left the balcony. I couldn't take it anymore. Just for the record, I spent a minute in the toilet and flushed.

The girl laughed when I came down. She didn't come to the balcony.

I had expected her to follow me upstairs.

"Innocence is a beautiful thing," Shibu said.

She waved the money I had given her. With a smile, she held it to my face. Then she shut the door.

Before I could change my mind.

*

25

"What happened?"

Shibu's eyes were wide open.

"I met the prince of Persia."

"What?"

"Nothing. He's an old man."

Shibu laughed.

"Let's go."

He walked away without me.

The temple was land-locked. It stood in the centre of a maze. Alleys and by-lanes surrounded the temple. There were walls on all sides. Several gates led to the premises. Each of them was camouflaged. The doors and walls were of the same colour.

But I didn't tell Shibu.

"One of the temple exits is connected to our building. It opens into the caretaker's backyard."

"So?"

"That's how he disappears. Mr. Ghosh goes through the temple."

"He takes a different route?"

"Only on the return."

"But why?"

"Maybe there's no reason."

Shibu walked ahead. We went back through a long trail of alleyways.

That's how I knew. Shibu had climbed out of my head. I didn't realize *when* he did, exactly.

✱

3

Two Years Later

*T*wo years passed. I don't know where they went.

Meanwhile Shibu and I grew up. Some distance grew as well.

We saw less of each other every day. Our easy brotherhood gave way to a measured acquaintanceship. I played solitaire with him in my head. But he didn't know it.

We joined the same college. Maybe it wasn't a co-incidence. Shibu enrolled when it was time. He shaved, he smoked. Gels defined his manhood.

But I didn't let him get away.

Shibu kept himself to himself. For want of better things to do, I turned to books and dendrite.

It was a happy phase. I released well-formed spit balls on wild men downstairs. I hated their bikes and swagger. Once in a while when I went to buy Gold Flakes for my father, I spread the legend of a long-haired dog that roamed our corridors. It was Shibu's idea. Soon the descent of my saliva was met with a quiet compassion.

Everyone loves dogs, Shibu said.

Meanwhile, my world became my window. It was small but it painted a pretty picture below.

The window was part of my father's chamber. His case papers were packed tightly in a bunch with black shoe-laces. They looked like wild flowers when they were tidy. The files were thin, made from cheap cardboard and coloured a slutty pink. No one bothered to trash them so they lay on the cold red-stoned floor, piled against a blue wall.

My father kept a news-clipping from the west coast with his papers. It was titled 'fair and lovely'. I didn't know what it meant or why he'd kept it, but I read it every night.

A light-bulb hung over the heap. The bulb was dim and flickered like a lost cause. I stayed up nights gazing at the filament in the light globe. It kept me awake.

A middle-aged woman was abducted Wednesday last, the news-clip reported. She'd been taken from a crowded marketplace. The cab driver had two accomplices, including a woman. The victim was robbed of jewellery and cash valued at a few lacs of rupees.

A tube of adhesive came cheap. Hardware stores sold dendrite opposite our building. When I came home from college, I rinsed the grime from my face and sat down for a quiet dinner. Dinner was a solemn ritual. We ate to keep ourselves alive. My father stared at news tickers with the T.V. on mute. My mother corrected answer sheets with a red pen. Once fed, they retired with a murmur leaving me exactly as I was before.

Meanwhile the cab driver drove through the suburbs, the paper said, while his friends collected loot at gun-point. The lady got dumped at a highway under construction. She'd lodged an FIR at the nearest police station. Maybe that's how my father came into the picture.

Squeezing out the glue on to my shirt, I settled down in my den. Often I wore full-sleeved shirts to get more surface area. I followed a silver clock with a nasty alarm to time my inhalations. When the hands on the black dial moved a quarter, it was time to sniff up the next kick. By two in the morning, I'd be swimming in the organic fumes of myself and the rest of the night was a blur.

I dreamt of the robbed lady sometimes. She purchased gold for her family. She carried heavy cash as well. Then she climbed into a shuttle car at the crossing near the main road. A few miles later, the driver changed routes. When the lady yelled, he pointed at a young woman. She sat next to the lady and wanted to be dropped off first.

I switched the light bulb on and off. It was a slow loop. I matched the bulb with the clock. Tick-tock, tick-tock; tick-tock, tick-tock. The tungsten came alive with the moving hands. The clock pressed the light with my thumb. After a while, the ticking got lazy. Time moved slowly. A lizard peered at me. It lived on the wall and saw everything. I noticed its eyes. They flickered in the glow of the bulb. Cold, cruel eyes, undeterred by circumstance.

The young woman didn't get down from the car, the paper said. Once the taxi entered the suburbs, out came a shiny black pistol from the girl's purse. Through the rest of the journey, the young woman collected the lady's cash, jewellery and cards. Later they drove into a highway and ordered the lady to jump at a drained-out canal.

In late autumn there was a nip in the air. Gods flew in from distant lands. Instinct brought flies to my room through an open window. The light lizard, fat with food, straddled the bulb where the insects roosted. It chewed the season down. I kept its black pellets in a silver snuff-box. The lizard dropped them at night. The pellets were crowned in white. It was a sickly white.

A photo was appended with the article. It showed the police-station where the complaint was made. The lady was flanked by two policemen in uniform. She wasn't pretty.

I preferred the girls below. Happy hours started at twilight. Chicks were served neat at my window. They never roamed in groups. When darkness fell, the wild bikers emerged and I stopped counting.

She was a thin woman with a face wearing an off-white sari. With the paper folded halfway, her pout disappeared into a corner.

My mother never wore white. When she returned from school, she found me dusting case-files or poring over yellowed bits of paper. At first the papers would crumble. They sporulated like amoeba in my nervous hands. Once the dendrite wore off and my motor skills returned, I read a sheaf from start to finish.

That's how I knew of Shibu's grandfather. He was a very rich man. I saw his will. My father had a copy among his files.

The man left everything to his son. His estate was in the name of Shibu's father, Shushobhon Dasgupta.

*

My father was struggling. He moved between Old Post Office Street, Esplanade and the Strand. It was a useless peninsula.

He spent his time reading. There wasn't much work. He pretended to be busy and missed his meals. At lunch time, he smoked small Gold Flakes and ran around the courts. But he didn't go inside. I never saw him eat. He wore his weariness heavily and carried it to his chamber near the City Civil Court.

The chamber was a cubbyhole built of wood and plaster. It had a whirring electric fan, a copying machine and a massive shelf which took up too much space.

On a good day, he sat behind a table and touched his moustache. Dirty teacups were drowned in a steel bucket on the pavement. Once a client arrived, he lifted a cup with a three-leafed shamrock and put it down on the bench.

It made me sad to look at him. Lots of things made me sad.

One night, I caught my mother sobbing at the kitchen sink. She stood over a piece of stained cloth near the tap. It was an old purple blouse with little fasteners hanging from the neck. She told me we would lose our house very soon. My father had borrowed money for his 'affairs'. It was a private business to supplement his income. He had mortgaged our flat.

"We need to buy it off the landlord," she kept saying while she ironed his shirt every morning. My father didn't say anything. He sat in his chair reading. The chair moved when he turned a page of the newspaper.

"Sandipan will do something."

My father was very different when he was young. His friends came from rich families. They wore Gandhi caps and fooled around the Esplanade.

My mother said he was dressed in a stiff starched *kurta* when they first met. Later he wore half-sleeved shirts and white trousers to impress her. He gelled his hair back but she knew it was oil. His comb had sharp teeth.

There was money. He smoked a meerschaum pipe with his friends.

My father had given away our family house in north Calcutta some years ago. I'd seen pictures of it. It had high pillars and a giant pool of water lilies. He had donated it for welfare work. It was his father's dying wish. The man died on a tin bed reeking of ethanol.

In the recent past, my father tried to sidle up to my mother's family. Some of them were high-ranking officials in the party. "It's pathetic to watch him," my mother complained. In the end, mercifully, he had given up.

We lived in extraordinary times. A smell of change hung around us. A prick of franchise in a booth, a daub of indelible ink, and a new era would begin. There was a promise of better things.

It was the change we all wanted yet secretly feared. Lest it become a monster, like the last time. A summer of discontent was drawing to a close. In the deepest corners of our wasteland, farmers fought with land and chemicals.

"Maybe things will improve once we turn past the wretched *left*," my father said turning the page to a new story.

The court was a special sweatshop. People whored around with little or no money. And far less scruples. I asked my father about his cases in hand. Somehow he always had enough.

Shady men met outside his chamber. They spoke grimly until my father passed some papers. At times they slipped a cheque into his coat. His pockets were loose, specially made with terrycloth.

He seldom got briefed. His matters weren't listed for hearing. No judge ever heard him in court. Some men who came to his chamber took him away in a ferry across the river. He returned late at night or the next morning.

Sometimes I sauntered across the railway tracks. That's how I bumped into Sebastian from college, who sat two rows behind me in class.

*

Sebastian Rudro Gomes was long and athletic. He had love curls on his head and a stupid mouth. I didn't know him well enough. Not anymore.

Like all colleges, our students mixed unevenly. Gangs formed on tongues and pockets. Our tastes were different. Fathers were either rich or poor.

It was a natural process mimicking the world. No one seemed to mind it. We were grown up.

However lunch made the mix sour. Food was a lousy attendant. During tiffin break a heartless map-man drew boundaries across the relief of our canteen. The lines were precise and everyone followed them.

When the bell rang crowds convened in small parochial groupings. We huddled together before a stranger could barge in. Birds of a feather.

Sebastian though was different. He ate everything.

Sebastian raided his father's pharmacy and brought back gifts for his friends. His father had a line of drug stores among other things. Once when Shibu got sick, he made a prescription for him. Sabbie had an elegant scribble.

Sabbie and I went back a long way. We were bench partners in school. Back then we shared trump cards and wrestlers with each other. There were graffiti and works of art that we composed with our nails. Sometimes our pee streams crossed the wall.

But our school hadn't taught us how to handle change. Sebastian Gomes dropped his middle name and a cumbersome innocence. It happened along the way while we were growing up.

When our class bench moved to a different floor, we moved our different ways. The sections were re-allotted. Sabbie and I became victims of a lottery. Our co-habitation dissipated into a friendship of the past.

*

The day I ran into Sabbie he was repairing old cycles at Chandni Chowk.

He said he worked part-time at his father's garage. His father had everything in small quantities.

Sabbie put a broken spoke on the floor. Then he cleaned up and tossed a pedal into a bin outside.

We went for a walk once he finished.

On the pavement, I kept bumping into Sabbie. I kept saying sorry. His pace was different.

"That's alright. I bumped into Shibu the other day."

It was a matinee show. Sabbie wiped a smudge on his forehead using a grease cloth.

"You went together?"

Sabbie threw the cloth with a shudder.

"He sat next to a dirty old man covered in vapours."

"Dirty old man?"

Shibu knew a dealer in Chandni Chowk by the name of Sulaiman. He supplied drugs to Shibu. I also knew Sulaiman ran a tailoring shop further north.

"That's the one."

"Doing what?"

"Holding hands," Sabbie chuckled.

They were rubbing a hard substance in the cinema.

We both knew Shibu well so we bonded easily. Sabbie was worried about him.

"The other day, I saw him in the student union hall. He was screaming on top of a bench, ripping pamphlets and burning clumps of grass. They chanted slogans like a bunch of killers. I saw rashes on his face, Sandy. The scars were horrible."

In two years' time, Shibu's face had become like a plastic sheet. His nose was blue and transparent. The tips were shredded with use.

I didn't say anything.

"That reminds me – he got a big one that day at the movies."

Sabbie spoke of scars and a piece of glass that Shibu possessed. He mentioned the old man in the next seat. Sulaiman the tailor sold his wares in a dirty shop at Rajabazar next to a party office.

I listened to him carefully. Shibu wouldn't last long. That's what it looked like to me.

It didn't matter what people did to him. He would die anyway.

*

We didn't have much else to talk about. There was a girl in Shibu's batch. She had freckles that drove me mad, "with desire," I said, enunciating the thought carefully.

I saw her every day in passing. She was at college and afterwards on the basketball court in a bouncy red skirt. But I'd seen her properly only once. It was on a lusty night last winter when we were drunk.

Her escort had passed out on dark rum. He lay on a bed snoring gently. White cream from a Christmas cake was iced across his forehead. His rum was strong. There wasn't another bed in the room.

She was alarmed at the prospect of a lonely night. She had hormones to spare. Finally she called a little boy from a corner. He licked the wine from her thighs under the cleaving mistletoe.

It fascinated me.

I smoked up on the terrace later that night. It was difficult to get the scene out of my head.

"The one with puckered lips, you mean?" Sebastian asked.

"Yes."

"She's bad news, sir."

"Why?"

"She's got frowning eyebrows. And her voice is hoarse."

"So?"

Sabbie looked around. "So?"

He made me sit on a staircase in the road. "This footage I saw, Sandy – of *them*, at it."

"It could be anyone."

"Someone installed a spy click in their love nest."

I glared at Sabbie but he ignored me.

"She runs across the room in a skimpy skirt. My friend Amit is in the video. He enters the room with a gun. The gun doesn't move. It grows big in her hand. Very big! Even his balls get heavy. There's a dent on the couch where he sits."

Sabbie closed his eyes and smiled.

It sounded disgusting in the middle of a road. The wall behind me had hand-drawn posters. They screamed for votes in different voices. A bloom of twin flowers sat prettily on a green patch. There was a faded sickle above an open palm, but it looked rusty. The change was about to happen.

"Are you gay?" I asked him.

"And that's when he lunges, tits in his face, yanking her pair with medieval tongs."

This time I stood up.

Sabbie stood up with me. His back wore a coat of slippers borrowed from the stairs.

"You know about last Christmas, Sandy."

"It was a spill. Her wine slipped."

Sabbie smirked. "Renuka likes muscular tongues."

"Tongues are *made* of muscle."

I brushed my trousers on the road.

"He screamed like an animal when he found out. Wine dripping from her skin."

People watched us on the street. A shirtless man with a belly chased flies at a sweet shop next to us.

"Let's walk."

I wanted to run away. The whole thing made me sick.

We went past a row of timber shops. There were many small offices on the road next to each other. I recognized some of the names.

Sabbie stopped suddenly.

I looked around. It was a long road with lots of people. We were standing near a window with blinds. It was hidden behind a gate. The gate was padlocked and built low on the ground.

Sabbie pushed it open.

There weren't any shops on the pavement opposite. The buildings on either side of the gate were deserted.

"What's inside?"

"Come."

"I think I should get home."

"Don't be scared."

It was his own apartment. His father had it spare.

"I let my friends use the rooms once in a while. For a small fee."

Sabbie had turned the space into money.

I followed him into a whitewashed corridor. There was no furniture, only some beads hanging from a rod and a couple of beanbags on the floor. Brown buffet lamps diffused a sleazy shadow on the wall.

"That's odd. I thought I switched them off."

Sabbie guided me towards another room.

The rooms were connected. There was more space inside. The apartment was L-shaped and got bigger as we went in. Further, a windowless wall looked over a foam mattress. It was mounted on a low frame with cushions to lean on.

The foam had softened in two places. The cover was warm. It looked like a recent imprint.

Someone was inside the flat.

Sabbie went to the end of the room.

"Wait, I'll switch on the light."

But before he could find the switch, someone bumped into him.

Sabbie recovered. He hit a panel near the door. The room was bathed in neon.

"When did you come in?"

I switched on another light on the wall. This one was white and fluorescent.

"You gave me a key," the other person said.

The voice was thick and raspy like a man's.

Sabbie turned to me and smiled.

"Recognize him?"

The other person looked at me.

"This is Sandy from my class. He wanted to take a look."

"Hi, I'm Amit."

He wore a pale salmon shirt with a high collar. His khakis were pleated in reverse.

Amit was a senior in college. He was in Shibu's batch.

Sabbie smiled and took us outside in the common area.

We sat on the mattress with glasses. There was a bottle of whisky under the lamps. Sabbie ordered some food and kept talking.

Amit was quiet.

I rubbed my back on the foam cover. It remembered my size. After two drinks I walked away.

They watched me on my way out.

*

4

Cats and Dogs

A few days later I was sitting at the Black Pearl on a high leather chair. That's when I saw Mr. Debangshu Ghosh again.

Once in six weeks, I woke up early and looked at the mirror. One hand rose to the head and inspected my hair while the other hand cleaned my teeth in silence.

Once I'd washed my face, I continued to inspect leaning on the ceramic basin. When my arm hurt, I stared at the *bindi*-dotted glass. The mirror separated my different parts. I kept staring at them.

Maybe it was time to remove my hair. Maybe I should let it grow. It wasn't an easy decision.

I didn't possess much but I was deeply attached to my hair. I loved the way it grew. It defined me.

"You can tell a man by his hair."

Shibu laughed at me.

It wasn't insignificant either, rising above external appendages – hands, legs and interesting things in between. No one spoke of de-balling; why was hair any different; why did we take renaissance for granted?

"The absence of pain," Shibu said wearily. "It's like taking off a wig."

"But there *is* pain."

"You are retarded."

Then, Shibu remembered his brother and looked away.

It was a stupid rule. I had to get my hair cut periodically. Whether I wanted to or not.

"Why can't people mind their business?" Haircuts made me nervous.

Shibu couldn't understand. "It's a bunch of dead cells, you know that, right?"

"I like dead things."

*

After a preliminary cold shower, I clipped my nails with a nail cutter made from shiny metal.

"That's keratin. Get rid of all traces." Shibu pointed censoriously at my fingernails as if they were poisonous.

I shampooed my hair at home. Shibu warned me about the barber's helper. "Don't let him grope you, those fingers have been everywhere."

He passed me his new body-suit for luck.

It was a Sunday morning. The Black Pearl was a short walk away. But it was a long way back, so I ate a hearty breakfast with eggs and milk.

A dirty hair-man summoned me to his chair. A tiny television set perched in a corner was streaming an old Hindi feature film. I shut my eyes to think of pleasant things.

The barber turned my head, adjusting its angle to suit his shears. Once in a while he passed me my glasses so I could check his handiwork. My new face looked ugly in the mirror.

"Mr. Ghosh, please have a seat."

It was the woman behind the reception.

"We have it ready."

My eyes were shut. I twisted my head an inch in the other direction. But the barber's clipper pinched me.

"What's wrong?"

"Nothing. Give me my glasses."

Mr. Ghosh was standing in the doorway. There was a large gunny bag in his hand. A walking stick stood next to him.

*

"I'm in a hurry Rita, I can't wait."

Rita the receptionist scurried into a small foyer of the salon. Idle hairdressers kept staring at the T.V. screen.

"Is everything alright?" my barber cried. His clipper scratched the back of my head.

Without my glasses, I couldn't see much. I heard Rita return from the inside room. "Thanks for waiting Mr. Ghosh."

I let my ears do the seeing. There was a rustling of burlap when Ghosh put an object inside. I heard a click of his walking stick on the stairs and then there was silence.

I waited a full minute. "That's enough," I jumped at last. "I don't want my hair shorter."

"Wait, I'm almost done."

"What are you doing?"

The barber looked at me. I was strapped to a chair in a white shroud. "I'm cleaning up behind your ears. Be still or you'll get a nick."

"What's left of my hair?"

"I have to taper off your neckline. Then I'll blend in the clipper section. Why are you asking?"

I hadn't tipped him before. Among other things, I was too young to tip. This time I gave him a crisp note from the books of a teller. The barber put his instruments aside and released me. I donated the rest of my money to Rita and fled.

I ran across the stairs into a heavy sun outside.

The barber's clipper felt raw on my neck. There was virgin skin above it. The sun pricked my ears with fresh heat. Meanwhile the streets were empty. Ghosh had melted in the sun.

After five minutes I reached a string of bookstores. Most of them were closed. Salesmen sulked at the counter. Everyone was pissed with work.

I lounged around the bookstores watching people come and go. The ones with money didn't have time. A few people took pity and glanced through old books on sale. But they had empty pockets. Small groups of neighbours gathered in pyjamas to discuss the weather.

A tiny teashop was balanced between two bookstores. The shops fell over each other. Debangshu Ghosh was sitting inside one of them.

When I looked closer, I saw he was inside the teashop. The man was sipping tea under a black awning. He drank from a ridged glass. His tea was milky even from a distance.

The awning's cover kept him hidden. But his shadow gave him away. The other walkers were stout. They fed on fried crumbs and oil. Ghosh's stick mixed well with the crowd.

The owner of the tea shop looked happy. He stopped smiling once in a while to address fresh demands. The batter was wiped with a dirty towel. The men sat huddled around their food. Licking their fingers with pleasure, the old men nodded at each other. Wattles on their necks went erect with every slurp. Their lips were hard and tight. It was a noisy orgasm.

I looked around the pavement. A flying cart pimped fresh sugarcane juice in a corner. I quickly ordered a glass for myself.

I leered at the sack which Ghosh carried. Meanwhile the vendor pressed a long stalk of sugarcane. The sack was coiled up next to Ghosh. It sat like a faithful dog near his feet. The body was built with a dense woven fabric. It had grown a belly since I saw it last. Whatever Rita had given him, it had fused well.

The eaters took their time. When at last Ghosh came out of the awning, I was three tumblers down. Any much longer, I would have puked into the gutter.

Debangshu Ghosh entered an overgrown park. There was no real cover, so he sat on a bench near the side. A large football field was strewn untidily across the centre with patches of grass. Its balding edges were lined with trees.

I hid behind the gnarls of a crooked acacia and watched him from the pavement.

I sweated a little. Maybe my scent triggered an unpleasant memory. That's what I thought when a troop of dogs gathered around me. They looked vicious.

The dogs barked loudly but I showed them a finger. That shut them up. I kept looking at the bench.

Mr. Ghosh rested with fatigue. He parked his head on the backrest. With his cere half open, he gulped in air. Sometimes he jerked and sat up straight, thrusting his neck forward. He looked around adjusting his parallax, bobbed west and east, and then reclined again.

"He's a pigeon in a human suit," Shibu said.

"Go, get him," I whistled. I stood outside the park on a pavement. The pavement was lined with stray dogs. But the dogs weren't interested.

They sniffed and snorted falling over themselves. I had to kick them away when they came too close. A couple of fragile specimens fled, but the others howled like a rebel outfit.

The dogs were powerfully built. They looked bigger than the strays I'd seen in the neighbourhood. Bushy tails swayed to their gambrels. Their muzzles were square. Scissors hung from them at a sharp angle. The ears were pointed like horns.

"Talk of the devil," Shibu said when I told him but it wasn't funny.

Tanned with saddles, and masked in black and brown, the rebels moved in a pack with their jaws showing.

I thought I should make peace with them. Accordingly I whistled a friendly song. Nothing happened. There were bubbles in my mouth. Then I made baby sounds. They barked again.

I bent down and touched their bellies. I tried to tickle them. All I produced were stiff ridges of hair. The ridges showed up on their hides. It was scary.

"Were their tails high?" Shibu asked me.

"Yes."

"Were their heads level? Canines bared?"

"Yes, yes."

"Then you must have pissed them off."

There was a collective tremor on the pavement. Alpha hides shook, my hands shook, and the air was thick with adrenaline.

"You should've run, stupid."

They drove me out anyway. I felt their teeth snapping at my ankles. The growls echoed in my ears like a receding storm.

First I let them scatter. Then I did a quick U-turn and walked ahead. It was a large park. There had to be other ports of entry.

I sailed around looking for a kink in the mainland. After five minutes I spotted a bruised wicket gate in a corner. It was hidden in creepers through a sudden break in the wall. The wicket looked unused.

I looked inside. The heat had driven all life away. The park was tranquil like a dead animal. Its grassy skin lay uprooted in large patches, replaced by a layer of ochroid earth powder.

The bench was empty. Mr. Ghosh was gone.

I sidled past the padlock, down a gravelled path leading to the benches. The path was sprinkled with cigarette butts, plastic and paper. The playground was to my left, and on my right, beyond a forested column, was the outer wall of the park and then the road.

The street dogs hadn't entered the mainland yet. A spire-peppered fence, rising above stock grids on the outer wicket gates had checked their entry.

Peering at the soft turf under my feet, I searched for clues. A layer of dust clung to the topsoil. It was mixed with banished half stones, forming a line of fine granule on the path.

Fifteen minutes later I found a piece of cord on the ground. The cord was thick. It was coiled around a pebble.

It took some effort to uncoil it. Once I had shaken its inertia, the elastic went limp. It rolled up indolently in my hand. A faint inscription on its face bore a name.

I put it around my waist. It formed a belt on my hips and held snugly. The band was flashy. Pieces of stretch cloth hung from the cord, ripped, like moulted snake skin. Underwear briefs maybe?

The cloth smelt funny. I sniffed some more until I could smell traces of ammonia and detergent. I caught a whiff of booze too.

I slid my pants down. I tugged my jocks off and slit its throat with a splinter. The cut was minor but the elastic escaped. It flew like a catapult. I fingered the broad cord in my hand. The texture was wet. I kept looking until I found a gash.

The mark was clear. It wasn't a razor's swipe. Nor was it the hack of a penknife. I kept kink out of it. Claws?

Or was it a human being?

Nails were delicate. They chipped easily. But they could be filed to ruthlessness.

Suddenly I caught a movement. Something moved near the corner of my eyes. It came from the bushes.

When I looked again, the bushes didn't move. The earth hurled along its orbit. It was a bright Sunday morning. Everything was normal.

But there was someone around.

I tiptoed across the walkway. The outer wall served as a bed for my spine. I moved through the perimeter towards the spot. When I was close but not too much I climbed a low branch. Through a cluster of dry leaves there loomed a clearing. It was a sudden burst of soil.

Mr. Ghosh was on his knees. He nursed a wound in the ground.

His magic basket lay deflated behind him. The sack was ten feet from my hypotenuse. It was crushed under the weight of a small power drill, a bolt and a wing-nut. The nut had a tall head and helical ridges around its diamond.

With cupped hands Ghosh cleared a hole in the ground. There was a pile of earth behind him. Next to the pile was a beheaded shovel. Its blade was balanced on the pile. The metal scoop was tanned with fresh mud. Next to it was his walking stick.

Walking stick my arse.

Mr. Ghosh didn't need a walking stick. The long handle of the shovel was dismantled. It was disguised as a stick.

Debangshu Ghosh was a common gardener. He was digging a ditch in the park. I could buy his story. It was a commissioned job. Did he want an approval? I could sign it if that's what he wanted.

I loved his little touches. His fingers pinched the dirt. Something was inside the hole. He twisted the object to make it loose and then he heaved. Nothing happened.

He got off his knees. The hem of his *lungi* was soaked. Mr. Ghosh touched the gunny bag. Some of its surface came out and then slipped back inside. It was a quick movement.

He slid his arm further in and fingered the cross stitch. A room was ready for the new guest. The hole in the ground produced a dazzle of white under his shovel.

Ghosh scraped the hole in a hurry. The more he scraped the bigger the hole became. Some of the edges came up. They were round and white. Then they got bigger.

The branch (where I sat) creaked under my weight. Ghosh would be out of the park in five minutes. He would take the white edges with him.

I came off the bark and checked the outer wall of the park. There were ledges on it but the wall had thorns. One could scale it with iron gloves. I didn't have any. The peak had pieces of splinter.

I made a dash for the far-end wicket. I ran a few steps and then the blinding sun hit me. It was a lot of distance to cover in the open. Damn.

When I crept back to the wall, I hit a pebble along the hedges. As it turned out it wasn't a mistake. The pebble struck a metal surface.

I flew blindly towards the sound. There, I met another wicket gate. The line of bushes hid me well. Finally I reached a broken pavement outside. The path was firm but it ended up in a dead lane. I found myself in a corner butted by houses on all sides.

I kept my head low and crawled through the pavement. The asphalt kept breaking in chunks. I patted the footpath. All of a sudden a cat came my way. It stood right on my face. I patted it too.

But the cat was no use to me. So I picked it up and hurled it over the wall. I heard its indignant hissing on the other side. Mr. Ghosh squealed. I let them get acquainted.

Ahead of me there was a mansion. It had false pillars bearing a facade. I looked at the columns until they looked crooked. Lumps of paint were congealed on their curves. The painting was done in a hurry. Lifting a chunk of bitumen from under my feet I smashed it against the gate. The gate had a kiosk attached to it. It made a big hit.

A security guard rushed out of the kiosk. He had a stick in his hand. The spotted cat may have been his. He looked as if he missed it. I picked up a larger lump of pitch this time and sent it flying. It slapped his jaw hard.

When I bent down to repeat, the guard sprang into action. He came like an arrow out of the gate. I chucked the piece of concrete across the wall but I didn't hear it land. It must have dropped on the sack of hessian. Good, that meant Mr. Ghosh hadn't left.

When the gate-keeper looked good to strike, I took to my feet. Making my way through the wicket gate I ran back into the park. The man followed me faithfully. I was hoping he would.

I took off Shibu's t-shirt while I ran and dashed towards the digging site. The guard held his jaw and followed me. When I was close enough I pitched the garment like a tent on my head. It hid my face while I headed straight for Mr. Ghosh. He stood in the same spot. He was glaring at the cat when we arrived. I saw his *lungi* through the thin threads of Shibu's bodysuit.

Using Ghosh as a centre piece I ran around in circles. The security man didn't get tired easily. He traced my motion arc for arc until we were caught in a centrifuge. A few rounds later we fell out of orbit like lost stars. I scuttled into the field and reached the other end. I waited while the sun hit my bare back and chest.

The guard gathered momentum. He closed down the distance quickly. Recovering my breath I darted in the opposite direction. He almost bumped into me. In a reckless attempt to turn on the run, he lost his footing.

I think he sprained his ankle. He fell on the grass. His feet wouldn't move. There was pain on his face. I tried to help him get up. He tossed his stick but he missed me by a yard.

The chase began all over again. This time it was much slower. By the time we returned to the digging site, both the cat and Mr. Ghosh had abandoned the park.

The piece of cord was gone too.

I wanted to check the hole in the ground. But the guard wouldn't let me. I ran out of the park into the safety of the road. I dispatched his stick to his office address. It hit the kiosk this time. There was a small crack on the glass cover where the stick landed.

Out of his sight, I pulled my vest out and wore it like a winner.

*

5

A Hole in the Ground

I reached the house in five minutes. I jogged half the way until my breath lasted. I draped myself over Shibu's small bell. Strands of cobwebs flew into my eyes.

But I should have left Shibu out of it.

It's funny. Somewhere along the yellow wall of our compound, before I went in through the gate, I actually considered digging the hole myself. Without Shibu's help. It would have saved me trouble. I wouldn't be wearing a beard today. God, how it itches when the river swirls at high tide.

Shibu's aunt came out with a comic book. When she wasn't being a bitch, Miss Shelley read bubbles and coloured strips.

"What's the matter? Is someone dying?"

In many ways Shelley was a piece of cake. But she was well baked.

At first she was easy to read. Ramrod straight spinster with oval-glasses at the neck; pursed lips and a frown; brow furrowed in eternal distaste; saris too starched to be comfortable. Every time she looked at me, I thrust my chest out and squeezed my belly. Sometimes I even stood at attention. She did that to you. She was that sort of a woman.

Yet she liked being a woman. Once every decade, I noticed her doe eyes behind thick horn-rimmed glasses. Her eyes were lined with *kohl*. They were sparkling. The austere edges of her face assumed an attractive boniness. Her neck was suddenly very slim. Some days, I even forgave the line on her lips.

But a decade is a long time. One had to bear her in between. Shibu hated Shelley. So did I. She was easy to hate.

Shibu's father seldom spoke to her when he came back. He didn't speak much anyway, unless he was drunk. He liked being drunk. It gave him a hysterical cheer. Sometimes he sang songs to his bottle and soused himself to sleep.

It was his house. He could do what he wanted. But Shelley was a trespasser. She had forgotten to leave.

We all have a story. I needn't get into all of that now.

"Please ma'am! Please!" I said to Shelley.

"Please, what? What do you want?"

"Please could you call Shibu? It's an emergency."

"He's sleeping."

Balls he was sleeping. Shibu doesn't sleep. Shelley almost shut the door on my face. But I pushed my way inside. I went straight to Shibu's room.

Shibu's flat was painted in yellow with big brown patches near the wiring. The interiors were brightly lit. The door led to a dusty shoe rack and swerved left towards a medium-sized sitting room with *batik* cushions around a television set. The T.V. was preserved carefully in a plywood cabinet with sliding doors. Years later, it was still brand new. It was one of those sets. They don't make TVs like that anymore.

A locked bookcase was pressed against the opposite wall. Wicker cane chairs with sunflower smiles held the *batik* cushions deep in their crotches. The bulging cushions sagged under them. To the right, a wooden dining table balanced an empty casserole and wax fruits in a uterus-shaped bowl. No one ate the fruits.

On either side of the bookcase there were two rooms. One was large and spacious. It was the master bedroom. Shibu's parents slept there when they slept together. The other bedroom belonged to Shelley. It was small and tidy, next to a balcony with three money plants. I'd never been inside the bedrooms.

The balcony was a narrow strip of tiles. It was always wet. There were pink bars which served as a trellis. Puddles of water played on the floor.

A high glass-topped table served as a feeding site for Surjosekhar, Shibu's brother. The table looked over the hanging money plants. The kitchen was on the other side. It was unusually large. The entire mezzanine was built around the kitchen.

Shibu's father Shushobhon trashed his bathroom with ripped tissue paper when he was home. He squeezed tubes of shaving foam near the basin. It looked like a toad's back. I felt sick in the bathroom so I washed my hands in the kitchen. It was a mammoth kitchen. Each time I came out of it, the apartment looked like a waiting room built as an afterthought.

Sturdy high-back chairs with buttoned arms were placed around the glass table. The table was in the centre. An imposing chesterfield in dark leather was set aside for Surjo. Shibu's mother would point at the traffic downstairs through the balcony. She made him eat his *Cerelac*. The glass on the table was cracked along the edges from Surjo's banging spoon.

The walls were largely bare except brown patches in the wiring and four picture-frames. The pictures stood above a Cavendish banana. The fruits were made of wax. They were kept near the casserole. The picture frames were set in a diamond on the wall. They didn't have people in them. Four large German Shepherds snarled, bristled, lolled and chewed, respectively.

Surjo was terrified of the pictures. He trembled past the wall and rushed into his chesterfield. The casserole was always empty. No one used the table anymore. The shepherds had it to themselves.

"Why do you have the frames?" I asked Shibu once. It made no sense. The dogs looked common.

They needed to cover the wall with *something*, that's what Shibu said.

Beyond the table under the picture frames was a short passageway that led straight into a bathroom. The brothers shared the bathroom. It had a high floor. I think the toilet was crooked like the rest of the mezzanine and the high floor was just a bluff. There were two cabin rooms at right angles to the passage, Shibu's and Surjo's.

Surjo had the first cabin. He seldom used it. Demons tried to choke him when he was alone in his room. A wall cabinet was embedded in the passage with stored pieces of silver. Shibu's door had a curtain.

When I walked into Shibu's room he was hiding behind a pile of clothes. I looked over his shoulder. There was a diary. I don't know what he wrote, I didn't ask him, but he penned his words carefully.

A little notebook lay on his lap. He wrote with his tongue out.

I remembered what Sebastian said in his father's apartment. "He's so futile. One day someone will just kill him."

"Come with me, quick," I told Shibu. "It's about Mr. Ghosh."

I slapped his diary shut and brought him up to speed. Shibu kept sniffing while I spoke. I tore a few sheets from his notebook and wiped his nose. I kept the torn pages with me in my pocket.

Shibu parted his lips to speak but I dragged him out of bed and took him to the road.

I scanned his face carefully when we reached the park. I couldn't say if Shibu recognized the spot. His features didn't betray anything.

When I finished, Shibu mumbled something about hidden objects. There was a list kept under his mother's bed. He said he knew the park well but I cut him off.

I didn't hear a word he said.

*

We didn't need rain but we got it anyway.

First we popped a balloon in the sky. It floated over our heads and then we pumped it. The balloon filled up quickly. It got big as a cloud.

Shibu met me on the roof with his almond nails. We waited for the right moment and pop went the balloon. The sun-dried city showered in the open.

Shibu said, "Let's go."

I looked at the road below. The tram-lines were covered in mud.

"It's mucky."

Shibu didn't care. He led the way later that evening, squelching a sea of filth beneath his feet. "Ok, here's what we do," he said at the wicket gate. "We'll work the dogs."

And then he walked away into the darkness.

I'm not scared of dogs. I avoid the louder ones or I whistle them away. But I didn't want to meet them at night.

"Bastard," I said scowling at the infinite darkness. "I should have pushed him off the roof when he was high."

A few minutes later Shibu returned with a broken sheet of iron.

The cattle guard at the wicket was slippery. A few bars had come loose, rolling like wind chimes in the mud.

"I need your help," he said.

The tablets on the ground were wide apart. Shibu managed to execute a long jump with a small run-up across the grid. He landed in an infant ox bow lake on the other side. Instantly he exploded in sludge.

"Fuck this mud."

"What now?"

"Pass me an end, bimbo."

I putted the short end of the iron sheet towards him. Shibu fixed it on the ground with pieces of brick.

"You do the same."

I found a heavy cinder block and dumped it on the spot.

"Now get the dogs."

The sheet was spread like a bridge over the cattle grid. "Why the red carpet?"

"Because dogs walk on their toes, dumbass. They'll slip through the grid. Now go fetch them."

I told him frankly that I wouldn't be able to get the dogs.

Shibu snorted. "Fine, sister. You sit here and pick some berries."

I stood in a corner and waited for things to happen.

The drizzle returned. There is nothing worse than fine, misty rain. Droplets fell on my head like drugged gnats.

I took my handkerchief and placed it on my head. Raindrops slipped from leaves above and tickled my neck. I slapped them hard and pulled the veil lower.

Shibu came back with the dogs. They stood in a line behind him. He looked at me and grinned.

"Forgot your umbrella, sister?"

"We need a boat. The park's flooded." The rain grew heavier still. Gusts of wind swept through the forest floor.

"I feel like Noah."

I can't identify dogs or other animals in darkness. My vision isn't perfect once the sun sets. The dogs looked identical. I couldn't tell one from the other.

"They look like a family."

But the pack ignored me. They moved in a stupor drugged by Shibu's charm.

The park looked different at night. The storm hid the landmarks completely. The football field had turned into a continental shelf. A bunch of sea monsters played on the field.

There was a path around the bushes. It was ravaged by stones. The gravel withdrew into its depths. An abyss of darkness had sunk the walkway.

The downpour intensified until we couldn't see three feet ahead of us.

"Should we go back?"

Shibu's face lit into a smile.

The dogs waded in the water uncomfortably. My eyes were useless in the rain. It kept streaming down my glasses.

Suddenly a whip cracked. Shibu heard it too. It came from somewhere on our right.

Through a curtain of water, there was some shaking. The bushes grew restless. A tree shook and fell on the ground. It was a young plant. The shriek was terrible.

I jumped.

"Ha ha ha." Shibu's voice flew like an unpleasant bird. "You're such a pussy, just like your father!"

I turned my head. Shibu stood behind me.

The rain was plated with silver. A curtain of water stood between us.

"Did I tell you? Tiptoeing around our flat. I jumped on him."

It was true. My father snooped around. But that was a different matter.

"He rolled down the stairs!"

The dogs howled at a gust of wind. They sprang forward with their noses on the ground. The moment passed.

It went uneventfully. I unclenched my hands.

We hold ourselves back all the time. But no one gives me any credit.

Prodded by an old instinct, the dogs lunged at the young uprooted tree. The storm ignited their senses. Twigs and branches crumbled under them. I heard the crunching of soft bark as it snapped through its centre. I closed my eyes for a moment. Not that it made much of a difference.

I'm looking at my diary as I write this. It's not an elaborate entry. I haven't written much about the night, which is strange. What I have done, I've drawn pictures along the margin. I can see the park. I can't draw very well but it doesn't matter.

The details are lost. Names of things and places, or effects of human actions elude me. But I remember *images*. The hand-drawn forms of Shibu under a halo. A pack of dogs at his feet. They speak strongly.

I'm glad I drew the pictures out.

When I opened my eyes, Shibu had unwrapped his windcheater. He looked like a god. It covered his synthetic head in a halo. The hood glistened like shiny paper.

The dead stalk floated along the submerged trail. Finally it careened into Shibu's knees and ran aground. Shibu raised a majestic hand.

I picked up the trunk and rowed my way forward. The oar got entangled in the littoral mass of stone and rubble. The forest floor was heavy. As a result our progress was painfully slow. The gravel on the ground, along with the lining of fine granule had come alive in a secret pact. They nibbled at our feet like piranhas, biting sharply through our canvas shoes. The darkness breathed life into dead objects around us.

I looked around the sides of the park. The boundary wall was struggling to keep its head up. On the unfavourable end of the slope, it barely raised its shoulder above the high water mark.

A few dogs became frisky near my feet. Strong, down-sloped winds quickly turned into a squall. New winds rushed into fjords of rock and slush.

"Can you see anything?" Shibu called out to me smiling like a deep-sea pirate.

Then the drizzle grew into a full-bodied torrent, stalling us completely.

Wet to the bone, the lead dogs snapped at everything that moved underwater. Paper cups and cigarettes hovered like particles in a giant washbasin. We stood in a huddle unable to move. One of the dogs caught a cold. It sneezed so much that we were covered in sediment.

"Let's move under the trees."

Shibu shepherded his flock away. In the middle of the cluster, there was a hollow trunk. We snuggled like worms around it.

Shibu spread out his arms. The dogs moved in closer.

I felt the putrid breath of strays on my body.

"Let's go to the bench."

I had to scream above the storm.

Finally the rain was on my face. I was glad. The water washed the smells away. My ribs were moist from rubbing against their coats. There were fleas on them. The fur chafed my skin.

Meanwhile I got stuck in a pit. There was a deposit of mud inside. It was sticky and refused to let go of my feet. I couldn't move unless I yanked them off the ground like a magnet.

When I arrived at the first bench, I took off my shoes. I spread them out and washed the bits of smothering mire that clung to them like memories.

Poising myself on the backrest, I looked at the vast stretch of marshland that separated us from the digging site. I let the rain fall on my head. It cooled me down.

Shibu joined me five minutes later.

"Want a puff?"

"No, thanks. I'm enjoying the breeze."

He slid his hand into his gabardine. "I don't mind another. It's stuffy." He looked for an unfinished joint in his pockets. The glossy twill on his thigh reacted like a reptile. Shibu's clothes were shining with wet fur. The dogs, on the other hand, borrowed Shibu's twill. Their hides were covered in fibre. It was a fair exchange.

Shibu protected his stick from the rain and stroked it with his fingers.

The dogs were restless. They stood around a cluster of trees as if they were tied up. They wanted to move.

"I'm sorry about the incident with your father," Shibu said thinly. "I couldn't resist it."

Next he produced one of those lighters that come in shades of yellow and pink. He juggled the plastic case before snapping it with his fingernail. The spark flickered and lit the cheap frame.

"Believe me, Sandy, it was *so* funny," Shibu said. "He was so funny! He looked like a clown in the stairway!"

The stiff blue flame shone like a beacon in the inky darkness. Shibu exhaled a new cloud of smoke. It smelled suspiciously like the last one.

"I tried it once before," he said twirling the stick between his fingers, "with Surjo. It didn't turn out as funny though." He took another puff, a long deep puff that came out through his nostrils and ears. The half joint in his hand sagged under its own weight.

"You've met Sulaiman, haven't you?" he asked me suddenly. "Sulaiman the tailor?"

"You took me to his shop."

"He gave me a fucking blue diamond."

Shibu started tapping the earth with his feet. I stared at him. Eventually he found a manhole.

"But I hid it! Shhhh, don't tell anyone."

There was a garden hose at the far end of the wall. Tracing the rubber for some distance, I found a nozzle. A few strays became interested and trotted up to me. I pulled the hose off the ground and took it to the manhole. The dogs followed me. I picked up the brass phallus and covering its mouth with a dab of my thumb, I let the pressure grow. Just when the dogs came close, I let my thumb go.

The strays froze on their tracks. I could see the fear on their faces. That felt good. Their snouts quivered like fishtails.

"Will you stop being a dick!" Shibu screamed.

I put the hose down.

"Revenge."

Directing the pipe towards the manhole cover, I rinsed the crust on the lid. Thick needles of water cleaned the grates on it. The fragments came off like a coat of paint.

"Now we need a crowbar," Shibu said.

"I'll look for it underwater."

"I'll help you."

Shibu wrenched me to the ground. In a few seconds, my head was buried in the marsh.

"There's the mud pack you've been looking for," he said.

"Fuck you."

Shibu gave me another clean jerk and sunk my body. When I raised my head after a full minute, my head was throbbing.

I washed my face in the brown water and then I stood up. "I know where to find a crowbar."

It would fit his neck. Between his gullet and the wind pipe.

"There's a stretch of wall on the other side. It has a hooked iron fence. Some bars were loose this morning."

I eyed the prominence on his thyroid.

"Then what are you waiting for?"

I swam to the other end. I unhooked a bar from the fence.

It was a powerful instrument. A brutal death. It could kill the way it was designed.

But I was a pussy. I gave the bar to Shibu. He secured the hook to one eyehole of the disc and ordered me to bring another. When I returned, he'd lifted one side of the cover.

"It's bloody tight."

I fastened the second bar to the manhole. My pull was weaker than his. The plate got stuck in the opening. Shibu wedged his bar in and levered it at his end. Then he came to my side and pulled the bar up.

"Let's do it together."

We pierced our crowbars into the cover and heaved. The disc moved but it didn't come off.

"On the count of three. One...two...three...pull!"

With a rapid burst of clicks and clangs, like the whistling of whales, the lid succumbed. A black pit stared at us from below. We drove the water into its depths. I recovered some fallen branches and swept the collected flotsam into the manhole. A few minutes later, we could see the wet earth where we stood.

"You know the general area, yes?"

"Around here." I marked a large plot of land.

"Why didn't you mark it?"

"I was chased out of the park."

Shibu inspected the area. He walked around the forest floor, tapping the earth with his feet. Suddenly, as if by magic he walked right into it.

The spot was intact. Shibu had found it.

He promptly set to work. With loud whoops he rolled on the ground. His feet were up. Then he crawled among the dogs and made barking sounds.

"What the hell are you doing?"

"I'm trying to be one of them."

"Why?"

"I'm training them to dig, stupid."

The dogs didn't know that. A great silence fell upon us. I roamed around the benches to fix the spot. Shibu made frantic gestures with his hands, mimicking the act of lifting mud. The dogs looked at him curiously but they didn't move.

"Trust me," he said looking at my face, "I've done this before."

"What do we dig with?"

Shibu took out an antique dessert spoon from his pocket. It was made from a sheet of dull silver.

He looked at the spoon and then at the row of dogs next to him. Suddenly he started gyrating.

The dogs stood up.

Leaping a few inches off his bottom, Shibu called out to them to absorb his infection.

The dogs retreated into a huddle.

It was pathetic to see him like that. Shibu behaved like an idiot. When I feel guilty about his death, I remember these incidents and feel better.

"Damn the fucking muck," Shibu wailed, winching his spoon up from the mud.

"Yes, I noticed. No shoulders." I pointed at the naked stem of the spoon.

Shibu pounced on a second set of dogs. This time he tossed the spatula into the forest.

Nothing happened. He looked expectantly at the dogs. No one moved. Wilting a little, he rushed into the trees himself.

A few dogs turned away.

There was a rustling of wet leaves in the distance. Shibu rummaged through the forest howling like a mad bitch. "I found the fucking silver!"

It was a sturdy spoon with a wide grip and a short, curved thread. The bowl was busty. Two closely spaced arabesque ribbons ran along its length across both edges of the stem. The relief shell lay at the end of the handle, faintly crested with a nude damsel. She held a thistle in her hands.

"You can't dig a hole with a naked woman."

"Watch me."

The damsel worked like a dream. The earth was soft. She stripped it bare in no time. Someone pulled a carpet from under her feet. The dogs joined in the digging with a flurry of sludge. Shibu twirled his wrists and whipped the hole like cream.

It was a grand gravediggers' orgy. Man, woman and beast had come together.

Shibu lit a joint and passed it to me. The smoke was beautiful. The rings were slow and heavy like the stuff in my head.

"You've been here before, haven't you?" I asked him.

He looked at me. I sat on the wet grass and let a dog nuzzle my feet.

"I don't mind telling you. You're my friend."

"If you say so."

Shibu rubbed his nails together. "One time I picked up Renuka from the station. I put her luggage in the hostel and brought her here." He rubbed his nails again.

A small white moon shone on his thumb. Renuka Sharma was the girl with freckles. She went back home every few weeks.

"She was on my lap," Shibu said.

I was high too so I burst out laughing.

"Forget it. You're not interested."

"She was on your lap," I prodded. "Go on."

Shibu re-lit his stick. It smelt of decaying flesh. I took a few puffs from him.

"She wore an orange spaghetti. I wanted to haul it off like a bed sheet. She called it amber. But it was orange, a most disturbing orange." Finally he left his nails alone. "I almost gave it to her. But then I hid it. I buried it somewhere here. It was orange."

I remembered one Christmas night not very long ago. Renuka had winked at me among many others. Then she went into another room. My eyes followed her arched bottom. I went through the door, tearing her clothes down.

But it was in my head.

She returned with a drink a few minutes later. Her hair was disheveled from the dangers in the other room.

"Stop!" Shibu cried suddenly. "I see something."

He slid his fingers inside the fissure and extracted a wooden box. It was shaped like a casket. Shibu tapped the soft lining on its face. "What do you think?"

I leaned over the hole and inspected the object. The sides were tattooed with ornate *Madhubani* carvings. It had a burnt finish. The lid was hinged to the base with clasps.

"Open it."

"It's airtight. What can it be?"

"Just open it."

Shibu worked the clasps carefully. Nothing came out of the lid. The air was filled with detergent and booze. It smelled familiar.

Shibu looked inside a small compartment. He looked relieved and then he shut the box.

"He didn't get it. Let's go!"

"What?"

"It's still here."

Shibu shrieked like a madman and ran out of the park.

*

6

Lock and Key

*T*he next afternoon I walked into Shibu's class during my break.

His classroom was near the end of a long corridor, butted by an empty lecture hall and a Physics laboratory.

A senior pulled my collar and took me out. "Where are you going?"

"Shibu."

"He's by the window in the corner."

I went inside and waited for the boy to leave.

"Where's the box?"

Shibu was surprised. He didn't like me in college.

"Come back later."

"Just tell me what's inside it."

"A key."

"What key?"

"I don't know."

Shibu took a large barrel from his sling bag and placed it on the bench. Licked by a deep patina, it was attached to a bronzed key ring. The ring was large as a handcuff.

"That's it?"

Shibu nodded.

"Are you sure?"

"No, there was a genie in a bottle. I left it at home."

"Did you check properly?"

"I was up until daybreak turning the box around. I couldn't sleep."

"Why?"

"Surjo was crying."

They said Surjo wasn't normal. Ganesh the caretaker told me something was wrong.

Surjo's hands were wobbly. They fluttered like wings. He had a small head and tiny cold feet. As if someone put icicles under his socks. He spoke little and cried a lot.

"What's wrong with Surjo?" I asked Shibu one day on the roof of our building.

The large vacant terrace was littered with plants and a giant hoarding mounted on parallel poles. Shibshankar used the horizontal bars of the scaffold to do chin-ups early in the morning. His name had been etched on the parapet to mark his territory.

"What do you mean? He's alright." His arms were flexed on the bar.

"He's not like you or me."

"We're different."

Shibu was a regular boy. He couldn't show love. But he had a soft spot for Surjo. He bought sweets for him with his own money. Surjo's eyes glittered when the smell of coconut hit their flat.

"He can't even walk properly," I complained. "He needs to be fed, dressed, everything. He just sits there."

Shibu pulled himself up with his hands.

"He doesn't play with us. He doesn't go to school. Hell, he doesn't even look me in the eye."

"Fuck off."

He finished counting up to thirty and got off the pole.

*

"That damned Shelley...she must have switched boxes," Shibu said in his classroom.

I looked at the giant key on the bench. I didn't like the mention of Shelley. "Maybe Ghosh came back. There wasn't anything else in the box."

"Where did you keep it?" I asked.

"I didn't let it out of my sight."

"Where did you hide the box?"

"If you must know, foxy lady, I kept it in the cupboard."

"What cupboard? You don't have a cupboard."

"I'll bang your face in!"

I was angry as well. "I need to know why the fucking box is empty." I dragged my words out slowly.

"Your aunt has a habit of going through your stuff. She found porn in your boxers."

It was true. Shibu didn't deny it.

"I want you to think about last night. Remember the details." I leaned over his bench pressing him to a corner. "I want you to give me a fucking guarantee that Shelley didn't spy on you."

Shibu didn't say anything.

"Why are you protecting her?"

He put the key back in his satchel. "Why would she spy on me? She's not mad."

"She *isn't*? Why do you think she's alone?"

"That's enough."

One of his fingers came up. It was a warning. Shibu was threatening me.

In my head I pinned his hand to a wooden board. I flashed a torch over his fingernails till I saw his pale blood flowing.

"Ever heard of genes? Did it ever strike you why your brother is mental?"

I had spoken too much.

A stunned silence followed. I tried to break it but Shibu grabbed my collar. The collar was large and stiff. I didn't wear a tie to college.

My throat came in the way. He shook me hard. Shibu had large hands and my throat was small.

"I'm sorry," I said.

It sounded like a whimper. Shibu held on to my collar.

"I didn't mean it."

"Of course you meant it." His voice was low.

"Let me go."

"First you letch at Renuka and then you bitch about my family. *My* fucking family!"

He relaxed his grip slowly.

"You thought I wouldn't find out?"

"Find out what?"

I managed to breathe out.

"I know, alright. I *know*."

I wanted to hear it from his mouth.

A cloud passed overhead. The sun went out like a flame. I couldn't see his face properly.

I went to the wall and switched on a tube light.

"Sabbie told me this morning."

I looked at Shibu. I wanted to defend myself but it was no use. Sabbie had done his job.

"I'll see you in the house."

I walked out.

I paced down the corridor. The floor was smooth. Many feet had dragged on it that morning. There was no colour left.

I looked at the passage up and down but there was only distance. Sebastian wasn't there.

I decided to look him up.

*

Early that evening I was at Shibu's door. His aunt let me in.

"Let's see the key."

Shibu was sitting on the floor. His arms were wrapped around his legs. He produced the object and looked away.

"It looks really old."

I spoke loudly so he would hear me.

A forest burned around us. Shibu had a stick in his hand. It wasn't nice.

"And it's sticky to the touch."

"Like your dick."

Shibu stared sadly at a waste-paper basket. It had fallen cherries and tobacco in it.

"Look. I don't know what Sebastian told you..."

"I don't want to talk about her."

I looked at the key again. It whistled when I blew into its stem. The key looked bigger in the smoky room.

I suggested trying the annex of the building. A line of storage sheds hugged Mr. Ghosh's flat. They were never open.

"Those garages are owned by Mr. Ghosh. Why would he hide the keys?"

Shibu opened a window and let the smell out.

"But suppose Ghosh is hiding something? The sheds are locked. No one knows what's inside them. It makes a great hiding place."

Shibu picked up the key.

"This looks familiar. I've seen it somewhere."

He held the key against the light outside.

"Where?"

"If I knew, I would say it."

The smoke refused to leave the room. I cleared my throat.

"Maybe someone removed an object from the box."

"Shelley wouldn't do it."

"How do you know?"

"Quit the drama. Face it like a man."

"*You* be a man. Ask the bitch where she hid our stuff."

"Even if she did, she wouldn't tell me."

All of a sudden the doorbell pealed three times. I quickly hid the box under the bed.

Two minutes later Renuka Sharma breezed into the room. She looked lovely.

*

Shelley lurked behind the curtains. From where I sat near the bedpost, I could see her eyes peep inside the room.

Renuka smiled politely at Shibu. I knew there was something wrong.

Shibu yelled from where he sat: "Do you mind?"

"I'm cleaning your father's silver," Shelley said.

"Please go. I need some time alone."

"Ask your friends to leave. That would be a start."

Shibu took the box and hurled it at the curtain. The box fell on the floor.

63

"That's my box," Shelley said.

Shibu went to the door and picked it up. "Get out. Go!"

Shelley looked inside the room. A silver trophy dangled from her hand.

Renuka turned. Her hips were bare along the midriff.

"First your mother and now you," Shelley said bitterly.

I drew the curtain across the door. My hands were trembling. But Shelley didn't bite me.

"Charming woman," Renuka drawled in her thick voice.

I said - we'd been talking about her.

"Liar."

"No, I swear we were!"

"Bitching I bet."

I blushed. On an impulse I looked at my watch.

The time was right. It could be a special evening. I dragged the two of them out of the room.

We ran downstairs.

*

In the lobby, we stood outside the generator room. "We need your help," I said to Renuka.

She smiled.

"We are following a man. He's mixed up in ugly things. This key was hidden by him in a park." I took the barrel out of my pocket.

Renuka whistled like a girl.

"He leaves the house in exactly five minutes."

Shibu woke up suddenly. "I knew it! I told you I'd seen it somewhere!"

He pointed at a keyhole behind us.

I turned and faced the generator room next to the staircase. The door had a petite frame but the hole was large.

"Is it big enough?"

"I've seen Ganesh lock this room. He uses the same key."

I slid the key in and turned it to the right. The flap opened. I pushed the door inside.

"Well done!" Renuka cried.

It was pitch dark inside the room.

"Does anybody have a torch?"

"Stop being a sister."

Renuka giggled and went inside. She brushed my arm on the way. Shibu and I followed her in. Then the door shut behind us.

"I like this darkness," she said.

Using our hands to gauge the room we inched forward. A thicket of cardboard boxes was wrapped near the door.

"I feel an almirah," Renuka whispered.

I took a step towards her voice. My shoes landed on her feet.

"Sorry."

"Give me your hand. I'll show you."

I stretched my arms on either side. Renuka moved my fingers to a block of wood. There were small carvings on it.

"Can you feel the double doors?"

I did feel them.

"If you go up," she tweaked my wrist higher, "you can see the outline. But the glass is missing."

Shibu took a piece of cloth from the top shelf. He stood to my right. I felt his arm when he put the cloth in his pocket.

Renuka lifted my hand above her neck. It rested on her shoulders.

"It must be a book cabinet."

She stood in front of me. Her body faintly touched mine. I could smell her shampoo.

We stood a long time like that.

Shibu slid his hands inside the framework. "The top rows have collapsed. The edges are sharp."

He flattened the bulge in his pocket.

We groped in the dark looking for different things. My hands touched a hard cylindrical object. Shibu found a box in his wallet and lit a match.

There were pieces of bone scattered on the top shelf.

Renuka walked ahead. Before she could get to the cabinet, she hit a wall. Shibu lit another match.

It wasn't a wall. When the match blew out, there was darkness. A growing shaft of light came inside the room.

The back of the cabinet had a connecting door. The door was wide open. That's where the light came from.

Debangshu Ghosh stood in front of us.

I turned and fled.

But Mr. Ghosh caught sight of Shibu. He spat out his name. I heard his voice from the stairs.

It sounded like a curse.

*

7

On a Dark, Stormy Night

In hindsight, I find it strange that Shibu and I didn't discuss the incident in the generator room.

It may have been because Shibu's grandfather passed away the next weekend. He died in his sleep in Murshidabad. Shibu's mother was terribly upset. She was fond of the old man.

Bani Dasgupta was pretty when she smiled. She got married at a young age. Shibu didn't look like her at all, which was a pity. He could have been handsome.

Bani bustled around the house. But her eyes gave her away. There were bags under each of them. She was a tired woman.

When I walked home on aimless afternoons, I caught her sniffing money plants in the balcony. She clutched the pink bars like a caged animal.

I didn't know much about her past. She spoke about it only once. It was a day after Shibu's father left the city. The house wore the look of a dead circus. It always did after Mr. Dasgupta was gone.

Cartons and polythene bags were strewn around the flat. Surjo kicked cubes of thermocol in the kitchen. There was a feeling of joy in his movements. It was scary. Cigarettes were stubbed on the floor. The smell of nicotine hung heavy in the air. Plastic cups smeared with alcohol and ash had been stashed under tables.

Mrs. Bani Dasgupta made me a glass of *aam panna*. We spoke about green mangoes that day. She described her marriage to Shushobhon. "I was a brat," she said.

A slice of mango lay on her lap. She sucked on it dreamily and put the pulp on a steel plate.

"My father-in-law has lots of land. But my husband fought with him and left."

Shibu spoke a lot about his grandfather. He was an old comrade, well respected in his time.

"He got along well with Shibu. Old men love boys. I sent Shibu back to Murshidabad from time to time. Of course I didn't tell my husband about it."

I asked her what the problem was.

"They fought about money. In the end he threw my husband out. Shibu and I had to come away with him."

She sucked her mango wistfully.

Shibu's father, Shushobhon Dasgupta, ran a shady business. He spent a large part of his life abroad. He went to the Deccan coast, to the Gulf, to Southeast Asia, everywhere a small ship could take him. I heard he didn't stay in one place for long.

"They won't let him," Ganesh told me.

"He collects more than he sells," my father told my mother.

"He leaves his scruples at home."

"Mr. Dasgupta makes money that can't be made."

"Shushobhon is a smuggler."

I heard a lot of things. Everyone was jealous of him.

At the end of each quarter, Mr. Dasgupta returned home from his travels. They didn't lock the door when he came. Not that they needed to. I was the only guest. When I entered he gave me a red can of Coke or a bar of milk chocolate. The chocolates were chunky, made from honey and almonds. He didn't remember my name. "Here's one for you champ," he said. I liked him.

Meanwhile Shibu made sure he didn't bump into Mr. Ghosh. I hadn't been spotted in the generator room. He met me a few times in the porch without any reaction.

Debangshu Ghosh collected bones. Was he a museum thief? If he hid them, the bones must be valuable. But something else bothered me. Why was there a smell of detergent in the cabinet?

Shibu wasn't interested. He joined a local youth committee and made new friends. He came home drunk like his father. I met him on the roof every morning. He handed me pamphlets for distribution. "The party requires more students," he said. We spoke of this and that and then we left.

There was nothing else we could do. In our haste to escape from the generator room, we had left the key behind.

*

Mr. Dasgupta came home after months.

Normally I joined Shibu on the roof with a cup of coffee. But that day I spent the morning with Surjo. I read fairy tales from a book while Bani got dressed.

All afternoon I stayed away from the house. Later I went to Sabbie's apartment. I got my hair trimmed once everything was done.

When I returned, the bodysuit on my back smelled funny. I changed into my own clothes and finished what I had to.

I made sure nothing remained in the den. I was scared my father would find out.

When I came home again later that evening, Mr. Dasgupta had arrived. I wanted to see his gifts. He'd been away a long time.

I imagined him standing with a beer near the cushions. He was a large man with a mass of black hair. A thin moustache was pencilled above his mouth. His eyes were bright. They shone like buttons in the dark.

Mr. Dasgupta spilled an ounce of beer when he saw me. It fell on his belly and he wiped it off. He rushed to his wallet next to the ceramic bowl. His fingers went inside a leather pouch with a smell of linseed oil on the tips. Finally he handed me money from a faraway land.

He could do any of these things. It was all in my head.

When I reached the mezzanine however, the door wasn't open. I bumped into Renuka at the landing.

"What are you doing here?"

Her hair was cut short. She looked like a boy.

"Trespassers will be prosecuted?"
When she smiled, she looked alright.
I winked at her.
"I wanted to check on Shibu. He left college in a rush."
"Ring the bell."
"He's not at home."
I knew that already.
"There's a strong smell of alcohol here," she said sniffing.
"It's his father."
Renuka made a face.
"Yes I saw him. He leered at me until he saw Amit."
I turned around. Amit came out of the shadows in the kitchen door.
"Let's go."
Renuka turned and walked towards the stairs. Amit went with her.
I followed them down to the lobby.
We passed the generator room. "Isn't that the one?" Renuka asked me.
Amit looked at the door carefully.
"Can you open it?"
Amit had a black bag with him. He put it on the floor. Thick metal tubes glistened inside the zipper.
He peered into the bag. With his hands he searched through the instruments. Renuka looked over his shoulder.
In the end he produced a knife that could skin a crocodile.
"I'll slide this into the doorframe and unclasp the latch."
"This is not my bra," Renuka giggled.
Amit shoved the blade between the door and the wall.
"Give me a hand." He turned to me.
I gave him my hand.
"Push. We can free the tongue. The door will come off."
"Why are we doing this?"
"Loser!" Renuka thrust her chest out. She leaned into the bag and passed me a hammer. "Here, smash it away."
I stood frozen on the spot. My hands were unable to hold anything else.
"Relax, I was joking."
They laughed at me.
I was relieved. My palms were sticky. Luckily I had a piece of cloth.

"Come Amit, let's go."

She walked out through the collapsible gate.

Amit nodded and zipped up his bag. He looked at me before he left. I put my hand in my pocket.

They went off into the darkness. I was left alone in the porch.

*

Ganesh the caretaker came ambling in through the front gate. He carried vegetables in a vegetable coloured bag. His eyes were tired and sweating.

He looked over his shoulder at Renuka.

It was easy to identify him in a crowd. He was the man with a dirty smile.

"I went for fifteen minutes and you let her get away?"

The street was dimly lit. A few shops hung lanterns outside. Office people with attachés held their saucers with one hand. Renuka walked past them. Some of them took a second look.

"What a fine pair," Ganesh said looking into the distance. "What did you do with them?"

"They didn't come for me."

"I hope Shibu had fun."

He wiped the sweat on his face.

"They've gone looking for him."

Renuka and Amit kept walking until I didn't know which was which. She wore pants like him. Hers were rounder but they walked next to each other. I couldn't tell the difference.

"Didn't Shibu *want* to see them?" Ganesh asked.

"Maybe he does but he isn't home."

"But I saw him."

I was surprised.

"Are you sure?"

"He came with a friend."

"Which friend?"

"I don't know," he said. "I haven't seen him before."

"Where are they?"

"They went to the roof. I heard them through the staircase."

"Are they still there?"

"I don't know. I went to buy groceries."

I went up to my flat. A sense of unease gripped me. I felt lonely. It kept growing on me.

I pressed a tube of dendrite in my den. I changed into a crisp shirt to hold the glue better. Its linen was full sleeved and spacious. The glue was quick. I didn't have time to measure my inhalations. I breathed in deeply and ran around the building, getting high.

I took a last look at the blue carbuncle in my hand. Shibu had given it to me. It looked as if it were contagious. I wrapped it in a clean cloth and went for a walk.

It was primetime Wednesday. Our cable connection was cut by the local guy. But he hadn't touched Doordarshan. Riding a small satellite, it pimped *Chitrahaar* in the streets. I fastened myself in front of the TV.

Fifteen minutes later, a violent storm broke out. My parents returned with a big umbrella. I was glad I was inside.

Window panes smashed against the wall. Papers flew like pigeons. My father rushed to switch the TV off and knocked a vase on the table. That brought my mother to the room.

"Get out of the way!"

I disappeared into my den. But she trapped me.

"Why haven't you closed the windows, stupid boy?"

"My files are soaking wet!"

Rain streamed inside the den. The water was doctored with fine grains of dust. Rags and discarded underwear were quickly draped under the window.

"We should have plastered this gap."

"It's leaking everywhere, what's the point?"

"Fill it in, fill it in."

"Don't just stand there!"

My parents tried to cover the house up. Meanwhile a tree got loose on the pavement. I saw its death from my window. It staggered and fell heavily, crashing a streetlight with it. The intersection was plunged in darkness.

The little bathroom shuddered in the storm. Chilling gusts of wind swept through our flat. My parents locked themselves in their bedroom. The rain came roaring in through an open vent in the kitchen, slamming the door repeatedly. A horde of noisy ghosts plundered our fittings in the dark.

I ran through the house and shut everything. The ghosts hid behind the curtains. I was careful to avoid them but my toe hit a wooden leg. A table toppled. Something heavy on it fell and broke. The sound was like an explosion.

Thankfully my parents didn't hear it. But my toe was on fire. I howled to make the pain go away. They didn't hear that either.

I limped to the kitchen to apply first-aid. There was nothing on the shelf apart from cold water. I couldn't see much in the dark. A large crack in the window let the storm inside. The curtains were limp and clung to the window. Its cloth flapped like flags.

Just when my ears were getting used to the noise, I heard a massive crash outside. The nest of capillaries above the building had snapped. Strangely no one else heard it.

I hobbled in pain up the staircase but I couldn't get far. Feeling the outer walls with my hands for support, I returned to the kitchen. The tap was placed high above the sink. I splashed some water over my feet. It made a mess on the floor.

I gave another ten minutes for the snapped capillaries to return. It was an elastic nest. It would roll back in time. Then I remembered Shibu on the roof. He must have heard the crash.

My toe felt better. I could walk without screaming. But I couldn't find a light anywhere. The windows on the stairway were either stained or missing.

I crawled upstairs. The staircase was like a waterfall. Rain came in through the missing glass. I assumed the roof was flooded already. Someone must have left the terrace door open.

I lost my footing several times but I didn't give up. I inched towards the melting glacier upstairs. When I reached, some of the distant street lamps were coming back and the space was suffused with a smoky glow.

The rain stopped suddenly. But Shibu wasn't on the roof. No one was.

I walked into the wet flooring of the terrace. A few familiar objects were lying on the ground. I picked up the ones I needed. A few others were useless so I let them be.

A line of dead plants lay near the parapet. They looked like human corpses. Shrivelled leaves and pieces of earth hid under the giant hoarding. The soil smelled funny.

The plants were difficult to distinguish. It was very dark near the corner. Besides, the broken pots were submerged in the roof. Two heavy metal poles lay above them.

Our giant hoarding had collapsed.

I saw Shibu's battered head peep out from under the hoarding. The whole mass had crumbled above him. Pieces of steel rolled on the ground.

Shibu did not blink. His mouth was slightly open. His face looked ugly.

I preferred him alive, I think.

*

The I-beam had collapsed on the roof. Shibu was dead.

I waded slowly to the centre of the terrace and identified Shibshankar's skull. His eyes were half closed. The hair on his head clung to their roots like seaweed.

I removed the flanges of iron from his chest. His ribs and groin were crushed by the sudden weight of the web. A piece of paper flew away. His empty jockeys were in his pocket. Bits of frame and plywood facing were strewn across his limbs.

The flooring of the roof sloped northwards. The water hadn't collected in Shibu's spot except in asymmetric puddles. There was a trail of blood all the way to a low wall where the drainage holes were embedded. Some of the blood had pooled around Shibu's body. Eventually it seeped through the porous adobe.

*

The iron poles had stood near a corner of the terrace. There was a low wall running around the roof. It was low enough to peep over. The hoarding above it pulled traffic on the road.

The large painted face of a lady lay sprawled across the turf. She sold luxury soap with a smile. She was the only one smiling. I felt like breaking her teeth.

I hadn't seen that part of the wall in years. It was hidden behind an iron joist. When I was ten I would crawl under the web and pretend that I was a caveman. The parallel beams had a low stair which made the parapet unreachable. But it didn't matter anymore. The sides of the roof had collapsed.

I could walk into air if I wanted. There was nothing to hold me back.

The surface had ruptured in the corner and gravity had done the rest. The place looked like a landslide. I saw a few lit windows in the distance. There was a hint of movement. It was nice to see life around.

Someone came and shut a window pane. I saw him clearly. His silhouette was outlined through the light.

I stooped over the broken parapet. Maybe Ganesh had come into his backyard? I knew he killed chickens in the dark. The rain would help him clean the blood.

The flagstones below were very still. There was no movement. Ganesh wasn't in his backyard. His door was wide open.

Then I saw Shelley downstairs.

I looked at her closely. My glasses came in the way so I wiped them dry.

Shelley was lying lifeless on the ground. Her head was crushed. A large section of the wall lay in fragments beside her.

While I kept leaning near the parapet, unable to take my eyes off the scene, I heard Surjo. His voice came from a window. It seemed a thousand miles away.

I wished to god he would stop crying.

*

PART 2

ANIMUS, THE MIND

8

Away

*M*y parents sent me away.

I was sitting in front of a muted television set. A sports show bored the crap out of me. It featured many balls of many colours. I quietly watched them bounce on TV.

My mother said to my father: "He's too young. He should go stay elsewhere."

She spoke to him as if I wasn't there. In some ways I wasn't.

I was wandering through a thicket with cardboard boxes. There was a smell of detergent around the bones. A large foam mattress was swathed in blood.

"What do you mean?" my father said.

"He could stay with Rathikanta. It's a nice house with a big garden. Besides, he lives alone."

Rathikanta was a cousin of my mother's, twice or thrice removed. His house was farther removed. He lived in the suburbs almost an hour's drive away.

I'd met him a few times before. He dabbled in politics and party affairs but he was largely useless. The older son of a statesman, he ran for elections and lost every time.

As a result he spent most of his time reading books – old fat journals and books of history put together in a grand manifesto.

"Why does Sandipan have to go away?"

My mother looked at him. "I think you know why." Her bangles clanked on her wrist.

"But Rathi doesn't even go to the bureau office."

"He has clout with the police."

"On account of his brother!" my father sneered. He loosened his belt and re-grooved the leather strap around his waist.

Rathikanta's brother was a big man in the police. He had been promoted recently after a change in government. My father didn't like him.

My mother looked at me strangely. "He will be well protected in Rathi's house."

It was the next morning. They hailed a yellow taxi and dropped me off at a beautiful house. It was very far away.

Flowers were lined up in front like nursery children. They beckoned in many colours. The chrysanthemums were yellow. Some were starched white in the sun. A noose of bougainvillea hung near the driveway.

Our cab wasn't allowed inside the gate so I dragged my bag through the gravel.

Crows with fluffy heads pulled out twigs from their nests. Their homes were damaged in the rain. The birds swooped down towards my bag cawing uproariously. Their hungry eyes looked for food. It was a bad omen.

I looked at the big bungalow in front of me. No one was home so I checked myself in. My parents didn't get down from the cab. Rathikanta knew I was coming. He ran his house like a hotel.

I stood before a big block of white. It shimmered like an eggshell in the afternoon sun, balancing a storey on its head. The second floor was newly built. The edges of the rectangle were domed like a pyramid. I looked the whole thing over. This was the asylum to help me forget.

I waved my parents goodbye. Shibu's skull lay smashed on the road. His eyes fixed their gaze on me. I jumped when the wheels of the taxi rolled over him and then I ran to save his life. But it was too late. Shibu was dead.

My mother's cousin Rathikanta lived with his daughter. They lived alone with about twenty servants. The servants came with the house.

Rathi's daughter, Bobo, was a solemn girl with large, solemn spectacles. She was a couple of years younger than me.

Rathikanta was a forgetful man. He was seldom home. His mind stayed elsewhere. There was a vague smile on his face, tickled at a joke he heard in London many years ago. He didn't bother me much.

Bobo was always around. She called me for my meals every day, leading me out from the guest room to the dining hall. We got along well. She comforted me.

There were many open spaces within the house. The ground floor was divided into halls and sitting rooms. All the rooms had chandeliers on the ceiling. They hung like grapes. The servants lit the lights one at a time.

At sundown, the servants retired to their colony. They stayed in a separate building.

There were brown wooden panels on the floor. They were built to absorb sounds. I could hardly hear any footsteps in the house. It was very quiet when Bobo wasn't around.

The guest room where I slept was part of a new block in the rear. It was equipped with bulbs and tube lights. I was scared to switch them off.

One day I was reading a book in my room. I don't remember the name of the book. The binding was put together by a man with a long needle. The soft black ridge was shapely and comforting. While I stared at the cover, Bobo plonked herself on the edge of my bed.

"I heard about your friend. I'm sorry."

My mother told her. She called every night. Bobo gently stroked the hair on the bed.

I hadn't spoken about Shibu after his death.

"Last I heard from your mother, they got a death certificate."

I didn't understand.

There was some trouble with the police. Shibu's father had to pay good money to get it done.

I couldn't keep quiet any longer. "It wasn't an accident."

In those few moments on the roof, I looked closely at Shibu's body. Lifelessness was a scary thing. It took me a while to realize he wouldn't move. I wanted to kick his parts back to life like a broken TV.

I walked downstairs after that. I slipped and fell on the waterfall, rolling down the last few stairs, but I felt no pain. I was covered in bruises from the fall. The stairs was comforting. They took my mind off things.

I walked into my flat and told my parents. They went to the mezzanine and informed the Dasguptas. Or whatever remained of them. Then they held hands together and went upstairs to look at the bodies.

I stayed in my room. I screamed and screamed but I didn't make a sound. A silent film unspooled itself around my head.

No one asked me questions. I didn't tell anyone anything.

I could have told them a few things. I could've told them about the gash at his ulnar where his wrist was flaked in a bright red moss. I could've told them about a piece of paper that I took from Shibu's pocket. I had slapped his clothes and head but the blood that oozed out was fresh – like the trail on the adobe.

The mossy prism on his wrist had dried up. Someone had wiped it clean with ripped briefs and stuffed them in his pocket.

I dictated some of my notes. Bobo listened with a severe frown on her face but her eyes hugged me gently. She kept stroking the threads on my bed.

I understood.

Shibu had slashed his artery before the beam collapsed on him. That was the idea.

*

A fortnight passed. The rituals were over. Everything was brushed under the carpet.

I spent my days sitting with Bobo in the garden, drinking endless cups of coffee. Sometimes we watched the sunset together. The chrysanthemums were yellow but they weren't bad. I'd grown to like them.

"It's strange, isn't it?" Bobo said one day. "It's too much of a co-incidence."

I was tired. The hoarding crashed and fell in the storm. It fell on Shibu killing him instantly. Next it landed on a wobbly parapet and dislodged the roof. A huge chunk fell on Shelley who stood downstairs.

"Simple."

"Why was Shelley standing outside in the rain?"

Bobo was young and curious. It would pass.

She put a small hand on my shoulder.

"I'll help you."

A cluster of overgrown weeds swayed in the distance. The gardener was bitten by a snake near the boundary wall. The snake had a mottled coat according to the servants.

"Besides," Bobo said, "my uncle is in the Force. I've asked him for help."

Closer to where we sat, the lawn was consistent. The ends of Bobo's hair spilled into the grass. A hothouse loomed above us. To our right there were flowers with a violent rush of colour. The flowers ended in a muddy plot near a break in the fence, leading to a cattle trail. It disappeared into a cluster of shanties near an unmanned railway track.

I couldn't resist it any longer. I told Bobo everything.

*

9

Confessions of a Bad Man

I returned to my dwelling house after a month. I missed Bobo.

My father was nervous. He jumped at trifling noises. His chamber was locked up. It stayed locked for a few days.

I sat my parents down one evening after dinner. "I heard the police came. What did they say?"

They fiddled with the remote. One of them tried killing the T.V. The battery was dead so I got up from my chair and pressed a button on the wall.

My mother cleared plates from the table. The greasy bowls were stacked into a pile. They called an engineer from the buildings department, she said. There were faulty welds in the hoarding. Of course the storm had contributed to the fall. According to the Met Office, wind speeds had reached a hundred that night.

My father sighed. He cleaned his spectacles using the shirt on his belly. "There was an immediate cause for the collapse apart from the storm."

My mother returned from the kitchen. The bolts on the hoarding had been tampered with, she said. Someone had unscrewed them on purpose.

I licked the gravy from my hands. Some of it was dry and stuck to my fingertips.

Shibu was the only one who went to the roof, I pointed out.

"And *you*," my father said putting his glasses back.

They hadn't told the police.

I reminded him that Ganesh went to the roof to water the plants.

"Have you seen the state they're in? He hasn't watered them in months."

He shook his hands. A small towel hung on a ring next to his head.

My father had hushed up the matter. A police investigation meant trouble. "They pry incessantly."

Shushobhon hadn't spoken much. The cops didn't like him. They smelled liquor on his breath.

It was Mr. Debangshu Ghosh who did the talking. "He speaks well when it matters."

In the end no one pressed any charges. The cops went back smiling.

"Some of them had extra notes in their arse."

"Don't use filthy language!"

I washed my hands and went to bed.

I couldn't sleep. I pictured the billboard as it stood once, when it was alive. There were two rows of catwalk just below the apron. They protruded slightly from the transverse. The catwalk was used by the maintenance crew as a platform when they came to paint a new face. Did the workers fiddle with the footings and support? They might have damaged the structure by mistake. But the hoarding hadn't been changed in months. No one went near it except Shibu.

Bobo was right. Everything was strange.

I got up from the bed and picked out a new toothbrush. I rinsed until the smell of food went away. Then I washed my face.

It was incredible: the beams had fallen *exactly* on Shibu's head.

The bristles on my toothbrush felt soft when I squeezed them. I cleaned the brush gently with water and soap. I changed my wet t-shirt and went back to bed.

There was a trail of blood on the terrace. I'd seen it. The trail hadn't rolled down the slope as it should have. The blood was heavy with dead corpuscles. There were stagnant puddles which meant that the gradient was inconsistent.

But the trail of blood was smeared *across* the adobe. It was a large area along the parapet wall. That meant a long period of violence. The way carcasses leave signs on a butcher's floor. And yet the fallen beams could have only given *instant* death...

Slowly my thoughts wore away. The shadows deepened and someone entered the room. It was Shibu's ghost. I expected him sooner or later.

It wasn't him. My father switched the lights on. He spoke from the door. "Are you awake?"

I pretended to be asleep. He stood for some time but I didn't stir.

He carried a newspaper clipping in his hand – the one from the west coast. It was hidden among his files.

*

I bumped into Mr. Ghosh one morning. I crept behind him and stood among his pigeons.

I was careful not to scare the birds. Ghosh made swallowing sounds in the back of his throat. That calmed them down.

Shibu would have done something in my place.

I missed Shibu's noises. On sunny mornings he went down on his hands and knees, pretending to be a wild animal. He had a good animal voice.

When it rained, he brought Surjo's banging spoon to the portico. He dunked it in rainwater and wiped the mud on his face. The water quickly swallowed the handle. Mud spread like lava over the spoon and coiled around the fingerboard. Rolling his eyes, Shibu leaped off his four-footed base with a scream.

I spent an entire morning on the roof smelling the flowerpots along the parapet wall. Someone had dumped dish washing liquid in the soil. It had mixed with alcohol and rainwater, choking some plants dead. I wondered if Ganesh knew about it.

Mr. Ghosh stopped feeding the birds when he saw me.

The pigeons didn't mind. As long as their wheat remained, they didn't care what he did.

Ghosh drew me aside to a corner near the gate. To my huge surprise, he started weeping.

"I killed your friend."

*

Two fat pigeons pecked at my feet. I let them so long they left my toes alone.

A rock pigeon forced its way into the crowd. I tried to avoid it but my leg hit the metal of the gate. The gate shook violently.

The milder birds got scared. They fluttered their wings and flew away. For once Ghosh didn't care. He continued to cry.

"In fact," I said, "*you* should have been under that hoarding."

"I was reading a book in the lobby."

"What?"

"That night," Ghosh said, "I was in the lobby."

He dabbed at his cheeks. Wrinkles gathered over his tears. "Surjo was crying upstairs. I heard him from the staircase. Shibshankar was on the roof."

"Why did you dislike him so much?"

"He took my dog away! Then he followed me. Everywhere!"

Mr. Ghosh forgot about the clump of seeds in his hand. They were packed like coins in a small transparent packet. The remaining pigeons pecked peacefully behind our cleft.

"Once I ate too much and went for a midnight stroll."

"Where?"

"To the park. Suddenly a naked figure popped out of the darkness. It went *Yeeee!* in my ear. This one," he pointed clutching his left lobe, "the one that works!"

Apparently Shibu tried to put a string around his neck. "He wanted to strangle me."

"You said you killed him."

Mr. Ghosh had his gun with him that night. He saw Shibu's shadow on the terrace. "I was taking aim when Shelley appeared at my elbow."

She was hiding inside the caretaker's room or complaining about the pump. Mr. Ghosh turned and thrust the gun in her face.

"At that instant I heard a crash and then it was dark. A big chunk fell from the parapet."

Ghosh fled with his gun before he could help her.

"Shelley sat in the rain waiting for the slab to fall on her head."

I drew away from the cleft in the wall. The broad open sunlight made patterns on the concrete floor.

"If it hadn't been for the hoarding, I could have killed Shibshankar that night."

Ghosh sobbed like a little boy.

✳

"What is this I hear about Mr. Ghosh's dog?"

That evening I went to meet Ganesh in his quarters. Ganesh was ill. He was huddled around a blanket when I walked in. He was shaking with heat.

The redbrick complex was a rectangle. It was stretched out long around its edges. At its base was the main gate with a yellow wall around it. One of its sides had a few outhouses, standing like old men with roots. Between the other edge and the yellow wall was a small raised passage way. It was harder than the rest of the flooring because flagstones were paved on the patio deck.

Shelley had fallen to her death on this platform. The concrete stretched deeper into the complex, ending in a small sanctuary where Ganesh lived.

Ganesh's quarters had a blank facade. His rooms were built into it. He'd added an outdoor kitchen where he killed his hens. He drained off their blood in a pit near his holy *tulsi* plant. Since a portion of the premises lay vacant behind his flat, he used it as a backyard. That's where the bodies were stripped. Having removed the skin and feather, he hung them out to dry.

A stunted tree grew around the facade. It looked ugly but it bore white flowers with yellow hearts in them. What it lacked in height it made up in its wide sweep. I sat for hours under the tree when I was a child, burping on the chips that he fed me.

Ganesh said, "Mr. Ghosh first started shooting pigeons to feed the animal." He sat up clumped under a mosquito net. His nose was red. "It was a rotten Alsatian dog."

"So he really has a gun?"

"Of course he has a gun. Would I lie to you?"

Mr. Ghosh had eventually killed the animal. It got too greedy. Ghosh couldn't sustain it anymore.

"Why?"

The dog ate well fed beef. Mr. Ghosh bought hunks of premium hide and then he got the bones pressed in a lab. Every afternoon the dog chewed on them, making sounds in its throat like a woman. Sometimes Ghosh got the bones hardened so that they wouldn't run out.

I asked Ganesh about the gun. "Can you kill a man with it?"

Ganesh laughed. It was a spring piston airgun with a cocking lever. Ghosh used lead pellets because they were effective with pigeons. They didn't make a noise. "But don't worry, he can't kill you!"

In any case, Ghosh had a permit for the gun.

"Mr. Ghosh told me the roof fell on Shelley's head."

"More like Shelley fell from the sky!"

Ganesh rolled on his bed. He tried to toss the blanket from his body but it was too big. He got thoroughly entangled in the process.

"Ghosh always wanted to smash Shelley's head himself." He went on pulling his feet and hips out of the blanket. "After his wife died, Mr. Ghosh had a scene with Shelley. Don't tell anyone!"

"Go on."

"Things got murky between them. His daughter Aparna found out. She hated Shelley like everyone else. She eloped with...a boy."

Ganesh paused. His eyes were angry for a moment. I could have mistaken it for something else. A dust particle maybe.

"Anyway, Shelley fell off the roof."

"Why didn't you say so to the police? They think she died in an accident."

"It *was* an accident, wasn't it?"

His face was flushed with fever. "How does it matter whether she fell from the roof or the roof fell on her?"

I caught Ganesh wiping his nose on the wool of his blanket before I left.

*

10

Sleuth

*T*he next evening I bunked college and went to meet Rita the receptionist at the Black Pearl. She was surprised to see me.

"Haircut already?"

Rita stood over a shirted man missing three buttons down the collar. She held his hair with one hand and slapped his open chest with the other.

She wasn't a receptionist at night.

"Mr. Ghosh sent me. Are the digging materials ready for tomorrow?"

"Of course they are." Rita removed her hand from the open chest. "They are always ready."

She sighed and walked to the office desk where she kept her bills and pen. "He's a strange man."

I looked around the parlour. The room was *full* of strange men. Some had scissors and hair on their fingers. I took a step back and let the light fall on Rita's make-up. Her face was smoky but her lipstick was traffic red, blurring the soft dip of her bow-shaped lips.

"Yes he's strange," I said. "What's with all this digging?"

"I heard some story about a dead dog."

The man without the buttons looked up. "It died in the park. Someone killed it."

Rita glanced behind her towards the room where she kept her equipment. I wasn't allowed inside the room. Men with broken backs disappeared inside every evening. Rita used her fingers and helped them relax.

"Who killed the dog?"

Rita removed a plastic gel from a fold in her blouse. "Maybe your friend killed him." She placed the pen in the pen stand. "That's what the shopkeepers say."

I remembered the stray dogs outside the park. They looked like killers too. Only Shibu was able to tame them.

"Mr. Ghosh buried his dog in the park," Rita said.

The man on the chair stood up and undid his buttons. Once he'd taken the shirt off, he walked past the reception into the other room.

"Apparently he digs up the burial spot once a month. As a mark of respect," Rita added, "he offers it flowers and bones."

A table fan blew a leg out of the inner room. She quickly hid the trousers on a peg inside.

I thought of the little carved *Madhubani* box. "Only bones?" I glanced inside the room. Rita stood in the way.

"What do you mean, *only* bones? How should I know?"

She snapped impatiently from the door, picking up a shirt from the barber's chair. The man was draped on a high table. Two or three bottles of massage oil and hair shampoo were kept next to him.

"It's not normal to bury a dog."

Rita closed the door behind her. I heard her strike a match. I think she lit his candle.

*

I called up Bobo and filled her in.

The bones we'd seen in the generator room were old chewing bones.

"Hmm."

"And the room is connected to Ghosh's flat, remember?"

"Yes."

The bones I'd seen in the park were either from a carcass or fresh offerings from Ghosh. That explained the difference in their colour. "And Shelley fell from the roof."

"What was she doing there?" Bobo asked me.

I didn't have all the answers so I hung up.

✳

Next I went to Shibu's flat. I stood a long time in the mezzanine inspecting the size of the kitchen. It stuck out like a massive nose along the staircase. The landing looked small in comparison.

The kitchen had a separate door leading directly to the cooking range. I tried the handle outside but it wouldn't open. Big greasy spots dribbled on its sides. The door was dusty with age but someone had oiled it recently. I walked across the landing and rung the bell on the main door.

"Why aren't you in college?" Shibu's mother asked me.

I left my shoes at the shoe rack and put my hands behind me. Shibu's picture wore a garland. A plate of sweets was kept in front of him. Small flies buzzed around it. Cobwebs from the doorbell stuck to my fingers so I flicked them down. They fell on the rack and Shibu scowled at his new sandals.

Bani Dasgupta sat down. She didn't say anything.

"If you want, I can keep some of Shibu's stuff with me," I said moving the flies from my face.

"I want to keep it."

A much bigger portrait of Shibu's grandfather framed in wood hung on a wall near the bookcase. It didn't have flowers around it so he breathed easily.

Shelley was completely gone.

"Why don't you take Shelley's books? I don't want them," Mrs. Dasgupta said.

"From the generator room?"

"Yes, I brought them upstairs."

I looked at the chesterfield where Surjo was sitting. A dirty grey handkerchief lay on the glass table. A plaster was taped across his left ear.

"He misses his brother," Mrs. Dasgupta said and left the room.

92

Surjo clutched the sides of his wing chair. He didn't bang his spoon because it wasn't there. I went inside the kitchen and got him a ladle to play with. In between, I checked the kitchen door which opened on the mezzanine.

It had two latches. One went up to my waist. That was unbolted. The other was higher and held the fastening.

Mrs. Dasgupta returned and handed me a heavy bundle. I kept staring at Surjo. "Is he alright?"

"It's my fault. I've misplaced his medication. I must go buy them again."

I stepped out of the door with my arm full of books and bumped straight into the coconut sweet seller. He was dressed in white as usual and carried a large covered tray on his head.

"This house is mourning two deaths. They won't buy sweets," I told him.

The plate of flies on the shoe rack hadn't changed in days. The shoes smelled stale.

"Yes, I know. I miss Shibu," he said.

"I miss him too." All of a sudden I burst into tears. Some of the water fell on the books.

"There, there." His tones were dulcet. "Would you like to buy some sweets?"

*

I left the sweet seller at the landing and went up to my room. The cartons of books were clearly labelled. At length I found what I was looking for.

Stuffed between the pages of an old Bengali magazine were some letters. Old letters written by Shelley to Mr. Debangshu Ghosh. I didn't read them.

So Ganesh wasn't lying. Here was proof. In my hands.

It was good to have proof. But why had she kept the letters? Why hadn't Shelley sent them to Mr. Ghosh?

The writing was in a steady hand with curly dots. The 't's were curved. Why were the letters *still* with her?

Maybe Mr. Ghosh read them secretly. But where did he hide them? Inside a hole in the park? Within a wooden box three feet below the ground?

But if he kept them hidden, why were they back among Shelley's books?

I rummaged through the rest of her magazines. After half an hour I found a box wrapped in an old newspaper. It had some carvings on it. I'd seen it before.

I got the clasps off and pressed the hinges. There was nothing inside it. I tapped the soft felt lining. It felt hollow. I tapped some more until the base gave way. I lifted the cushion and found a big basement at the bottom of the box. A few clips and rubber bands were stuck together.

Shelley had pulled the letters out.

How did she do that? She must have taken them back the night we found the box.

Shibu was a careless fool. I was right all along.

✱

The next day I hailed myself a cab.

Two hours later, Bobo and I sat in her garden with large mugs of coffee.

"Okay, let's see what we have," she said. "Ghosh had a dog. He loved it like a child. It died in the park."

I sipped my coffee.

"He stores bones, he saves letters, he hides keys. But why?"

The coffee was good. I let Bobo continue.

"And, why isn't *she* curious? Mrs. Dasgupta. What does she know?"

I promised Bobo that I would speak to her again.

"Then there's Shibu's father. What's his story?"

✱

11

Words

*A*fter Shibu's death his family fell apart.

They left dirty boxes outside the door. The windows were shut most of the time. Shibu's room was locked up.

"If it's shut I feel he's inside the room. It makes me happy," Bani Dasgupta said.

We tried to keep him alive in our own way. Shibu's parents went to the country every weekend. But I had nowhere to go. Without Shibu the house wasn't much fun.

The police came to our redbrick a few times. I heard some rumour about the case being re-opened. Bobo said – Shibu's file had reached her uncle in the Crime department.

Sebastian and I were sitting in his hostel room late one evening. He kept the room even though he had an apartment of his own.

We didn't use Sabbie's apartment anymore.

"I feel weird every time I sit on the foam mattress."

"This is where he sat," Sabbie said pointing at the cushions. "That's where he ran. I remember the light on his face, Sandy."

It was just a shadow from Sabbie's buffet lamps.

The first rainy day after Shibu's death we felt like a smoke. We hid under a window on the ground.

"Do you get girls over?"

I looked at the spacious room teasing the end of my tobacco. We didn't have filters but Sabbie made a good roach.

"Oh yes!" Sabbie laughed and twirled the weed. "You want one?"

"Renuka wanted to speak to you. I asked her to come."

Sabbie's face changed in a flash.

"You should have asked me first!"

He licked the rolling paper angrily.

I looked around his room again. It was a square with a large four poster bed pushed to the centre. The bed defined the room but it didn't fit in.

"Is there a problem?"

"I don't like her anymore." Sabbie set the weed on fire. He puffed deeply, once, twice, and then he broke into a coughing fit.

"Easy," I said.

"You talk to her alone."

I'd brought Shibu's handkerchief with me. It was soaked in booze and washing powder. I wanted to give it to Sabbie but he wouldn't take it.

"It's not safe with me."

Renuka walked in suddenly.

No one spoke for some time. The weed was good. I looked out of the window and admired the shape of leaves in the distance. Tall trees tripped on themselves and fell in the backfield. A couple of tailorbirds followed a branch outside.

Renuka asked Sabbie: "Did you tell Sandy about what we discussed?"

Sabbie blew out. A cloud gathered above his face. "I was about to."

He passed the joint to me.

"What's this about?"

I inhaled with my mouth full.

"Shibu and I broke up." Renuka put a large bag on the four poster bed. She sat cross-legged.

"When?"

I balanced the cherry at the end of the burning stick. Sabbie had told me but I wanted to hear her facts.

"Just before he died." Renuka put her feet down.

"He died accidentally. Stop blaming yourself."

Sabbie took the joint from me.

We were playing games with each other.

"I'm not blaming myself, I'm blaming *you*!"

Renuka tossed an open bottle at Sabbie. "Shibu was fucking suicidal but you didn't tell me!"

The bottle shook with fury.

"Take her away for god's sake!"

Sabbie was drenched near the window. "I don't want a scene here!"

I led Renuka away into the next room. I held her hand. She was remarkably easy. I let her stand for a moment.

"Fuck it, it's all over now."

I held her close to my body. The shampoo was still there. She put her head on my shoulder.

"No one's blaming you, I promise."

Renuka looked up. "Why have you brought me here?"

"Shibu's mother knows about the suicide," I said. "We could keep it that way."

A small piece of paper nestled in her left breast.

"I want you to have it." She tossed her head towards the cleft of her top.

"What is it?"

"I wrote a letter to Shibu a few days before his death."

"Does Sabbie know?"

"He could tell the cops later. Shibu posted the letter back to me. You understand?"

"Yes that will do."

Renuka looked into her clothes and handed me an envelope.

*

The words were typewritten but barely legible. Shibu had scrunched up the paper in rage. The writing was impersonal. There were creases across the fold.

I held it against the dim light at my father's dictation table.

"Dearest Shibu:

This is my last letter to you.

I stole your diary from the satchel when college ended. I don't know if you ever found out. I wish I hadn't taken it.

Anyway, I read it all. Every fucking word. I licked it clean.

You should know what that means. I could end the letter here and say goodbye.

But I will continue.

It was a lovely day outside. You wanted to go for a walk and meet the amazing shoe-shine boy, the one with the big box of wax.

And suddenly you got angry. Anger is always your excuse. It puts your mind to rest.

You couldn't keep still. You couldn't use your imagination. It's too damned hard, you wrote. So were you.

You rifled through the newspaper. No good. Fucking newspaper. You rushed to the shoe rack – some grey-scaled curves caught your attention. You pulled out a scrap of paper. A vernacular daily. The one your aunt used to wrap her watermelons. It reeked of compromise. You turned away in disgust when you smelled your palm. The stench stuck to your fingertips like labels: your father's wet gumboots, schools of gaping smelly fish, fibres coursed with lignin and black liquor.

And suddenly a vague memory stirred. Not yours, mine. I remembered you telling me about the time you moved into the city. You ran to the roof at dawn to catch the morning dailies. Rolled up chronicles of joy. Newspapers delivered by the cyclist with a strong arm. Your landlord had a leaking pump so the roof was full of puddles. You picked up the dailies from their wet beds and dried them in your room. In front of a stuttering A.C.

Every pimple faced youth I knew in school lived on the stuff. But people grow up. It's not fair.

There's nothing left to say.

I understand. You won't ever change. It's sad. You deserve this.

I'll leave you alone.

-- Renuka

*

I looked around the little room. It was next to a bookstore. The clerks had left the corridor leaving me alone with their papers and briefs. My father was still in his chamber working on a will. I wanted a ride back with him.

My hand was caught between the typewriter and a reading lamp. I pushed the lamp to make room for my elbow. The memory of clacking ribbons stuck to my ears. I read the letter again.

It was powerful stuff. Bobo would be happy.

*

I found myself in Sabbie's room again three evenings later. I had a few things to clear up.

Sebastian was kneeling beside his bar. His room-mate had removed the lesser gods from a shelf and put some bottles instead.

I saw a slim flask with a flared lip. A urine coloured beverage formed its contents.

"Did you know about this letter?" I dangled the creased sheet before him.

He peered at the Bookman font.

"It's from Renuka."

Sabbie understood. "Yes I know about the letter, inspector."

"Why didn't you tell us?"

"Shibu showed me the letter. We went drinking the day he died. He was upset about something. After three shots he read it out to me."

"How long was he with you?"

"He left soon. He had to get somewhere in a hurry. That's what he told me."

"That's not all, Sebastian Gomes."

"Shibshankar had to post the letter back. Fuck off inspector."

I wrote his statement down. Shibu went to the post office drunk and mailed Renuka's letter back to her. The story hung there.

"I'm not taking sides, Sabbie. Shibu was my friend."

I put the letter back into my pocket.

"He was my friend too."

"Balls he was."

Sabbie lay on the ground staring at the fan. The floor was cold so he slid under the bed.

"Did you give Shibu's diary to Renuka?"

"Maybe I did."

"So Shibu killed himself because of you. Well done."

I said that and left. He was drunk. I wasn't.

*

A few days later I ran into Mr. Debangshu Ghosh at the gate. He was getting ready to leave.

"My daughter wrote to me," he told me happily.

I didn't have anything nice to say. I went up to my room.

Shibu was on drugs. What kind of drugs? Were they dangerous? Could he have died of an overdose? Can a healthy boy kill himself? He tried it twice before but he failed both times. Besides, no one knew about it. Did the story hold? What did Sebastian tell him when they drank that night hours before his death? Could Sabbie have pushed him over the edge?

Did Shibu think of *me* before he died? Renuka was on his mind. She was an angel. They said she was a slut but I liked her. I liked her breasts. The small of her back fitted my chest. I wanted to protect her.

Shibu would have died anyway. He wouldn't have survived the weight of the hoarding. The fates were angry with him. It was a night of innumerable deaths. He was *destined* to die. Everything was a result of cosmic incidence. No one should be blamed.

I went back to the gate. Mr. Ghosh was moving out. Crates of furniture were tied to a van. His door was locked securely.

Ghosh put some rope around a chest of drawers. The shelves were wrapped in bubble.

"What is it?"

"I know why you're leaving. It's the police."

He laughed. "I'm visiting my brother. I'll be back."

Ghosh went back to his rope and passed an extra length under the bubble wrap.

"Why do you have a gun?"

Mr. Ghosh tied a knot around the heap. "Pest control. It's my father's."

He made another knot and pushed the package towards the van. "He used it in our village near the border. What's wrong?"

"You lied to me. Shelley was *on* the roof that night. With Shibu. You killed her."

Mr. Ghosh handed money to the driver of the van. He put the remaining notes back in his wallet. The driver counted the things in his carrier and tossed a plastic shroud around it.

"I didn't kill Shibu."

Mr. Ghosh walked towards the passenger seat.

I ran after him. "You told me Shelley was downstairs."

He got into the front of the van and closed the door. The driver made an entry in his register.

"I *saw* Shibu that night."

I banged on his window. The driver held a small cigarette in his mouth. His ash fell in surprise.

Mr. Ghosh rolled his window down. "You don't understand. I saw him on the roof that night."

The driver took the cigarette out of his mouth. His register was tucked behind a vanity mirror.

I banged on the door of the van this time. It almost made a dent.

"He *pushed* Shelley off the roof, alright?"

A blue pen fell from the mirror. It landed on the driver's lap.

I stepped away from the door.

The driver looked relieved. He picked up the pen and put it back in his register.

"Why didn't you report this?"

Mr. Ghosh shook his head. "The boy is *dead*."

The van purred excitedly. The exhaust blew giant smoke rings on my face and went out of the gate.

*

Later that evening the bell pealed three times. Shibu's mother stood at the threshold.

"Please come in."

No one was home. The lights hadn't been switched on. It was a gloomy, quiet evening. My fingers reeked of paper and glue.

Bani stood at the door. "The police think that God killed Shibu."

"Yes?"

"He didn't." Her voice was steady. "There was a letter."

"I know."

I passed a finger across my nose. The paper was still with me.

"No one else should know."

I nodded.

"Why did he do it?"

She looked at me.

"Shelley died that night too. I wonder."

Her eyes were puffy. She needed cucumber. Thin slices of cucumber cut into discs with seeds at the centre.

Bani didn't come back that evening. When my parents returned they found me in my room.

I don't know when I passed out. I slept a long time in the den.

I dreamt about Shibu. He asked me questions but I didn't know what to say.

A demon, erect like a man, crawled out of my head. I don't remember his face. He dangles his thin legs from my shoulder. Sometimes I listen to him.

And then I wake up in a cold sweat.

Months later people still ask me about Shibu. "Did he kill himself?" they say. "Why?"

I tell them the truth. "It was a dark stormy night. Anything could have happened."

*

PART 3

ET CETERA, THE OTHERS

12

Meeting the Parents

I mustered courage in a bottle one night and went back to the mezzanine. I had to let Bani Dasgupta know a few things.

The brand new TV sat in its plywood cabinet. The coffee coloured doors were shut. The TV was switched off.

I sat on one of the wicker chairs. Mr. and Mrs. Dasgupta held my audience.

I looked at the bare walls. There were brown patches around the wiring and four picture frames above a wax banana. The dogs were still there, snarling, bristling, lolling, chewing, like they always did.

It was the same dog. It had to be.

"Is it yours?"

*S*hibu's father looked at his wife. He licked the foam from his fifth *Kingfisher*. Four empty bottles stood near the bathroom door.

"He was a good dog but he was frisky," he said.

It was one of those days. I wanted to see how drunk he was. I asked him what frisky meant.

"Nothing."

"You see, champ, doggies get together and frisk each other."

He drew whiskers on his face with the foam.

Bani Dasgupta said, "I wish you wouldn't talk like that."

She left the room.

"I called him Beer." Shushobhon smiled at the ceiling.

A large belly button slipped out of his shirt.

"Dogs should be dogs. Not agents of man. No?"

"I don't know."

"Beer was a good dog. But he lost it."

A low wail came from Surjo's room. It sounded like a police siren. Mr. Dasgupta turned to his bottle.

"He got into all kinds of trouble."

"Meaning?"

"First he attacked other dogs. Then he pounced on people. I was about to get him fixed. But I had important work."

"What did he do exactly?"

"Shibu went to the park and let him loose."

The door at the bedroom moved a little. Surjo cried again.

Shushobhon looked angrily at Surjo's room. "When will he grow up?"

"Should I check?"

"He gets wet. He soils his clothes. The day Shibu died, Surjo peed all over himself. I found his clothes in the bathroom. Bani told me he turned on the shower by mistake. Ha!"

Surjo was wheezing in his sleep.

Mrs. Dasgupta came out of her bedroom. "What's the matter with you?"

Shushobhon stood up. He saluted his father's picture and went inside. Bani looked at Surjo's door but his wheezing had stopped.

"Can I speak to you?"

We were alone.

She looked at me surprised. Her eyes went to the clock on the wall. It was past midnight. "Yes? What is it?"

Ask her about Surjo, Bobo told me in my head.

"He's not been keeping well."

I asked her if he'd caught a cold.

"It's this rotten season. Health suffers. Frail health more so."

I asked her if he got drenched in the rain.

"No of course not," Bani snapped. "I wouldn't permit that."

"Mr. Dasgupta told me he went under the shower by mistake."

She looked at the door. "Yes, that night."

When they returned from the terrace, she found him in the bathroom. He was standing in his clothes under the shower. She had to drag him away.

"There was a letter," I said.

"I told you."

"What do you know?"

"It was addressed to Shibu. It came from a girl."

"What else?"

"A friend of Shibu's told the police. But it was much later. Once they re-opened the case."

She looked at me kindly.

"He was weak like his father. But Surjo is strong. He'll recover."

*

In the interim Bobo visited our building. She didn't meet me or anyone else.

"Be careful," I told her.

"I'm just a little girl."

"That's it."

"Don't you see? No one will notice me."

Bobo made a list of questions. I fingered the list in my head.

Mrs. Dasgupta was sitting in front of me.

"What were you doing when the storm broke out?" I asked her softly.

"I was sitting in the bedroom. Shushobhon slept through the storm. I had to wake him up when your parents came."

That sounded alright. Mr. Dasgupta had just arrived. He must have been tired from the journey.

"And where was Surjo?"

"*Surjo?*"

"Yes?"

"He was tucked in his room. I put him to sleep after feeding time."

"You don't know when he woke up?"

Mrs. Dasgupta looked upset. "Excuse me?"

"Surjo was awake when you came down from the roof. You told me he was under the shower. So when did he wake up?"

"I don't know."

"Did you know about Shelley and Mr. Ghosh?"

Pause. "Who told you?"

"People are talking about it."

She had heard a rumour after Shelley came to stay with them. "But it died down. People talk. I didn't speak to Shelley about it."

I ticked a few things on my list. "That's all," I said.

"Is the interrogation over?"

Bani smiled at me.

"I'm sorry for the trouble."

"What about Surjo?"

I wished her a good night and left.

*

13

Storm in a coffee cup

$\mathcal{T}$he next night I couldn't get sleep. I went downstairs and borrowed a bottle from Mr. Dasgupta. He gave me a poly bag to smuggle the booze out.

I poured out a glass for him. But Bani didn't let him leave the house.

I fiddled with an empty casserole on the dining table. I counted the wax fruits slowly. No one had touched them. Good. A bunch of blue grapes sat next to a banana. I didn't want to take chances.

Shushobhon Dasgupta came back from the bathroom. His wife retired to bed. I thanked him for his help and left.

Midway through the bottle I got drunk. I took a large knife and a blue grape from the mezzanine then I went downstairs. I wanted to do something fancy.

The lobby was dark. It was after midnight. Ganesh had locked the collapsible gate. I sat on the couch near the giant mirror and sharpened the knife. The metal shone brightly in the float glass. I saw the generator door in the light of the blade.

The door was ajar. I went in through the storage room past the generator. The wall with the connecting panel was two feet away. Beyond the panel was Mr. Ghosh's flat.

I slid the knife inside the joint and pushed. The tongue gave way. I heard a click somewhere. I pushed harder and thrust the knife inside. It was a loose latch.

The connecting door opened.

The lights and fans had disappeared from the flat. Empty brackets hung on the wall. There weren't any bulbs or switches left.

A giant hook crawled out of the ceiling.

The few remaining furniture was wrapped up. There was a musty smell in the air. I stepped on something soft but it quickly moved away. Nobody was hurt. I'd brought the bottle with me. I sat in a corner to drink the rest.

A curtain was draped across the window. With the knife, I slashed the curtain to shreds. Some light from the road outside let me see what I was drinking. It was whisky. The bottle was almost full.

The incense stand was in front of me. When I was younger, I had visited a set of royal stables. It was part of a ruined palace. That was the first time I had smelled horse dung. I could still smell it. The sandalwood sticks weren't there. But I could smell them too.

Below the incense stand was a low stool. Something glistened underneath. Like a flash of silver.

When I bent down the flash was gone. I hunted for it and scooped out dirt, pieces of thread and a dead cockroach. Half eaten bodies were strewn on the floor. I bent lower this time and pushed my leg in. A squishy thing rolled over my ankle. It spat out the silver and then it was gone.

I picked up a lizard tail. A piece of stone was tied around it. The stone seemed to be broken. I took it to the window and held it against the light of the bottle. It was a shard of glass. It had three heads along its edges. I felt the substance with my fingers. It wasn't stone or glass. It was broken in half or into many pieces. I didn't have the other pieces so I looked at the three heads. It seemed to be part of a star shaped object.

I put the star down and drank some more. The bourbon was making me sweat. I fanned myself with the curtain. Bits of cloth spilled out and flew into my bottle.

I tried to make a clean cut but the curtain rod fell down.

Grains of paraffin wax spilled out from its hollow. I juggled them in my hand and put one in my mouth. It tasted fine.

But I wanted to pee first.

I stumbled towards the bathroom. The commode was in a corner. I slipped on a pool of water and fell on my back. Someone else was inside or there was a leak. I pressed hard on the flush. It didn't work.

I wiped the wet stain from my shirt. A rubber flapper sat on the flush box.

The flapper was worn out. I picked up the ceramic lid of the commode and looked inside. There wasn't much water left. Some more wax was packed at the bottom. Dry marbles of paraffin were stuck together. A few shiny splinters from the three headed object had collected along the sides. Stuck to one of the splinters was a slip of paper. It had a number on it.

I put it in my pocket and left.

*

"What's your theory?"

Cupping both her hands, Bobo enjoyed the warmth of her coffee.

We walked down the cattle trail. Squirrels played around us. They hid among the flowers when we strayed too close. It was a beautiful afternoon.

The ground was soft. Rain had moistened the earth. The grassless trail was ravaged by hoofs of many sizes. There were criss-cross lines of alluvium across the trail, drawn by cyclists.

"That letter was sent back to its sender just before his death," Bobo said softly.

The trail rose and went along the shoulder of a hillock. An ugly ravine stretched before us. I ran up the hill and almost spilled my coffee. When I looked behind me, she was still standing.

I climbed down and came beside her.

"Why did he send it back?"

"Maybe he wanted to protect her." I noticed a few hairline cracks on the sediment. The ground was dry at the foot of the mound.

"Renuka gave you the envelope as well. It's post marked."

I picked up a pebble and tossed it to the other side.

"Nice of her to keep the envelope."

I heard the pebble fall across the ravine.

"What if Ghosh *actually* shot him?"

I wanted to change the subject.

"Seriously?"

"I didn't get a chance to inspect Shibu's body. The police would have found a bullet but the matter was hushed up. Besides, Mr. Ghosh spoke to the police himself."

Bobo nibbled the chain around her neck. "And Shelley?"

"You think Shibu pushed her down?"

"It's *possible*. In what position did you find Shelley's body?"

I looked down the ravine. "She wasn't face down."

"She might have fallen backwards."

I held Bobo's hand and dragged her through the slope.

"Wouldn't she have screamed when she fell?"

We almost tripped on a bed of leaves.

"Wouldn't someone have heard her?"

"It was a noisy night," Bobo said. We came to a stop. "*You* heard the hoarding fall. No one else did. Because you stood near an open window. The others were locked inside their rooms. Their windows were shut. They heard nothing."

We crossed a small bridge. It was made from planks pinned together. The path looked pretty.

"And then there's the issue of timing," Bobo continued. "When did the hoarding crash? If Shibu pushed Shelley *at the same time*, it's doubtful anyone would have heard her."

I sipped my coffee. Our cups had collided on the slope. The coffees were mixed up. There were pockets of Bobo's milk in my mouth.

"One other thing," she said.

"Yes?"

"The lobby is in the centre. Surjo was on the mezzanine. There's a staircase between them, plus the kitchen. Surjo was on the other side of the building two storeys above the lobby."

"*Then Mr. Ghosh couldn't have heard Surjo!*"

"No. I tried it."

I sat down happily on a ledge. "So he's lying." The rock was moist under my pants.

"On the other hand if Mr. Ghosh *was* sitting in the lobby, why did he go outside?"

"In the rain?"

"Yes. It doesn't make sense."

Bobo walked ahead and hit her toe against a fishplate. We had reached the train tracks.

*

14

Stone

$\mathcal{S}$hibu humoured me in small ways when he was alive.

It's not healthy, he once said, to appreciate the manhood of other men.

"Why, what's wrong with it?"

"Fuck off." Shibu stared at me and walked away.

*

But I wasn't joking.

I allow myself to admire a male form from time to time. "It's like worshipping a god."

Shibu's anatomy was well-arranged. It inspired me. I wanted to get big like him.

However it wasn't easy.

It involved a lot of work. I'd seen Shibu do pull-ups on the terrace for hours. The apron below the hoarding cringed under his weight.

But Shibu was selfish. He didn't let me use the hoarding.

Back in my flat, I hit a solution. One day I took a grinding stone from the kitchen. It was a fat object that crushed poppy to a pulp. I kept it in a corner of my den. Shibu called it a Plan B dumb bell.

After he died, I left his bush alone. I didn't have a choice. Accordingly I looked for the grindstone.

I hunted amidst a sheaf of files in the den. It was the world's biggest paperweight. My father's white bond discards were kept under it.

The files were bare when I unlocked the room. Their black shoelaces were ripped out. A stale, wet smell hung from the ceiling like a punching bag.

My father's news clippings were gone. The scrapbook called 'fair and lovely' left a mark on the floor where its brown cover had peeled off. The legal whites were strewn in disarray. The woman on the west coast had been abducted again.

Something else was missing. My stone.

I hadn't entered the den in a long time. Not since Shibu died. Were the papers on the floor when I fastened the windows that night? Or did they fly away in the storm?

My memory was a blur.

I went to the kitchen to ask my mother. To my surprise, the grinder was sitting next to her.

"Give it back. I want to do weights."

She stared at me. "I bought this a week ago. You lost it or what?"

She rolled the new stone on a slab.

Its surface was pock marked. The stone was smeared with chilli and coriander.

I came out of the kitchen and went to the telephone.

"Strange," Bobo said, "when did you use it last?"

It was some time ago. "A couple of months."

"Does your father know?"

As it turned out, he knew too much.

*

At first his reaction stumped me.

My father jumped a few inches from his chair.

"You're becoming a problem child!"

I wanted to do weights. I flexed my arms to explain.

"Do push-ups instead."

He returned to his paper.

My father knew the case was still open. Newspapers blew up the issue. Shibu's grandfather was a well known man. His daughter and grandson died the same night. Not only that. He passed away himself under mysterious circumstances.

People stirred the topic further. There were theories and debates in tea shops. A media house alleged foul play. Maybe the new party was wiping out its rivals? Someone should protect them. At least their families should be saved.

Rathi's brother had been assigned to take up the matter. Ministers asked him to send a report to the government.

There were many reasons why my father disliked him. Rathi's brother was a snob among other things.

"Men like him can't be trusted. They can't hold the past. Always looking for new friends."

After his promotion Rathi's brother avoided family gatherings. The women stood in groups and bitched about him.

"Mixing with us will be a waste of time."

"It's easier to pretend we are strangers," they said.

I stared at the paper in my father's hand. An ugly thought hit me, all of a sudden.

"Did Shibu take the *shilnora*?"

"I don't want to discuss Shibu."

I nodded my head. I was used to his orders.

He lowered the paper a couple of inches. "We found it."

I gave him a blank look.

"Mr. Dasgupta found it on the roof. We hid it before the police came."

"Where?"

"Now it's gone." He made a gesture like a magician.

The stone was found on the terrace in a dry state. Since it was lying under a cover, it didn't get wet in the rain.

I asked him *why* he'd hidden it.

"Your fingerprints could have been there."

"But the police might find it useful. We should get the prints checked."

"I got them checked."

He looked at me quietly. We didn't speak for a long time.

"I paid money. No questions asked."

My father had shut himself in a dark place with Mister Five Fingers and compared the fingerprints.

"We found exact matches."

Mine would match all right. I had used the stone.

"Yes but *when* did you use it?"

It looked bad. A heavy stone found at the crime scene with my fingerprints on it.

"But Shibu's prints would be fresher."

"Why?"

"Because I didn't touch the stone that night. Shibu did."

Apparently the finger man could not verify the timing. It was worth a guess but he wasn't sure. He was a hush-hush chap.

"He told me it was impossible to testify the relative age of prints." Some of the marks had developed quicker, implying they were newer deposits. But the finger man wouldn't enter a witness box. "It's a matter of evidence."

"What else did he say?"

Fingerprints on non-porous surfaces, if left undisturbed, can last a long time. The *shilnora* for example.

"But wouldn't the rain wash them away?"

"Yes but it didn't. The object may have been used under dry conditions."

I didn't like the word 'used'. I asked him what he meant.

"There were traces of Shibu's blood on it."

*

Mister Five Fingers had sold his story. Fingerprints could be retrieved from any surface, even from articles underwater. So the rain wasn't a big point.

"What else?"

"My fingerprints were there too. I held the object with a handkerchief. But it wasn't thick enough."

He looked sad.

*

"Did you do it?" Bobo asked me.

"What?"

"Did you kill Shibu?"

I laughed loudly.

"Your mother told me an extraordinary thing the other day."

It was a lie. My mother didn't speak to her.

"She saw a thin track of blood on the stairway. From your door, all the way to the roof."

"So?"

"On the night of Shibu's death."

"There were *two* murders. Can't there be a little blood?"

"On the *stairs*?"

I didn't know what to say.

"When your mother went to the roof, there was blood in the stairway. Where did it come from?"

It may have been my blood. "I slipped on the way down. Maybe I got cut and spilled some."

"I dabbed your body when you came home. There were bruises and bumps on your back. No cuts."

"Then how did the blood get there?"

"You brought it with you."

"How?"

"It was Shibu's blood on your body."

I steeled myself. "That's not what happened."

"Your mother says you shut yourself in the kitchen after you returned. What were you doing inside?"

The bitch. She thought I cleaned myself in the sink.

"Your clothes are missing. You burned them that night."

I looked at her. "No one will believe you Bobo."

That was the problem.

*

15

Bobo

*R*enuka waved at Surjo from the road. He stood in the balcony without his mother.

Her smile was wasted on him. She was useless without a dick. Surjo waved back, drooling on the salmon pink bars.

"Poor child, he can't help it," Bobo said.

Sometimes I couldn't help drooling either.

*

A small shadow formed on the money plants. Bani Dasgupta came to the balcony. Surjo spat on the clothesline and turned away.

I followed Renuka on the opposite pavement.

People stared at her hips. A few white-capped men left their bikes on the sidewalk.

I merged with the traffic. It was good to watch her from a distance.

Then she went inside the redbrick. The concrete path led her to the *tulsi* pit in the back. She took some dead flowers and wrapped them around her palm.

I hid behind the wall and watched her.

Renuka picked up an empty plastic bottle and went to the pump. A small tap was working on the ground. She filled the bottle and put it to her lips.

I didn't leave the cleft. When Renuka emerged from the pump, it was difficult to recognize her. She had a long piece of muslin on her head. It was white in colour, loosely woven around her hands.

She looked like a photo in my father's chamber.

Her nose was sharp. With her hands she tweaked it some more. It grew like a carrot. A thin parchment came out of her purse. She rolled her fingers at the edges. Then she put the sacred cloth to her forehead.

I watched her. The purse grew tight. It hugged her hips.

In a quick moment Renuka kicked a door near the wall. It was a thin plate of metal with a hook. A wire was attached to it. The door was shut. She clutched the hook and put a leg on the wall. Then she swung herself between the two surfaces.

In a second, she was sitting on the ledge.

She took off her shoes and jumped to the other side.

I came out of my cleft. She was inside the temple already.

I walked back to the porch. Ganesh had locked his door. He wasn't home. His backyard was empty. Where did the white cloth come from? Maybe it was folded under his *tulsi*.

A long time ago I saw a woman at the temple. She had long hair. I remembered her buttocks. They were round under her sari.

Renuka's hair was short. Like a bag of worms. A fringe rose at the parting.

Long hair and short hair.

*

A couple of days later, I went to Bobo's house. I reached late.

Bobo looked at her watch. It was a *Timex* with a pink rim. Jasmine and Aladdin embraced each other. Their harems billowed in the desert. The dial stretched across an elastic band.

I took off my shoes and sat on the grass.

"Why is Mrs. Dasgupta lying?"

I put my hands up.

"Why were Surjo's clothes wet?"

"Shower."

"What made him go there?"

Bobo went inside and fetched a paper. "Let's put down what we have. We'll start with you."

I was ready.

"When did you enter the building that night?"

Her father wasn't home. The servants had a day off. There was no one else in the house.

We were alone. In a big quiet garden. I stared into the distance.

"Give me the exact time."

I couldn't say. When did I get home?

"A few minutes after eight."

"Shibu was on the roof." Bobo wrote that down.

"I spent a few minutes talking to Renuka. I reached my flat quarter past."

"Shibu was alone on the terrace?"

"I didn't see anyone go up."

"Unless someone was there already."

It was possible.

"Ganesh the caretaker said Shibu arrived with a friend."

"It must have been Sebastian."

"What does that prove?"

Nothing. He must have left before the storm.

"Unless Sabbie killed Shibu earlier."

"Ganesh saw him. Sabbie wouldn't take the risk."

"What about Ganesh?"

He went to the market. Where was he *before* that?

"Let us imagine for a second Ganesh did it," Bobo said.

That was easy. Ganesh was an evil man.

"He finds Shibu tottering inside. He goes to the terrace with a friend. And then, the friend leaves."

Here was a great opportunity. If Ganesh quickly went to the roof and killed Shibu, people would suspect the friend. No one saw him leave.

"What about Shelley?" I asked.

"Shelley. Shelley. Always a problem."

Perhaps the two murders weren't connected?

Two murders, two killers. Separate motives.

"Now let's return to your story. You switched on the television." Bobo paused and checked her notes. "That'd be eight fifteen or thereabouts. The show ended and your parents returned."

"They brought the storm with them."

"Around quarter to nine, the power went off. Correct?"

The street was shrouded in darkness.

Bobo made an entry in her table. "When did the power return?"

It didn't. Not until morning. The storm blew the lines. We lit candles and hurricane lamps.

Bobo noted the details on a sheet. She used big cursive letters.

"Don't worry." She closed the pen firmly into a groove. "The next few days will change everything."

*

16

The Rat

*O*ne day I grew up a little.

"I can't sit on my arse all day and wait for things to happen," I told Shibu, waking him gently.

Shibu wore his favourite bodysuit and slept on the ground. When he heard my voice, he stirred.

"I have to get them."

There were other people behind Shibu's death. I was convinced of that.

I had to find them out.

I picked out a shirt from the laundry basket. It shook in my hands. The shirt reeked of bourbon. Some paraffin was caught in its threads.

A slip of paper fell from the pocket. A broken star fell out too, but I didn't look at it. I dialled the number on the paper.

It was a Bombay extension. It put me through to a man in *Zaveri Bazar*. I heard the clink of golden bangles across the line. Silver toys played with each other.

"Mr. Ghosh from Calcutta," I said, holding the star and khaki together. The light of day came in through the kitchen. It fell on a ripped shoulder in my hand. "Where's my uniform?"

I didn't get a big reaction. The man in the market put me on hold and looked through his orders.

He didn't cover the mouthpiece. I heard a lady shouting at him. She kept shouting until she stopped being a lady.

"No one by that name," the man said and closed his order book.

I tapped on the wall. "Someone else made the order." I picked up a pen. It doodled on its own. "He's got a name. He may have used it."

Three bearded lions were etched on the star. Some khaki cloth was still stuck to its edges. "There was only one parcel for Calcutta."

The man opened another book.

"Check the last two months."

"Just one entry here. We sent it to Behrampore. Is there a problem?"

Behrampore was a city in Murshidabad district. It lay to the south of Murshidabad town, a few hours from Calcutta.

"It's not arrived yet. Confirm the dispatch address please."

Someone tossed a ream of textile at his end. It landed with a thud on the phone desk.

"You know best," he said. "We have your money."

I scratched the emblem on the phonebook. The pen was still in my hand. I looked at the drawings on the star and copied its motif on the last page. I drew a horse and bull at the base. They chased each other around a wheel.

"This was a private police tender," I said. "I have your last job with me. I want that uniform *now*."

"We get lots of orders. Who is this?"

"I was looking to buy some gold as well."

"Anjali? Is that you?"

"Who?"

The line went dead.

I replaced the earpiece on its cradle.

Mr. Dasgupta's bourbon wasn't finished yet. I got some ice out of the freezer and made a huge peg. I downed my drink before the ice melted and threw the bottle in the kitchen. I shoved the casing under some vegetable skins and covered it with cartons. I washed my glass in the sink and tossed the ice cubes.

My breath was pungent with the long shot. I lit a cigarette at the stove. The cubes disappeared while I watched them. I left the water on the basin. I sprayed some capsicum inside the kitchen. The can went to my trousers.

I went to a vase on the wall cabinet and took the artificial flowers out. I selected a bundle of crisp notes, put a new toothbrush and a pair of slippers in an overnight bag and left the house.

I left a note for my parents.

I reached Sealdah in time for the *Lalgola* passenger. At the station I bought half a dozen oranges. The man at the counter gave me a window seat. I spent the next five hours peeling fibres and dreaming of Renuka. I hurled the orange hides outside. The road was made with crushed stone and it flew under my window. Someone came and sold me more oranges. Small mandarins, shrivelled like nuts on a corpse.

The gentleman next to me looked familiar but I didn't know his name. He handed me a small paper bag and asked me to use it.

The seeds were sticky. Plop, they fell on the paper. Plop, plop. They didn't look enough so I gave him my fibres as well. The fibres stuck to the window. The wind held them in position.

The train stopped twenty times or more, but I didn't get down. Finally we pulled up at Murshidabad town. The wooden sleepers were strewn with oranges.

It was dinner time when the train reached the station. Everything was small and dark. I walked out and went down a paved road until I came to a hotel. They gave me a room on the top floor with a key and a bed. There wasn't much else in it.

I washed my feet above a clean potty and went down to eat. The menu was simple but I ate five times my portion. A man in a maroon overcoat settled his bow and asked me to get out. Billing was shut and it was closing time.

I didn't leave him a tip. I didn't give him my name either.

I selected three toothpicks at the main counter. The saunf was free. A person sitting at the table flicked a seed from his paper and put the bill on my tab.

A shelf full of maps hung above the toothpick stand. I looked around the counter and asked for the way to Mr. Dasgupta's estate.

"The old man that died," I explained.

The man at the counter looked me over. He produced a toothpick of his own. It was bigger than mine. Another fennel seed came out, this time from his teeth.

"I'll show you the mansion tomorrow."

On the road outside the hotel, I smoked five Flakes at a go and went to sleep. The cigarettes didn't light up properly. The filter clung to my lips.

My room was small. A window opened out to a low ledge into a balcony that didn't exist. The bed was big enough for two people without making anyone uncomfortable. A chair stood in a corner. A small side table hosted chlorine water and two pieces of biscuit. The biscuits were soggy. Dogs and guests weren't allowed. It was a rule.

I woke up around three in the morning. Someone was snoring outside. The lights were switched off. The switchboard was next to the door. I sat up in bed and listened closely. A glow of day came in through the window but it was still dark.

I realized the snores were coming next to me.

When I put out my hand, it hit a man on his mouth. He sneezed and woke up.

I ran to the door and switched the lights on. Another man sat on a chair. He was drinking my water. There was a steel jug on the table.

"Good morning," he said. "Where's my diamond?"

My clothes were on the floor. They had searched my bag.

The biscuits were gone. Someone was wearing a perfume. The room smelt pleasant.

The man on the bed rubbed one eye and got a knife out of his pocket.

"Say hello to your friend."

He had a nice smile for a man with one eye.

The man at the table had expensive shoes. He wore a green t-shirt with short sleeves, taut like young skin across his body. His chest heaved when he breathed. His neck was fat with red strings around it. They looked like cowbells.

"Listen, sonny."

The one-eyed man on the bed threw his knife across the room. The blade swished past my eyes. The two-eyed man caught the knife and snapped the switchblade shut.

"I have friends. They tell me things. Bani sent you."

That didn't make sense. I let him talk.

"I came to say hello. But I see no dog. I see no stone. All you feed me are two lousy biscuits."

He looked at the empty saucer on the table and spat into it.

The man on the bed got up. He adjusted his trousers, moved his balls left to right, and sat down again.

"You see him?" The man in the green t-shirt looked at his partner. "He's got one eye."

His breathing was heavy. The t-shirt was very tight. Its synthetic frills hugged his chest.

"I let him keep that eye."

He kept the knife on a pleated flower woven into his denims.

"He begged me so I spared him."

The man in the t-shirt passed a fat hand through his hair. His hair was silky. A blonde wisp fell to his forehead. It was dyed.

"I could save your eyes, sonny. Just show me where Shushobhon kept it. I'll drive you in my car."

I chewed my nails. They had switched the fan off. The room was stuffy.

"It's not in Murshidabad," I said.

It sounded like a setback.

"Then where is it?"

"I don't know."

The man in green tweaked his pants. The switch blade came out.

"Mr. Ghosh has it," I said quickly.

The two men looked at each other.

"The police chap?"

"Maybe."

"I don't believe this!" The green man's breasts turned pneumatic. For a moment I thought he would faint.

He kept the switchblade on the table and smashed my plate to pieces.

No one picked it up.

"Do you know how much that stone is *worth?*"

His spit fell and bubbled on the floor.

"I don't believe this. I screw his wife and he's still lying!"

He went to his partner and made him stand up.

"What do I do now?"

The one-eyed man blinked. "Break his legs and parcel him, boss."

That sounded like a good idea. The knife was on the table. It could be opened again.

I took the capsicum spray out of my pocket. It wasn't difficult. I had an eye less to spray. The green man struggled hard. I took a picture out of his breast pocket.

I closed the window, packed my bag and shut the door. I locked them up in the bathroom on either side of the squat pot. Their heads were shoved in the potty where their screams couldn't be heard. Then I slid the latch outside.

The switchblade came with me on my way out.

The man behind the counter paced up and down the lobby. I saw him from the last flight of stairs. He looked wide awake so I went into the canteen at the back. I wriggled out through the fire exit.

I walked around the hotel through a patch of gram. It grew in a narrow strip of garden next to the road. A black Ambassador car was parked under a streetlight. The bulb wasn't working.

A man sat behind the wheel listening to the radio. I got into the car and sat beside him.

"Let's go. Mr. Dasgupta's house, please."

The driver looked at me surprised.

I pointed at the ignition. He followed my hand but he didn't move.

I brought out the knife and held it to his head.

"I'm in a hurry."

The driver responded this time. He revved up the engine. The car quickly picked up speed. I had a local map from the hotel. It was spread out on my lap.

"Let's not take the route past the police station. I might slit your throat."

He braked. We almost hit the windshield. He took a u-turn and drove in another direction.

After fifteen minutes, the car stopped in front of big iron gates. Litchi trees and mango trees dotted the landscape. We stood there for some time.

"This is it," the driver said.

There was a familiar name on the nameplate. It was engraved in brass. Vast tracts of land led to a house. There were narrow pathways on the terrain with bushes of mulberry. A smell of water hung in the air. The rear of the mansion overlooked a bathing *ghat*. The wall on the west was hidden by acres of mango. There were dead silkworms on the mulberry leaves.

It was a difficult house to miss.

I took out my spray and used it freely. The driver screamed in pain but I shut him up with the knife. I nicked his earlobe. It was a light nick. His ear was soft under the blade.

Once he was locked in the boot, I took the wheel. The gear grew like a stick from the steering column. I took a left turn. Then I turned right and left again until we reached an old tree. It grew big jackfruits.

I unlocked the dickey and took the driver out. The fruits were hard in patches. They knocked him senseless. I drove back the same way and killed the engine a feet from the gates.

The mansion was very old. The gate was locked with a battering ram. A man slept on a mattress on the ground.

I decided to climb the gate.

It was sturdy. The iron didn't make a sound. There were several places to put my feet. My leg got stuck once but I swung over.

The man slept alone. I woke him up gently. His head was bald.

I let the blade shine on his face. It was wiped and cleaned. I used the skin of a pocket.

His eyes shot up to his forehead.

"Where is Debangshu Ghosh?"

The name made no sense to him.

"The policeman who wears everyday clothes." I pouted my lips to look like him.

He recognized me. "He left."

"When?"

"Days ago."

"Where did he go?"

"He went back with the others. They finished their work."

I swung the knife on his face. "Who else? Give me names."

"Two ladies and the man in a black coat."

"Names."

"They were from the police. He showed me a badge when he left."

"Lady policemen?" I slid the blade down his gullet.

"Yes, with boy hair and big breasts."

I wanted to spray him too but my balls hurt. I didn't fancy another ride up the gate. Instead I asked him to open it for me.

He stared after I got into the Ambassador. I saw him through the rear view mirror. He soaked in the number plate carefully.

I stayed close to the river. Mango orchards passed me by. The car dipped south until there were swamps everywhere. When I saw the river, I swerved left and reached a railway station. I parked the car and threw the keys down a drain.

A cycle rickshaw stood next to the platform. There was a man inside. I woke him up.

"Take me to Behrampore."

I handed him a hundred and went inside the cart.

The carriage went past wetlands and then we hit a state highway. The dawn broke in waves in the distance. The cyclist kicked the pedal hard.

After a few minutes, he put me down in the city. It was near the post office overlooking a strip of red water.

A square field lay opposite the office. There were courts in the neighbourhood. A jail stood beyond the field but it was shut.

We were outside a police station. I paid the cyclist another fifty.

"I need your help."

I handed him my broken star. It was wrapped in a khaki cloth. "Ask the man on duty for Mr. Debangshu Ghosh. Show him this."

The man felt the soft beige cotton on his palm. He looked at me.

I showed him another fifty. "They will pay you a reward."

He took the star and went inside. I hid behind the hood of his rickshaw and looked at the station.

He gave the star in the receiving section. One man was awake. The receiver heard the name and asked the cyclist to wait. He picked up a black phone and made a call. His face was tight when he put the earpiece down. Very slowly he left his seat. He walked around his desk and struck the cyclist.

It was a hard punch on the shoulder.

The man fell to the floor. The policeman picked him up and slapped his face. The man squealed and pointed at his rickshaw. I saw the policeman peep outside. He let go of the cyclist and put a whistle to his mouth. In a moment, the entire station was awake.

I jumped on the rickshaw. The handles were uneven but I took up position quickly. The hood rattled above me.

The saddle was uncomfortable. The plastic was very hard. Its foam kept creeping out from the seat. My arse hurt so I didn't sit on it. I pedalled towards the river and hit the main road. A few men in uniform followed me. I heard their shouting. Police whistles screamed behind the rickshaw.

Luckily they didn't have a van.

One man cycled but the other constables came on foot. I went past the jail until I was along the riverbed. I pedalled fast while the whistles grew soft. Eventually they died down.

At last I reached a jetty. There were ferries stalled around it. I pushed the rickshaw into the water. Then I hid in the bushes and waited but no one came for me.

I was tired. My calves screamed for air. But I couldn't sleep. The jetty smelt like a pack of hyenas. The ground was slippery where I sat.

Finally I got a boat.

I met my co-passenger from the train. He wore office clothes this time. He stood on the deck, away from a crowd of men. He looked at me suspiciously.

"Do you work in Murshidabad?"

I didn't say anything. Pointing at the mansion, I turned to the bank. The building looked massive from a distance.

We stood quietly in the ferry. Blind dolphins made waves in the water.

"I ferry across the river every morning. I take the train back," he said.

I leaned heavily on the railing. Drops collided against each other in broken symmetries and sprayed over my face.

"A man like that fills me with disgust." He stared at the bathing *ghat*. "Calls himself a Marxist!"

Strings of sweet water, reminiscent of freshly spawned fish, fell on my nose. I could smell *catla* and *rohu* shoaling under the river.

"I'm a Marxist too. But look at me." He rose above the deck like a snake. "He used his father's name to make money."

I sniffed the air again. There was a catfish somewhere. It smelled like a wild animal. Rows of crazy fish, swimming upside down, swelled the dark waters beneath us.

Suddenly he dropped his voice to a murmur. "He's a rogue. He killed his father."

I collapsed on the deck. After a few minutes I fell asleep to the soft moaning of the river.

✶

Many hours later, my mother woke me up. "Rathikanta wants to speak to you."

I hate being woken up. It gives me a headache. The whole morning gets fouled up. Several coffees later, I'm still in a bad mood.

I walked in a trance to the sitting room. All the tables bumped into me.

Sleep needs to be broken gently. It follows the laws of inertia. My body needed repair. Some cells couldn't be fixed at all. They had to be replaced with new cells.

The brain isn't a machine. You can't put it on like a switch.

"He's waiting. It's urgent," my mother said.

I was sure it was Bobo on the line.

I shuffled across the room and put the receiver to my ear. "Hello?"

For some strange reason, I always say hello when I pick up the phone. Why is it a rule? It's like 'dear' when we write letters. Dear Shibshankar, how are you?

"Come immediately," Bobo said. "I have something."

I took a shower. It didn't help. The water stung my eyes. I picked up a cake of soap and made lather on my body.

"Why were Surjo's clothes wet?"

I stood in the stall. "Shower."

"What made him go under the shower?"

My hair was a mess. I spread my arms out.

"Maybe Surjo was on the roof that night?"

I dried myself with a large towel. "Why would he go there?"

The towel cleaned my armpits slowly. "What did he do on the roof?"

✶

I wore clean clothes and jumped into a cab.

132

Bobo's garden looked like a jigsaw puzzle. A bunch of leaves interlocked in the distance. Their branches wandered like amoebae, making loops around the trees.

I joined Bobo on the grass.

"Mr. Ghosh is an informer."

Bobo adjusted her glasses. A sheaf of papers rustled under her arm. The papers were pinned to a clipboard.

She acted cool.

"That's what I wanted to tell you. He works with the police."

Bobo went inside to fetch another coffee.

My thoughts returned to Surjo. Was Bani Dasgupta hiding something? She was a shrewd woman. She could think on her feet. If she found Surjo in wet clothes, what would she do?

Did Surjo carry blood on his body? Maybe he left a trail on the staircase. Was that what my mother saw?

Bobo came back with a fresh cup.

"Tell me how this helps us."

She sipped her coffee.

"It's difficult to connect Ghosh with the deaths."

"You mean he had no motive."

"Why would he kill anyone? He doesn't have protection."

Bobo paused.

"Not anymore."

*

17

Surjo

*I*t was a Sunday. The Dasguptas weren't at home.

I bribed the cleaning lady and picked up a key from their shoe rack. The key opened their main door.

Sabbie had given me an address. It was a small house. A man with handy skills lived there.

"I know this guy. He's good," Sabbie said.

I met the man in his garage. Very quickly, he made me a copy. It looked exactly like the real thing. He was expensive but Sabbie paid on my behalf.

*

Later that evening, I put the original back on a peg above the shoe rack.

I went back to my flat and ate a light dinner. I waited for the TV to get switched off. The light in my parents' room got switched off too.

Late in the night, I heard crickets in the backyard. The noise came from the *tulsi* pit. I went down to Shibu's flat and stood by their door.

Switching off the mezzanine lights, I tried the new key. The door creaked but not too much. I killed a tiny blue light inside the sitting room and checked the kitchen door.

Surjo's room was far away. I took some water to the bed. A few drops fell on his hair. It wasn't enough to rouse him. I let the jug tilt and splashed his forehead. It was a hot night. The water tickled his skin.

When Surjo woke up, his room was dark. There was only a thin beam from the passage outside. He followed it out to the sitting room. I waited for him to enter the kitchen and then I plunged him in darkness. The bulb in the passage faded away.

Surjo dropped his glass. It was made of plastic so no one heard him. More water fell from it, this time on his feet.

I lit a torch and let it glow around the door. I walked to the midget door, opened it, and strode into the darkness. The trail of light fluffed on the staircase like a bride. Surjo came into the landing. He followed the light like a moth. The torch danced on the wall.

I walked one step at a time, slowly, shining the torch above me. The bulb on the staircase dimmed to a trickle. I heard Surjo stumble on the stairs.

Once I reached the top, I left the torch on the floor at the entrance to the roof. I went inside and smashed the only bulb that hung there. I broke it softly so that the pieces fell among the potted plants.

It was completely dark. I went out and picked up the torch. When I swung it, the light caught Surjo's eyes in the arc. Then I switched it off and waited.

It was a dark stormy night, without the storm.

Surjo joined me on the terrace. I stood in the shadows with a cap pulled over my face. He reached the centre of the roof in short jerky movements. Good. If that's what he wanted, I would give it to him.

I grabbed a shard of glass from the broken bulb. From behind him, I held his neck and let the glass touch him.

But Surjo wheeled around and grabbed me.

When he turned, he was someone else. A mad light shone in his eyes. Quickly, he took charge of the situation.

I got scared.

Surjo freed his hands and caught my wrist. He pined for the glass splinter. There was a force in him that destroyed my balance. His closed grip was hard as iron. But his open grip was worse.

Surjo's snaky fingers crushed mine. I danced in pain but I didn't show my voice. He giggled when my hand started bleeding.

It was like a game for him. His stringy muscles closed around my shoulders like a python. Slowly, he crushed my collar bone.

I couldn't shout for help. Even if he choked me to death, I couldn't explain anything.

Using all my strength, I pushed him back to the parapet. Then I stepped away and stood without any movement. I gave him a minute to calm down.

But Surjo wanted to play some more.

He charged and hurled me into the flower pots. I fell in a heap, more out of shock than anything else. My arms hurt. He may have recognized me. The cap was off my head.

Finally he ran out through the terrace door. He took my torch with him.

I went to the mezzanine after five minutes. Both the doors were shut.

I searched my pockets. The new key was gone. I must have dropped it in the scuffle.

"Anything's possible," I told Bobo later.

*

"See that shop?"

Bobo pointed to a shed in the corner. A three-point crossing lay ahead. It was near our building.

"Debangshu Ghosh used it as a hiding place."

The shutters were down. Bobo steered me across the kerb. We stood behind a stationary car and watched the shop.

A smaller opening lay to the side. It was planked up. There was an empty space behind the shop but it was locked.

"We should check it."

The planks weren't boarded with nails or anything else. They were set in a pile in front of the opening. Bobo made me take them apart along the flank. I put them on the road one by one. Then we peeped inside.

There was a small room. It was connected to the main shop. Perhaps it was used for storing supplies.

"Look."

Behind a pile of aromatic oils, an old man was sitting on the floor. He sat on a prayer mat with his arms folded like an alabaster bust.

"Hello?"

He ignored us and kept sitting.

"Maybe he's praying," I whispered.

"Or he's deaf."

"Hello?"

This time my voice was louder.

The man's beard was pressed against his shirt. The neck was covered in dirty spots. His beard was red and white in colour.

We stepped in closer. The prayer mat was near the end of the room. The man was turned towards the wall. From the back, we could see his collar. It looked a little wet.

I touched him lightly on his shoulders. The rest of his clothes were dry. But his body was getting stiff.

He was dead, whoever he was.

*

Bobo and I walked back once the police had cordoned off the shop.

The streets were empty. We walked past our building and stopped near a man with a burning fire. I ordered a cigarette and two glasses of tea.

The police said he was poisoned. They had taken him to a morgue. Someone put his blood on a slide and confirmed that.

A bottle of small blue pills lay by his side. It was kept under the prayer mat.

The skies were overcast again. The awning above our heads was made from a sheet of black canvas. Bobo sniffed the air. It had monsters in it.

"We are close," she said quietly. "I can smell it."

"What do you mean?"

"Surjo was on the roof that night."

I took a sip from the ridged glass. There were grooves at the bottom. The tea was very sweet.

"Number two: Bani Dasgupta. Perhaps she was on the terrace as well?"

"Did she push Shelley off the roof?"

"It's possible."

"Or maybe Surjo killed Shibu."

"If Mrs. Dasgupta knows anything, she's covering it up. Then there's *Mister* Dasgupta."

"Him too?"

Bobo fingered the base of her glass.

"He's not the murderer. But he's a man with secrets. He knows more than he says."

She paused.

"Four. *Your* parents may be involved. They returned late. Were they on the roof that night before the storm?"

"Motive?"

"No motive. Not much is known about your father. Five."

I smiled at her. It was my turn.

"You weren't on the terrace. That's what *you* say. Did you have an opportunity to get there? Yes. Did you have a chance to plan the murder? Yes. Do you have a motive?"

"No."

I ordered two more glasses.

The air was thick with moisture. I felt a shadow on the dark canvas overhead.

"Next there's Mr. Ghosh. He admits to seeing Shibu on the roof. Right before Shelley's death. That makes him the last person to see Shibu alive. Other than the murderer."

"Ganesh?"

"It's unlikely he killed both Shelley and Shibu. But why was his door wide open? Did he have access to your house?"

"He has a key to each flat."

"Then he might have stolen the *shilnora*. What if he put the murder weapon on the roof? And Shelley was found near his door. *In* the backyard."

"Is that relevant?"

"If Shelley was killed by a blow downstairs..."

A few large trees swayed on the opposite pavement. The first raindrops fell into our glasses.

"That's done with the building. What else?"

Bobo lifted her feet. She had taken off her slippers on a pair of sticks. The sticks were placed on stone slabs.

"Who went to the terrace with Shibu? That is the question."

138

"I don't know."

*

"Isn't that where Indrojit was hiding?"

A few policemen stood near our gate. They had come from the shop where we reported the dead man.

Bobo and I hid behind the wall and listened. The policemen spoke among themselves. We heard three of four different voices.

"What do you think?"

"It's that man Indrojit."

One of them pointed at the redbrick.

"But he got out recently, right?"

"Tried for murder."

"Twice."

"He was a pet dog. Party protection. We couldn't touch him."

"Was he connected to the dead man?"

"How? It was just an old shop keeper."

"No it wasn't his shop. I asked around."

"Then where did he come from?"

"I'm looking into it."

"But Indrojit was hiding *here*. This is pretty close."

"He might come back."

"Yes."

"Why?"

"His father lives in this building, stupid."

"Ganesh Kumar Sahoo."

A junior policeman put a tissue back in his pocket.

"Should we pick him up?"

"Later."

"Why, do you know him?"

Bobo and I looked at each other.

*

PART 4

BACCHUS, THE GOD OF WINE

18

Pink Elephant

I often surprise myself. It makes me feel young.

"Are you sure?" Bobo said clutching my shirt.

I pushed her away. We stood near a flight of stairs in an open space. At the foot of the stairs, men of all ages flocked around a caged enclosure. It was a liquor shop.

At the end of a long queue, I slipped some money through an opening.

The bottle that emerged from the other side was heavy, wrapped in an old newspaper. I admired its stout shape. The lines were straight. No angles, no curves. Clearly a man's drink.

I held Bobo's hand and took her to a porch on the road. The lid on the bottle was hard but it came off when I used my teeth.

"Don't drink *here*!"

Bobo looked around the quiet neighbourhood. The street dogs hadn't woken up yet. Meanwhile I stared lovingly at the open mouth of the whisky. Mashed grain, barley and rye. Beautiful.

We sat comfortably on the floor. It was someone else's porch.

"Wait till you see what I do," I told her.

The first drop of whisky went down like fire.

"Be careful, don't get drunk."

I took a giant swig. The fire rolled into my throat. Sparks rose in the belly and went straight to my head.

I felt alright.

"You won't pass out, will you?"

I looked at the bottle again. A red stag stood on a cliff across the label. It had big antlers on its head and its mouth was open. We had a connection, the stag and I. I raised the whole thing and gargled.

It was a quiet street. If you listened carefully, you could hear a radio. Bobo's pen scribbled on a notepad. The silence of middle class, the rustle of petticoats. And then I heard the purr of a patrol car.

It was a closed police van. An inspector's sleeve dangled from a window. The sleeve was made with white poplin.

They must have smelled the liquor. Did they follow me from the booze shop?

Two constables at the back wore nice cottons. They all looked at me.

Drinking on the road is frowned upon. No matter. I finished the bottle in one swig. Then, with nothing better to do, we ran like children. On the way I kissed the stag goodbye and threw him inside a bin.

The jeep didn't follow us.

It was dark by the time we reached. The redbrick building was quiet.

"I'll leave. It's getting late," Bobo said.

I stood alone at the gate for some time. Maybe I was high. That was a good thing.

*

Ganesh was inside his room.

A stick was placed in a corner. A chair stood next to the door under a pile of clothes. A desk was attached to the wall. It was full of junk, the way desks are.

Papers were stuffed inside large registers on the table. Off-white broadsheets peeped out of the registers. Two table clocks next to each other gave separate times.

Ganesh sat on the bed leaning over a table.

The second table was low and shabbier. A few brown paper envelopes were opened out on the surface. Ganesh was copying the contents of a typewritten page into a large sheet.

I didn't knock.

"Hello Ganesh."

I looked smart with my hands on the door.

Ganesh was surprised to see me.

"What is it?"

I closed the door behind me.

He quickly pushed his papers into a cupboard. It looked like a safety vault, the ones found in cheap hotels. He locked it and put the key in his pocket.

"Were those from Renuka?" I asked.

Ganesh stood in front of me with his hands on the chest.

"I saw her use your backyard," I told him.

"You're drunk."

I picked up his clothes neatly and put them on the bed. The chair was empty in two minutes.

"Or are they from your son? Prison letters?"

"You are drunk. You have to leave."

"Don't piss him off," Bobo said in my head.

I put on my best smile. "He's here, isn't he?"

Ganesh wanted to say something but he hesitated.

The whisky was acting up in my head.

"Was Indrojit in the building when Shibu died?"

No answer.

I kicked the chair next to his desk. It fell on the floor. Bang.

Ganesh didn't move.

I screamed in pain. The chair had large wooden legs. One of them crushed my big toe.

My voice bounced on the wall but it stayed inside.

"No he wasn't here," he said.

This time I jumped on the bed. I stepped on his clothes with my shoes on.

"Don't scare him," Bobo screeched.

Too late.

It wasn't me, it was the stag. The booze was doing its job.

"I'll call the police. They're looking for your son."

Ganesh walked across the room slowly. I stepped back on the bed. His hands were hidden behind his pants.

When he reached the edge of the bed he touched my feet.

"Indrojit didn't kill anyone. I swear."

Ganesh folded his palms and looked at my shoes.

"You're lying."

"He *saw* it happen. He has good eyes. It was very dark but..."

"What did he see?"

"Shelley fell off the terrace. That's what he told me."

19

Prince of Persia

*T*he next day I woke up with *Maggi* on my breath.

I had devoured two packs of *Maggi* the previous night.

My mother was asleep when I returned. The rice was kept on the table but it had grown cold and sticky. Stale food gives me a headache.

I'd brushed my teeth after dinner but the *Maggi* stayed with me.

The curtains were drawn. I rolled over on the bed. Suddenly I realized there was someone in the room.

I kicked the bedsheet away. Bobo stood in a corner near the door.

"Did you know about this?"

Bobo handed me a newspaper clipping.

It was a thin piece of paper. It was dated two years ago.

"What is this?"

"Read it."

I saw the coffee in Bobo's hand. It was bigger than mine. The mug was brown and bell shaped. A row of letters stood at the base.

She had taken it from the glass cabinet. But the cabinet was locked. Only my father had a key.

I turned to the paper. 'Fair and lovely', it said.

Bobo didn't say anything.

I read the words under the title. The heading was in bold like the writing on her cup. "Fair and Lovely."

The letters looked bigger than I remembered.

I read the article. It reported an abduction from *Zaveri Bazar*, a crowded market in Bombay. The victim lived in a housing society. She was a part-time nurse.

My father kept the paper in a glass cabinet. But it was locked.

The woman was middle-aged. She was dumped in a canal. The car went around in circles across the suburbs. The roads were quiet and deserted. Blah blah blah. It went on for another paragraph. I could quote the words if required.

It was the same story. I knew it by heart.

Bobo had taken the paper from the cabinet.

I sipped my coffee.

"Look at her picture."

I looked at the photograph in the article. Her features were familiar and then they eluded me.

"I don't know."

I put the paper down.

"Read the second article."

*

When I walked out of the backyard the previous night, I needed to pee very badly. The stag had mixed with my blood. They didn't like each other very much and wanted a way out.

Then I had to rush to the garage. My father's *Fiat* was parked inside with the canopy drawn out. I made sure I didn't wet the tyres and unzipped my trousers.

My father kept packets of *Maggi* in the car. I saw one of his pink folders through the window. It was caught in a ridge on the backseat where the leather bore dimples like a baby's butt.

I read a name on the file several times. It didn't make sense.

My father kept the car keys with him in the house. So I used a scale instead to unlock the *Fiat*. A long screwdriver acted as a wedge in my hands. When it stabbed the doorjamb, the door leaped out of its frame. The gap was big enough for the scale to slide through.

I got a spare tyre from behind the tool kit in the garage, stood on it and raised the lock at an angle near the roof of the car.

Once the door came undone flapping like a loose skirt, I looked through the file. It was shocking.

After ten minutes I went up to my flat. I took two packets of *Maggi* with me.

*

Bobo sat in front of me.

Overleaf, there was a copy of another news article. It was from the same newspaper. This piece was smaller.

It referred to the previous report. Two out of three suspects had been found. The third, a young woman by the name of Anjali, was still absconding. The police believed she fled from the region.

Neighbouring areas had been alerted. There were other charges against her. Posing as a nurse, she had drugged patients in the past especially old and retired couples who lived alone.

Using a variety of drugs – sleeping pills, barbiturates, etc. – Ms. Anjali disabled her victims before looting them.

A badly taken mug shot of Ms. Anjali was provided with the article. It was two years' old.

It was Renuka's picture.

*

She was younger in the photo. Her lips were coarse.

But her eyes were the same. I had seen this picture for the first time the night before. It was kept inside my father's file in the *Fiat*. I didn't know how he had a copy.

*

"She didn't do it."

Bobo's eyes twinkled when I said that.

"*You* wrote the break-up letter for her, didn't you?"

Quietly I sipped my coffee.

"Why?"

How could I refuse Renuka? Why should I bother explaining that?

"The police re-opened Shibu's file," I said. "Then they picked up Sabbie. He was grilled for hours. Renuka was scared they would grill her too."

"But you made a mistake."

"How?"

"A paper is fixed to the back of an envelope when you send a mail. By registered post."

"Yes, the post office does that."

"Apart from the date and address, the weight of the parcel is inscribed there. I checked the number of grams on the slip. It was heavier than a letter."

"Like what?"

"Copies of the news reports maybe? Someone was blackmailing her."

"She didn't do it," I repeated firmly.

*

A few minutes later, Bobo and I jumped across the wall in the backyard.

I looked across the temple compound. There was a building on the other side of the wall. It had an open turret along the flank. But the balcony was empty.

"That one."

I pointed at the staircase. It went up like a beanstalk above the neighbouring buildings.

"Will the old man remember?" Bobo asked me and I didn't reply.

We ran towards the opposite end and climbed above the camouflaged door.

The name was plated in onyx next to the gateway. The letters were spaced elegantly. 'Persia' it read left to right. I rang the doorbell three times in short sharp bursts.

The little girl at the entrance opened the door and held it for me. She wasn't little anymore. There were dark circles under her eyes. With them, squinting like a panda, she measured me carefully. A pack of cards lay clutched in her hand.

"Is the old man around?" I asked her.

Her face changed while her eyes grew bigger. "Aren't you the potty boy?"

"Yes." She had recognized me. Hooray. That was a relief.

"No."

I didn't understand. "Sorry, what?"

"He isn't around."

"We need a quick word with him. Please."

"You heard what I said?"

The girl's voice was shrill and sufficiently curt. The high quivering voice of puberty. "You can't meet him," she said shaking her head. Her thick hair smelled strongly of coconut oil.

"Why what happened?"

"He's dead, that's what happened."

*

We stood at the door for a long time.

Finally the girl made way for us and Bobo and I stepped inside. Together we went up to the balcony. The stairs had been cleaned recently with a series of footsteps but the handrails were stained forever.

The open view stretched around the neighbourhood. We stared at the redbrick building in the distance. Our terrace looked bare without the painted lady on top.

"Remember when the hoarding collapsed?" Bobo asked her.

"Oh yes. It was a horrible night," the girl replied.

"That was the worst storm of my life," I chimed in.

The girl stared at me.

Then she blinked. "Oh yes. The storm."

"Did you see anything?"

"I saw the hoarding fall like an elephant."

"There's a light on that terrace." I pointed at the redbrick wagging my finger near the top.

"You might have seen a few other things?"

The girl looked at the empty space where the soap lady once smiled on the billboard. Then she spoke quietly to Bobo.

"It was late in the evening. The people on the rooftops were acting funny as usual. They walked in circles around the antennae and water tanks."

"What time was this?"

I heard a scribble on Bobo's pad.

"A little after seven. I heard the big clock chime fourteen times."

I looked into the old man's sleeping room. A grandfather clock was encased in a big black bonnet. The dial had big roman numerals on a white background.

"Go on."

"A little later, I saw two boys come up."

She pointed at the roof of the redbrick where a few potted plants stood near the parapet wall.

"They were young boys."

*

The pen at my elbow stopped working.

It was a ball point pen. I heard Bobo scratch furiously but the words wouldn't come out. The ink had run dry. Its oil sat heavily in a plastic barrel refusing to move.

Another pen emerged from Bobo's bag. This was a roller ball with a fine grip. Soon the sphere at the tip drew out her thoughts. The curves on the sheet were new and precise.

Bobo said: "Boys?"

"One of them I'd seen before."

Bobo stopped writing.

"Was it him?" She pointed at me. I smiled at her.

The girl smiled back. "No this one was broad. He was draped in a caftan."

"And the other guy?"

"They were far away. One of them was barely able to walk."

"Why, did they fight?"

"No. He just sat there on the roof for a long time. I think he was leaning on the parapet."

"Did the other boy stay back?"

"I think I saw him leave after a while."

"But he didn't return?"

"No."

"And no one else came to the roof in between?"

"A plumber arrived later. When it was dark."

"And before that?"

"Not much. A woman came up to hang clothes. She was kneeling near the sick boy. And then the storm broke out."

The girl had run downstairs after that. Once the winds crashed against the staircase slamming doors and windows, she had left the balcony. There were clothes which would get wet in the rain.

"I unplugged appliances in the kitchen. The TV could blow up if there was lightning. When I returned to the balcony, there was a plumber on the roof. He had a helper with him."

Bobo used her cursive hand on a small writing pad. She drew a line across the page. Very carefully, she copied the facts one below the other in bullet points.

In the other half of the sheet, durations for each activity were noted in blocks of ten minutes. Then Bobo sucked on the clipper and calculated the timing of the storm. Rolling her nails on opposite phalanges, she made an estimate and wrote it down.

"Plumber you said?"

"Have you seen him before?" I asked the girl.

"No he was a new person. He had a big spanner in his hand which he kept waving around the low wall. I assumed the pipes were embedded in the parapet." The girl marked a thick section of air with her small hands to show the size of the spanner. "In the end he wiped it clean and left."

"What was he doing?"

The girl shrugged. "Fixing the pipe I suppose?"

Suddenly Bobo started shaking. There was an insect on her left foot. It must have come from the collected dirt in the staircase. The corners were full of filth and soot.

The itch started on her knee and crawled up her thigh, shamelessly slipping under the pleated skirt. Thankfully the skirt was long and sensible. She rubbed her legs, scraping, grazing the floral prints around her hamstring but it went through the hem like a beetle.

I turned away with dignity.

The girl stared at her but Bobo walked out of the house without me, scratching like a dog.

*

20

Reconstruction

I met Renuka late one night the following week.

She wanted to meet me in a crowded place. Where we stood, there were little pillars around a green expansive meadow. Stray horses stood in groups chasing flies with their swishy tails. The horses weren't too big. Their nostrils were flared in the dark and so they looked ominous. We heard them stomping the earth with soft hoofs.

Renuka and I walked away past a maze of standing buses. The buses had stopped running for the day.

"Tell me," she said.

Renuka stood in a wet open space. The rain hadn't dried up completely. The spot was badly lit even in the open. The only light came from a sex shop nearby.

There was a small wooden board on the pavement. There was a set of lamps on the board placed in a line. The shop hustled tropical oils, magic tablets and sperm. The sperm cells had been extracted from a Royal Bengal tiger, the vendor screamed. There was a bottle of syrup that made you go hard with passion. Another juice enhanced a woman's breasts twice over. Three spoonfuls every morning.

I turned to Renuka under the sex lamps. Her hair was shaggy with a cowlick in the centre. She looked very tall when she stood sideways. I took a step towards her.

"I have your *shilnora* with me." She smiled and pointed at my pants.

"Were you on the roof?" I asked her.

"Maybe."

"Did you do it?"

"Why do you care?"

"People are asking me."

Renuka jumped out of the way. A young man on a moped charged towards her. There was a big puddle nearby with a pool of still standing water.

But she didn't get splashed. Her ankles had the lightness of a *ballet* dancer.

There were many lights on the Esplanade. Renuka smiled and disappeared among one of them.

"You'll never get me Sandy. Ta ta," she said and walked away.

*

I took out what I had in my pocket. I aimed it at her head.

Renuka didn't turn back.

From my spot I had her covered. My palms closed around the soft parts of her flesh.

Renuka moved slowly in the distance.

The newsprint was in my hand.

I looked at her profile in the black and white photo. She was young when the article was written. Her lips were raw. Like thin slices from an overripe fruit.

I folded the paper and put it back in my shirt.

*

Once Renuka was gone, I felt my pockets. The lining was firm with fresh weight.

I touched them again. This time there was a jingle. The keys I had brought with me were still inside.

I walked down Old Post Office Street in the dark. The High Court was dead this time of night. A couple of mad men slept on the pavement. I jumped over them and opened the main doorway at the end of a passage.

Five minutes later I walked down the long corridor with a torch. When I reached the end, I unlocked another door and went inside. Then I latched myself in.

I knew where my father kept his documents. The flashlight in my hand was weak so I got a bulb going. A stash of legal papers was hidden under the table.

I took the false plank out. The papers were signed and stamped. Someone had registered them with a lot of money.

Fifteen minutes later, I found what I was looking for.

★

It was a large white hammock. I hung it between two trees in Bobo's garden.

Bobo sat on a rug with pads and pens. It was a nice evening, dark and mysterious. One side of the coffee tray was mine.

"I recorded the little girl on the balcony," Bobo said.

The coffee was bitter. A large flask with a thermostat lay on the side bearing more coffee.

Bobo had hidden a walkman in her underwear. I sat up on the hammock to hear her words better.

"What if Sebastian slipped something in his drink?" she said.

"I'm listening."

"Rohypnol enhances the effects of alcohol. Roofies. The date rape drug."

"And barbs are used as anaesthetics." I read it out from Bobo's notes.

"How did he *get* the drugs in the first place?"

"Forged prescriptions?" I told Bobo about Sabbie's father and his line of drugstores.

"Hmm. Sleeping tablets maybe. Barbiturates are used for epilepsy."

"And assisted suicide." It was all there in her notes. She had copiously produced reams of material from a medical journal.

"Isn't Surjo on barbs?"

"For his seizures, yes."

Bobo frowned and thought for a minute. "Did Sabbie leave the building that night?"

"The little girl said so. Play the tape."

"Why didn't he kill him on the roof?"

"What?"

"Earlier in the evening they went to the terrace together. Sabbie was alone with Shibu. Why didn't he finish him off right then?"

I didn't understand what she was saying.

"Let's say Shibu was sedated," Bobo said slowly. "He was weak. His impulses were slow. In a little time, he would be inert anyway."

"It wasn't dark yet. On an open terrace, that would be a huge risk."

Bobo looked at her pad.

"Sabbie left at seven forty five. Twenty minutes later, you arrived in the building. Then you met Renuka and Amit on the mezzanine."

"What were they doing on Shibu's staircase?"

Bobo continued with the time table.

"Around half past eight, the billboard collapsed. Hmm. Did someone tamper with the nuts and bolts?"

I told Bobo about Amit's big bag outside the generator room. "He has a hammer that can cripple the foundation."

Bobo took another sip of her coffee.

"Why did she cut her hair?"

"I cut my hair too. It doesn't mean anything."

"She's a tall girl." Bobo frowned. "It may've been *her* that Ganesh saw, not Sabbie."

"What about the girl on the balcony?" She specifically mentioned *boys*. Only boys."

"She was too far away to notice the difference."

"Renuka didn't do it," I repeated. "She told me."

"If she hid her boobies inside a jacket, no one would know. She'll pass for a boy from a distance."

"Come on!"

"And her hair's a mess. Curly like Sabbie's."

I gave up. There was no point telling her. I left the hammock and re-filled my cup.

*

21

On a Dark Stormy Night, Again

*T*he rains came like silent death. Suddenly the winds stopped blowing. When the downpour intensified, we collected our things and ran inside.

A few minutes later, with a roof on our heads, the garden looked beautiful. We sat on a marble floor and ogled the naked raindrops beached on the plants.

Rathikanta kept potting sheds in the garden. They were covered with sheets of hard iron. When the drops fell on the metal surface, the rain turned to noise. A pair of skeletons made love on the corrugated iron roof.

Suddenly the lights went out. In a flash, the house was bombed to darkness. The street lights vanished as well, extinguished with one stroke, all at the same time like a mass killing.

"A dark stormy night," I murmured.

The coffee was warm. Insects emerged from dark corners on the ground. The earth was hungry and wet, smelling of wild passions.

"Why do you think it's her?"

"Renuka Sharma." Bobo pronounced the words carefully, hanging on to each syllable.

Her name sounded strange in Bobo's voice.

"Someone stole my father's key. Did you take his papers out of the cabinet?" I asked.

She didn't say anything.

"You didn't suspect Renuka before. She may be a thief. Not a murderer."

I pulled my feet out from a rug and felt the soft wetness of the garden.

"She'll look good on your uncle's CV, that's why," I told her.

Little insects clung to my legs. Some of them nibbled my toes but the bigger ones got stuck in the hair around my calves. I flicked them carelessly on the grass.

"He says they'll tail her undercover," Bobo whispered.

I laughed. "You're piecing photos together and framing her, that's all you're doing."

"Rubbish."

"Forget about the motive. What do you know about her?"

I walked to the pillar where she sat. Bobo was slumped on the floor with her files around her like a roadside vendor.

"Sabbie was on the roof," I said. "Maybe he killed Shibu and Shelley both. Where does Renuka come in?"

Bobo rubbed two pebbles together near her ringed feet. The rainwater had flowed into crevices on the floor. The mosaic tiling gleamed in the dark.

"If you want to protect her, that's not my problem," she replied.

"Just because I wrote a letter?"

"Never trust a horny boy." Bobo sighed and put her head against the pillar.

*

It was time she knew of other important things. Maybe that would help her understand. I told Bobo about the *shilnora*.

"You saw the doctor's certificate?" she asked me.

There was a copy lying in my father's file which he kept hidden in the *Fiat*. I saw the medical report. It didn't mention a head injury. Excessive bleeding from a wound, it said.

"But Mr. Dasgupta got the report *made*. There was money involved. I don't trust the version."

Then I remembered something else. "What about the lady in the picture?" I asked Bobo.

It was attached to the first news clipping that she had shown me. There was a photo of the victim. I didn't recognize the woman, the one that was abducted.

"I was checking whether you knew who it was."

"Don't lie to me Bobo."

She leaned against the pillar and said nothing.

I grabbed her file from her hand. From inside the house, I brought a kerosene lamp out. I took the file with me in case Bobo tried to hide it.

There were many pictures in a separate folder. Her uncle had sent mug shots of Ganesh and Indrojit Sahoo to his brother Rathikanta. There were photos of other people too. The faces looked like ghosts in the flickering lantern.

A gust of wind shook the lantern. The flame danced and shone brightly.

Suddenly a face leaped out in the veranda. It seemed like a trick of light in the surrounding darkness. Then the features of a woman, sombre and weather beaten, settled down in my hands. It was a face which had seen strange things. I stared at the face unable to take my eyes off her as if I was hypnotized. Bobo looked away.

I took the file alongside the news clipping and compared the two. I held them side by side.

There was a photo of Aparna, Ghosh's daughter. I checked the face against a blown up image in Bobo's file. Separately, a mug shot was pressed into a compartment with a label. I saw her face in the flicker of the kerosene lamp.

The photograph in the news article was different. It was taken outside a police station. The complainant stood with a copy of the FIR flanked by two men in uniform.

It was Aparna's picture, when I compared the two.

So the robbed woman in Bombay was Aparna. She, who was abducted, looted and left on the road by Miss Anjali and her friends. It was Ghosh's long-lost daughter Aparna.

Someone had labelled the photograph. It looked like Bobo's writing unless she inherited her hand from her uncle. The label read, Aparna *Sahoo.*

*

"What does this mean?"

I spilled a lot of coffee on the floor. My hands were shaking nervously.

"There's a *third* clipping," Bobo said. She pointed to another file.

I whipped out the scan from an envelope. It was a long article. There were graphs on crime levels over the past year in Bombay and photos of ugly men and ring leaders. Among them the police were looking for a girl of twenty five. Her latest 'job' was a staged kidnapping. She had robbed herself at gun point from *Zaveri Bazar*.

Bobo looked at me.

The woman in *Zaveri Bazar* had manufactured the abduction. She had claimed insurance money and made off with the booty as someone else. What's more, Renuka was Aparna. With a plastic nose attached to her face and a false forehead. They were one and the same person.

"She's everywhere," I screamed.

*

Fifteen minutes later we were on the road.

"Can you drive?" Bobo asked me softly.

I pressed hard on the accelerator. Rathikanta's *Gypsy* was old and bruised but it answered well to my treatment.

"The parts are stiff," I told her. Then she saw me use both my hands when I changed gears.

"Do you have a licence?"

"It's lying somewhere."

"Look out!"

A truck went past the hood of the *Gypsy* at full speed.

"Don't take your hand off the wheel!"

It was past midnight. We had an hour's drive ahead. The weather was bad to say the least. The wipers weren't any good either.

"I can't see anything."

Bobo held a silver chain around her neck and prayed some gibberish.

"Neither can I." The *Gypsy* had a rocky ride across its chassis. The four wheels wobbled together. Its gait was tilted slightly to the left.

I asked Bobo to hold the chloroform steady in her hand. "Don't let the bottle break."

It was pitch dark. The lights on the highway were switched off. Slowly my glasses fogged up in the intense humidity.

"Make me a coffee, Bobo. I'm sleepy."

"This isn't a canteen. Just drive."

The flask was in the backseat.

"Please pour me a cup Bobo. I need it."

I cracked my window and let the rain in. Bobo fiddled with the thermostat and cupped her hands on her lap.

"Why do you keep chloroform in your house?" I asked her leaning towards the window. Thankfully the coffee didn't spill out.

"The gardener makes pesticides."

We had picked up a bottle from the potting shed. The fumes in the bottle were strong. Just the thought of it tickled our senses.

The coffee helped us through the journey. When we reached the redbrick, it was around two in the morning. The rains were less intense in this part of town.

I went into the compound through a side gate. Maybe there were cops watching the main gate at night or maybe they had fled in the rain. Why take chances? Bobo entered with me through a narrow passage past the garage.

The backyard was completely flooded. Ganesh had locked his door. We went around the rear of the building where the sewage had clogged up.

I tiptoed to a large window on the wall. It was above the *tulsi* pit in the backyard. Ghosts of half eaten chickens lay strewn on the floor.

Sometimes Ganesh left the window open.

The panes were shut but the window wasn't bolted. The winds had only closed them down.

I hoisted Bobo on the ledge above the *tulsi* pit. She opened a panel and slid inside Ganesh's quarters. Then she gave me her hand.

It was a large room with a radio box and furniture. In addition there were pieces from a motor engine, a few cardboard packages, a broken almirah and slabs of marble resting against the wall. Ganesh was in another room.

We peeped through a connecting door which was wide open. He was slumped on the bed under a thin sheet.

"Let's knock him cold."

I took out a handkerchief with a grey border. Bobo uncorked the bottle. The syrup smelled sickly sweet something like a tequila shot after a night of drinking.

She quickly shut the lid.

"Please don't pass out."

I splashed the liquid on the handkerchief. The cloth soaked it in hungrily. It was a thick fabric with dense loops across its face.

I went behind the bed and covered his eyes with one hand. I lifted the sheet a little and grabbed his mouth with the cloth.

Ganesh woke up with a start.

His mouth was wide open. The fumes went through his nostrils and throat while he struggled vigorously. He breathed in the toxic fumes, coughing like a sick man, wheezing, gasping for fresh air under his blanket.

I kept the cloth pressed hard under his nostrils.

Bobo stood next to me and soaked a second cloth with the bottle. This was a tissue with pink flowers on it. The edges were rounded. When she passed me the cloth, I smothered Ganesh again, this time stuffing the edges into his open mouth.

A few seconds later, Ganesh was lying on his pillow completely still.

"Is he dead?"

"We don't know." I looked for his keys around the bedside. The drawers and door pegs next, then the other room. Bobo searched the tables. We couldn't find it. Obviously the key wasn't kept in a regular place.

I checked his pockets. There were trousers everywhere lying untidily across the furniture. The legs were flopped on chairs or around low tables. His shirt was hanging in the bathroom. The underpants were in a bucket under the washbasin.

But the key wasn't in any of these places.

Then Bobo looked under his sheet. "Maybe he sleeps with it?"

I moved Bobo aside and removed the cover. *Voila!* Two sets of keys were tied on a string around his pyjamas. I took the smaller chain out.

The cupboard on the opposite wall opened easily. It had money, bills and a big packet. The packet was white in colour with a wire netting around the mouth. It had bundles of currency notes tied with small white strings.

Bobo passed me another key. There was a vault on the upper safe. I turned the key around in the opening. But the door didn't budge.

"It must be double locked."

Bobo passed me the last barrel from the keychain.

Finally the panel yielded. Inside, there were stacks of paper. Thick fat bundles of A4 sized sheets and *stacks* of other printed material.

It would take a year to read them all.

Bobo fingered the bundles carefully, feeling the sharp edges around the tips. The documents were stapled together and arranged neatly along the corners of the vault. In addition they were fastened with a plastic wire.

I went to the other room and brought a few plastic bags with me. There were hundreds of them kept inside the cardboard boxes near the window. I passed Bobo a packet and started undoing the bundles.

Bobo pushed the papers forcefully into the packet while I held it open. She groped the stacks from the vault along with loose stapling pins on the floor of the safe. The pins were bent and crooked, some of them darkly rusted near the ends.

Some of the piles of paper were stuck together. Rubber bands had melted in the heat of the vault and trapped one bundle with the next. It took some care to disengage them without ripping the edges.

Meanwhile a shadow emerged at the entrance of the room. Someone had stealthily crept inside Ganesh's quarters without us noticing.

He came in through the main door. The man obviously had a key of his own since the door was locked. The tables, shelves and chair tops were a mess. The drawers had been opened out like matchboxes. Several cartons and polythene containers had been turned upside down.

The man looked puzzled. That's when I saw him.

Bobo swung around with piles of paper and a plastic wire on her wrist, hanging like a limp dick. The packet fell from my hand. Bobo lost her grip on the last bundle and the documents dropped to the floor one by one like a solid fountain. We heard him breathe heavily where he stood near the door.

"Indrojit!" Bobo hissed.

He kept looking at us without saying anything.

The first thing I noticed about the man was his moustache. It wasn't a moustache really, more like freshly sprung whiskers on the face of a wild animal. They drooped in a bunch of hairy pea pods under a slim, flat nose. When he breathed out, they rose above his lips.

We're fucked, I thought.

Indrojit Sahoo had a timid mouth, the way a mouth looks once it's eaten something. He scratched the wood on a table absently using two long fingers leaning against the surface.

I waited for him to say something. He picked out a *beedi* from his left ear. Using the same two fingers in a quick twiddle, he lit the *beedi* with a matchstick.

Magic, it looked like magic.

Smoke blew out through the room like a special effect.

Ganesh didn't mind the smoke. It had a leafy smell to it, something pleasant and soothing.

The light in the room grew brighter. Shapes emerged from the shadows when our eyes got adjusted to each other.

Indrojit scanned my face carefully.

I stood rooted to the spot like a clay figure. My time was running out fast. I couldn't move, I couldn't run. And the *beedi* wouldn't last forever.

Then Indrojit looked at his father. Ganesh was lying comfortably on the bed. He slept like a baby.

Do babies snore? Ganesh wasn't snoring.

Indrojit flicked the *beedi* from his lips. It landed very precisely on his father's face as if he meant it. Hissing a little, the burning stick bounced off his cheeks in sprightly embers.

But not a stir from Ganesh.

His son took out some wax matchsticks from his pocket. He threw the whole bunch at the bed.

Indrojit had a good aim. The matchsticks landed on his father's forehead. Then they rolled down the bridge of his nose like worms on a rainy day.

Ganesh didn't wake up.

Indrojit went towards the bed. At the edge of the bedpost, he sniffed suspiciously and looked at us. The sheet smelled sweet.

Raising an arm, he slapped his father's face.

No reaction.

Bobo fiddled with her skirt.

"Let's go."

Indrojit Sahoo tore into the bed cover and stared at Ganesh. He didn't move a muscle. His body looked like a corpse except he wasn't stiff.

And then, Indrojit charged at me like a bull.

I heard Bobo's voice when his whiskers were flying in the air. Indrojit lunged across the bed. Over his father, he rammed his body into mine.

I tried to shield Bobo from the attack. My hands hit the wall behind me. My head hit the wall too.

I felt a sharp collision. I saw the cupboard, the ceiling and the floor in no particular order. A pair of bathroom slippers lay by the bed. The ground was moist.

The fan moved very slowly.

His whiskers were the last thing I saw.

*

I sat up in a dimly lit room.

My eyes were stuck in my head. I could see little furrows in my brain. With some effort, I put the eyes back in place. They fitted the sockets nicely.

I was lying in a bed against a blue wall. My back was propped up with pillows. The door at the other end faced the bed. It was latched.

Someone had locked the door from the other side. I didn't know that.

It was a small room. I looked through the window next to the pillows. There was a view from the third storey of a building.

In the middle of the room, a high shelf was set against the wall. A giant music system sat there with speakers. It looked like a new set.

Below the shelf, there was a stool with a remote control. Opposite the shelf, on another low stool, a girl quietly swung her legs.

I sat up on the bed.

The girl was colouring her nails. She stirred a little when she saw me but she kept polishing. She wore a short skirt. I saw her legs in the dark. They were dark too, with a prominent lump on the calf showing well formed muscles.

There was a small erection in my pants.

I couldn't see the colour of her eyes. No one had seen her eyes in a long time.

A small chair was placed at my feet. Two empty beer bottles and two glasses were kept on it. Rings showed on the surface of the chair. There weren't any coasters in the room.

It wasn't a classy place. I looked around the sparse interiors. The girl's halter neck was coloured a bright turquoise. The vest had a smocked back. It had elastic seaming in the front. I could see both sides of it. It rested on the back of her chair.

It was exactly her size. The vest would fit her nicely when she wore it.

I couldn't take my eyes off her.

"You should leave. It's been a rough night," she spoke for the first time.

Thank you, ma'am. I got off the bed, tied my laces and went to the door.

"Stop looking." Her voice was thick.

I tried the doorknob quickly. It twisted in my hand and kept twisting without doing anything else.

"The door is locked."

"Get out of the room."

I tried the door again. This time I used both my hands.

When it still didn't yield, I checked if there was a latch or maybe a chain near the handle. But when I put my eyes to the keyhole, I couldn't see the other side.

"I can't open it. What should I do?"

She blew on her nails. Her udders heaved when she did that.

There was a pair of heels on the floor but she found only one. It was painted brightly with a shiny finish. She slid her ankle in using her fingers. I looked under the bed, found the other shoe and passed it to her.

"Thank you darling," she said. "But you still have to pay me." She had a lovely smile with the shadow of a dimple but her cheeks were too thin to form creases in the right place.

"What for?"

The girl slipped her foot into the other heel. Then she clasped it around her ankle and stood up.

"Darling, don't make me beg. I sucked your cock all night."

I blushed furiously.

She spread her fingers wide. "Make it quick."

I looked at her wrist and her open palm. She wore an imitation watch. It was studded with small sparkling stones. Like her shoes, they were too bright to be real.

I looked at her fingers again. There were five of them.

"That's the rate."

She wanted five grand for the night. Desperately I tried the door one last time hoping for a miracle. No result. Then I checked my wallet. All I had were coins in the coin compartment.

Meanwhile someone banged on the door outside.

"And two thousand rupees extra for the beer. Special price for you because I love you."

That made no difference to me.

She came to the door and snatched my wallet. Her stride was like a wild cat, hunting. I looked at her bare breasts but I didn't touch anything. The nipples were dark, grainy, with the edges blurred into the soft rise of her tits. A few coins slipped out of the leather compartment. Nothing else. The dull brown cover of the wallet touched her naked body.

She tossed my wallet through the open window.

"Where's my fucking money?"

I cocked an ear but I didn't hear the wallet fall. Shit. It had my cards and ID in it.

"You thought I was for free? Motherfucker."

She looked angry. I liked it. Her boobs grew bigger when she heaved.

"I can get you some money from home," I said.

She slapped me smack on the face.

"You want the cops to come, don't you?"

Right then I heard footsteps outside.

It was time for me to take my hands off the door. Using both of them, I caught her wrists instead.

"They're looking for the man who brought me here," I told her.

My face was very close to hers.

"Which man?"

"Is something wrong?" Someone spoke at the keyhole outside. It was a heavy man's voice from across the locked door, on the other side of the room.

"Not yet."

"Ring the bell if there's trouble."

I checked my pockets. There was another tissue soaked in chloroform. It was a little stale but it would do under the circumstances. I had saved it for later. Thank you Bobo.

The girl had thin arms. She could be taken without any trouble.

I held her neck tightly. In one clear motion, her feet came off the ground. She bit the flesh on my hand with very sharp canines but I held on.

"Stop!" My hand started bleeding and then the blood splattered in the thinly crumpled sheets on the bed.

I pushed her to the window sill. It was a good drop to the ground. There weren't any grills either.

"One whore less no one will notice. If you bite me again I'll push you down."

I stuffed the tissue in her mouth. I didn't have a rope so I used her bra. Her hands were tied behind her back. She kept the skirt on, I let her wear it.

I picked up the remote and pressed the 'Power' button. The music played on full volume. Then I climbed on the bed and looked out through the window.

There was a heap of garbage downstairs.

Garbage is soft. It's like a cushion. Good. It would break my fall.

I climbed out through the window. I held the ledge and swung outside clinging to a thin cornice.

No, I can't do it.

I turned to my left. There was a pipe within an arm's reach. Holding the wall with one hand, I gripped the pipe's cylinder. It was a thick, hard cross-section made of withering paint and metal.

But my hand slipped before I could wrap my fingers around the pipe. So I let go of the grip and moved upwards. My fingers found the knob of a valve instead. It was a big knob with rough rounded seals. I coiled a thumb around one of the seals.

Finally I got a firm hold. There was another window near the valve. It looked into a smaller room. The room was empty. Thank god. I didn't want to scare a fat old man in the middle of coitus.

I cupped my hand firmly around the seal. The ridges on my palm fitted the valve. I used my sweat as a plaster. Then I left the ledge, got both my hands together and squeezed the pipe.

I looked at the garbage heap on the ground below me. There was a chance I could make it. Preferably in one piece. But it was just a chance.

I dropped down one floor. I used my feet for additional support. My fingers did the slipping. The scratches on the wall leeched into my body. My chest was badly grazed while I slid against the facade of the building. After a minute's struggle I turned my head and looked down again.

An old mattress was lying in the garbage dump. There was a pile of used plastic next to it. The cotton stuffing came out through several holes in the mattress.

There were holes and there was cotton. Cotton was good. It didn't kill. I closed my eyes and let go.

*

It wasn't a thud.

When I landed, the cotton stuffing flew around me like flies. It was a bad mattress. No wonder someone threw it away. It gave the clients a bad back. When they carried their sores back home, the wives got suspicious.

The mattress didn't hold my back either. I fell and slid down its lumpy body all the way to the end of the garbage dump. I rolled down the slope like a soggy tennis ball. The mattress dipped towards the boundary where a pile of bricks from a construction site were laid out in stacks. In the end a heap of compost broke my fall before I smashed my head on the partition.

I stood up and felt my parts. They needed to be checked for proper functioning if at all I used them. My spine would never be the same again. But I was alive.

Through a connecting arch, a gate led to the main corridor. A couple of policemen stood at the entrance. It was the only way out of the garbage dump.

"Come here," the constable said.

Meanwhile his friend finished an early breakfast from a brown paper packet.

I picked up a disposal bag from the heap. It was a black and layered plastic lying in a corner against the partition wall. Big refuse was stuffed inside it like confetti.

I saw myself in the constable's eyes when I reached the entrance. The look on his eyes gave me away. There was disgust on his face, an ugly masque around his ears; the hands were distant and unfamiliar. I almost choked on the garbage but he wouldn't touch me.

The pants I wore were tattered and greasy, squishy in patches with children from the garbage dump. My shirt was stained with blood and bruises. A large part of the soiled garbage had stayed with me.

I walked up to the policeman and pushed the bag in his face.

The constable recoiled in shock and shooed me away.

I took a turn on the main road once I got out. I had retrieved my wallet from the garbage dump from a fold of the broken mattress. There was a debit card inside it. I crossed the road, entered an ATM and took some money out of the machine.

It was a new morning. Noisy groups of vendors sold coconuts on the pavement, stalling half the roads near the main intersections. I stepped into a taxi and asked for Bobo's house.

An hour later when we reached, a new servant opened the door. I hadn't seen him before.

"Is Bobo back?"

I looked at the clock. 6:15 a.m.

"Bobo?"

He looked at me amazed. "Are you alright?"

Impatiently, I walked through the sitting room and sent a maid inside to wake her up.

"Tell her it's urgent."

The lady in the kitchen set the table for me. I showered and ate four eggs and a jar of lemon marmalade. I must have walked to the guest enclave thereafter and washed my hands and mouth in the attached basin but I don't remember any of it.

Many hours later I woke up in a dark room.

The room reeked of memories from the garbage dump. My clothes were stuffed inside a laundry bag in a corner which overlooked the rear of Bobo's garden. It was a nice cloth bag taken from a fancy hotel sometime during Rathikanta's travels abroad. I tossed the whole bag into a pile of leaves in the garden and closed the window.

But that didn't get rid of the smell. I went to Rathikanta's study to see what was going on. Maybe he had seen or heard something new.

"Bobo is lost," I told him once I was inside his study.

He rose from his armchair and greeted me warmly.

"They picked up Indrojit Sahoo at Sealdah. He was about to board a train," he said.

That was a relief. I didn't fancy being trapped inside a whorehouse again. "And what about Bobo?"

"And they also got a warrant out for Shushobhon Dasgupta. For the murder of his father."

I was wrapped in a bed sheet because I was out of clothes. The sheet almost fell from my waist.

"Bobo?"

Rathikanta sat down in his armchair. "Go get some sleep. You're not well."

*

22

El Último Doppio

*B*obo was sitting in the porch when I stepped out the next morning.

"What the hell are you wearing?" she said hiding her braces with her hand. "You look like a clown!"

I pulled Rathikanta's *kurta* out below my boxers. Its white linen flowed into my legs.

"You're smelling!" Bobo moved away when I tried to hug her.

"It's a long story, never mind. You tell me. What happened?"

"Indrojit Sahoo confessed in police custody. Shushobhon had hired him to kill his father."

Apparently the police found a dated will where the old landowner had left all his money to Shushobhon.

"Have they arrested him?"

"No he's disappeared."

"And what about his sister Shelley?"

"Shushobhon killed her as well. He thought the estate was split fifty fifty between the siblings."

"Then who killed Shibu?"

Bobo smiled and twiddled a pen at my face. "Tell me horny boy, who?"

"For the last time," I said, "Renuka didn't do it."

*

PART 5

MEA CULPA, MY BAD

23

Emma Rose

*T*he next day was the worst day of my life.

It started well, the sun shone brightly on our faces. I found myself below a sprawling staircase in a crowded building. The steps lolled like a tongue from the outer facade. My father, meanwhile, hid behind a white *Omni* van.

A dirty corridor extended above our heads. We stood next to a tree near the foot of the staircase. It was a big tree wearing its leaves like a loose petticoat. There were squirrels and fruits consumed by each other. Flowers polished their bushy tails in the sunlight, gleaming with fur and pollen.

It was a fine morning except we were at the hospital.

My father pushed me towards a drugstore near the parking lot. Shushobhon was inside an emergency ward. He was either concussed or asleep. Someone had sapped him on the head.

Residents walked past us like zombies. They had been on emergency duty through the night. Some of them were monitoring outdoor admissions. They came from the casualty block, swapping ghastly stories and the morning news tucked under their sleeves.

Some junior doctors fed coffee to each other. The coffee came from the teat of a scarlet vending machine in a corner, where the main porch was darker.

"Unhealthy," my father said, looking around.

A girl spoke about putting a tube into a man's chest. Someone else screamed for resection and clavicles, gently sipping on a Styrofoam cup. There were white gowns everywhere.

I ordered for a coffee. It was handed to me in a plastic glass. Once it was crushed, I felt better.

We went up a staircase lined with urine. The urine was stale and dry. Well dressed ward boys wore white shirts with a small blue patch on their pockets. The shirts were perfectly pressed. Some other boys roamed around the staircase in shorts carrying catheters.

"He's in here." My father pointed to a room in the corner. We picked up Shushobhon through his armpits from a low spring bed. No one stopped us.

Shushobhon had multiple fractures.

"Sideways collision with a vehicle." My father helped me carry him down the stairs. "He was lucky it wasn't head on."

*

Mr. Dasgupta was a mess.

His face and lips were mixed up with each other. They had the same colour. His teeth were missing until he smiled.

But he wasn't smiling.

My father purchased a bottle of mineral water at the drugstore. He added salt and sugar, shook it and poured the contents into Shushobhon's mouth. Some of his colour returned. The contours on his face emerged like a Cheshire cat.

Shushobhon stared at the faded buildings around us and passed a hand through his scalp. The hair was as thin as a wig. Someone had pasted it on his head in a hurry.

"My father died," he said.

We reached the bus stop on the road. Shushobhon struggled with his feet. His elbows kept sliding off our shoulders while we supported him and he limped dragging his other foot on the tar.

I called a taxi. A bus wouldn't do under the circumstances. He was too heavy. Moreover his leg was set in a cast. Shushobhon balanced it gently on the floor mat.

"Take me to the godown," he said.

The driver looked at us.

My father and I looked at each other.

Then Shushobhon leaned over and gave directions to the cabbie.

*

After a while a big gate came up on our left.

It belonged to a factory unit. There were rows of shutters on the arch closed like a ghost city. Right there we got stuck in traffic.

"Can I get down for a minute?" Shushobhon looked at my father. "I'll be back before the light changes."

"Why, do you want to pee?"

We were past the crossing of Coolootola. Surya Sen Street stretched before us.

"I know this place." Shushobhon pointed at the big factory gates. "Emma Rose?"

The name sounded familiar.

"Who?"

My father hadn't met Emma.

"He's a nice guy."

My father was confused.

"He's a man?"

Shushobhon was puzzled too.

"Who?"

"Miss Rose."

Shushobhon laughed.

"Emma Rose makes shampoos."

We looked at each other again.

"Is shampoo a code word?"

"Emma Rose is his trade name."

"Is he normal?"

"It's a beauty company! They make hair care products." He turned to my father. "Haven't you heard of Airy Fairy?"

"You must be joking."

"The ads are everywhere!"

"I missed them."

"It's a good shampoo. You should use it."

"Of course," my father muttered.

Shushobhon turned to the driver.

"Can you crawl near the kerb for two minutes?"

The driver pointed at the road. It was bumper-to-bumper traffic. The lights were red. "There's a procession ahead," he said.

"Great. Pick me up at the crossing."

Shushobhon got out of the car. We watched him limp into the warehouse.

"I got a call from Bani Dasgupta this morning," my father told me once the cabbie left the car.

Shushobhon had been struck on the head. It wasn't an accident. He was found on the road with a split forehead two nights ago.

"We need to get him to a safe place."

"Yes, he's acting funny," I said.

Before the lights could turn, Shushobhon returned with sachets and bottles under his arm. The procession ahead was trickling thinly with its violent chorus dying down in the distance.

"Here, egg-based and eggless, both varieties."

Shushobhon unfurled a russet casing from his pocket, more orange than brown in colour. Inside, there was a grey coloured container without a label. The wrapping was sticky. He made my father touch it.

"This is shampoo?"

"No, it's sperm."

The print on the wrapper was tiny. I could barely read the words but the spelling was terrible so I let it go.

I wiped my fingertips on my knee. The driver zoomed ahead past another crossing once the traffic was released a few minutes later.

We crossed old teashops on Mirzapur Street. They had blue walls. Lazy men dipped their toasts in milk, now dark with strands of flour floating in its depths. The bread got soft with every sunken crumb.

Finally the driver pulled to a stop near a lamp post. Expertly he put his vehicle between two bikes crouched on the pavement.

I opened the door for Shushobhon when we reached. It was inside the Rajabazar market.

*

The river Hooghly comes from a playground in Farakka.

Farakka is a quiet place near the border. Bengal almost disappears at its neck. Ganga gets bored with the feeble border choking on itself and threatens to leave the country.

Lucky for them, they have a child. It's the last romp of the Ganges in West Bengal. She's born at a barrage in Farakka. Hooghly is a blessing for the state, giving it shape and strength in its feet.

A man-made canal feeds her regularly. There are small tides to play with at Farakka. They stand in a line and tickle her feet under the barrage.

But Hooghly soon leaves the dam, flows southwards and tries to find her own way.

A strange delta awaits her at Jangipur. A ferry is leaving for the plains but it's too crowded. She doesn't know what to do.

Meanwhile Ganga abandons Bengal for the pursuit of Bangladesh. Suddenly there's no one to look up to. The river Hooghly goes out of control.

She is lost and *sans* direction. It's a wild reckless existence without its mother. She sleeps in strange places. Her banks get bigger every night.

And one day all her silt explodes.

Somehow she collects herself. It's painful but she recovers slowly. Under a different name, she leaves for the district border.

But it's not easy to change so far from home. The past haunts her. She drifts back and forth, disrobing like a common slut at Berhampore and Murshidabad town. Her lakes get left behind in the melee.

Then it's a battlefield at Plassey. The air is thick with the blood of brave men. She falls for a worthy hamlet but he lets her go. With a broken heart, she slips towards the sea.

Rolling down steps of the Burdwan border, the Hooghly hurls ribbons of distress.

Finally the rice eaters fall to her charms. They dismiss her romps as a fertile past. Satisfied, she brushes past Diamond Harbour into an island towards the ravishment of Bay of Bengal.

At Calcutta, the Hooghly hangs like a necklace. On one shoulder, a goods yard disappears into the Botanical Gardens. Taking hold of the other, the Grand Trunk Road plays with her body pushing the town of Bally away, fanning the incense across its banks. Between the expansive collar bones, the city's breasts are full.

Rajabazar, where we were, is an itch on the breast.

The itch gets worse all of a sudden. It has to be scratched from time to time. It's embarrassing when the gentlemen on the street are watching. But there aren't too many gentlemen in Rajabazar.

Shushobhon stopped us at a shop in the market.

I knew the shop. Shibu had taken me there a long time ago.

*

A blind tailor stood guard at the entrance to the shop.

He cut reams of cloth near a high step which served as a foyer to the entrance. A woman came wailing down the street begging for alms in a high nasal voice. The tailor groped a fistful of loose change scattered in coins on his table and handed some to her. She took the coins without a word.

He wasn't really blind. I saw him blink at her touch. Besides, I'd seen him before and Shibu had told me all about him.

Three rows of concrete were engraved below the foyer and paved the way upwards. A black collapsible gate stood at the peak like a moated castle. I caught a tendril and swung Shushobhon through the black accordion. Some grease oozed on the way but I wiped it off with my fingers. The swirls of shampoo had dried up and my hands were clean.

From the gully, I looked into the shop. Set far above the ground in a pillar-wall, the station was set smack against a canopy of windows. Shushobhon seemed safe inside.

"I'll tell you," my father said, taking a walk with me. We went past other shops in the gully, towards Narkeldanga. "A man died in a shop near our building some days ago." It was the one with a white beard, who was poisoned with little blue pills when Bobo and I found him.

His beard was coated with a red silvery ash. It was a false beard anyway. There were streaks of someone else's blood on it.

"That was Mr. Dasgupta's father," he told me. "Shibu's grandfather, the man with all the money."

*

I waited but I didn't say anything.

We stood for some time looking into the distance. My father peered in the direction of a local police outpost. Butcher shacks lay beyond the canal behind our back. Ghettos flocked like sex warts, glistening with heat and vinegar but they had survived the passions of wild men before our time. They bore the ravages of a bitter history.

The blind tailor in Shushobhon's shop lived in those shacks, he told me later when we were alone.

His ancestors had come from Lucknow many years ago. They had hustled Milch cows through the chicken neck of Bengal, swimming with their cattle downriver. Back in the day, Murshidabad was past its years of imperial glory. Intriguers and spies abounded the terrain, as did wives and concubines in palaces and appurtenant chambers.

The blind tailor opened out his cloudy eyes.

One day someone shot someone else and the court eunuch was charged with murder. The tailor's ancestors had to flee with the cattle tied in a line across a strong rope. "They were our livelihood, not food," the tailor sighed. Nevertheless everyone thought they were butchers.

I asked him about the long way from Murshidabad into the shacks of Rajabazar. It sounded like an impossible journey.

They had crossed the Hooghly on a rainy night. The banished Nawab of Oudh sat on a pensioned mound of earth in Metiabruz where lawyers thrived with wise men; there were horse traders and dealers of hide and buffalo horn; some sold opium and indigo.

"Things were brutal back then," the tailor said, "in many ways." Kites fought with groups of cocks and quail next to a reptile house. Frogs were trapped in small pieces of silk which were scented with flies the night before, and then they were slipped inside cages. The cages were full of poisonous snakes with scales and long forked tongues. Some men became cutters of diamond or made gold and silver lace; some kept stables. A few others turned to wig-making or built coaches and palanquin. But things didn't work out for them in the end.

"My fathers were butchers," he said bitterly, "and butchers they would always be." The royal chandeliers burst one day: they fell jingle jangle on their heads across the decaying teak mixing with the rest of the earthy mound. The men sold their last carpets, ate succulent potatoes with rice instead of meat, and then they fled straddling the waters of the Hooghly. Finally they waded into the city of Calcutta in the dark through the river, trading their cattle and hopes across the canal.

They had picked up a sky-blue Persian *feroza* on the way among other things.

*

The canal was behind us. It smelled of burning workshops on the left.

It was a late afternoon on a windy day. There was a nip in the air. Tumult and noise lay to the northwest where the workshops burned through their narrow chimneys. The main crossing was close but it was still far away. A tram depot was waiting nearby.

My father's *Fiat* was parked on the main road very near the crossing. We got into the car. He had the whole thing planned out. "Let's go for a drive," he said. "I'll drop you back."

Two middle-aged boys sat on the backseat with little stars in their eyes. One of them rode a bicycle. My father let him come inside once he lost his wheels near a corner shop.

My father kept talking.

Shelley had taken my father to Murshidabad when the old man Mr. Dasgupta was sick. Shushobhon hadn't yet returned from his trip abroad. This was a while ago maybe a few months into the previous year.

The boys on the backseat didn't have anything to say. We understood each other through the quality of our silence.

I asked my father, "What happened at Murshidabad?"

"Mr. Ghosh and his daughter were there as witnesses. Shelley asked me to draw up a will in her favour." This was before the old landowner passed away.

"I thought Mr. Ghosh's daughter ran away from home?"

"She was required at the estate in Murshidabad. We needed two witnesses for the will. So Debangshu Ghosh wrote to his daughter and brought her along to testify." There wasn't anyone else they could trust since the whole affair was conducted secretly.

My father drove fast and kept going around in circles. The wind whistled through the half-open windows and ravaged our hair.

"What happened after that?"

The boys behind sat quietly like poisoned mice. Maybe they'd fallen asleep. The ridges on the leather seat were plump with great brown buttocks of fat flowing into one another.

"There was something fishy going on," my father said screeching to a halt at an IOCL filling station with a garage attached. "I suspected coercion although I made sure Shelley didn't inherit anything."

Big snouted pumps dispensed fuel and petrol in a line in front of us.

"That's when I sent word to Shushobhon," he said. "I asked him to come immediately."

I watched a liveried attendant do his job. He pulled out a tentacle from a flat-nosed station and thrust the nozzle hard, pushing the hose deep into a lidded hole. The car took the beverage meekly.

"Why were we told that he died?" Someone had obviously sent word from Murshidabad. "Who spread the rumour of his death?" I asked my father. "Bani told me back then Mr. Dasgupta had expired. She mourned his death for days."

"I did," my father said, his eye poised carefully on the rolling display of the pump.

"You did what?"

The last stuttering drops of greasy petrol were injected into the camshaft. They slid into a locked up womb of the car, ready to bloom later from a toothed belt of the *Padmini*.

"I spread the news of his death," my father said taking some money out of his wallet to pay for the petrol.

I caught one of the backseat boys staring at me. He had a sly smile on his face. His feet were bare and covered in corns.

He looked cool when I glared back. "Stop checking me out, okay?"

A violent blush exploded on his face.

"Why did you do it?" I asked my father.

The boy put his hands behind his back, self-conscious but still carefully attentive.

"We needed to." We got back inside the car.

My head was spinning slowly like the closing minutes of a ferris wheel. I quickly collapsed in the backseat. The other boy sat next to my father.

I hadn't observed the other boy until now.

He was a dark-eyed sullen creature, a trifle hunched, clutching a tattered grey sleeve under his arms. He looked straight ahead through the windscreen.

Once my father asked him a question but he muttered two or three words in response without giving himself away.

"There was a huge risk to the old man's life," my father said.

"Five more minutes. Thank you."

The Other Boy timed his enunciations perfectly when he spoke. Not a single syllable was lost in the wind. He chose his words carefully – not too long, precise, like a pine anther dispatching rare pollen in the forest. For effect he stared at his partner.

"Besides, there was money involved." My father turned back and explained it to me. "Money."

The boy sitting next to me slapped his friend's shoulders at the crossing. We were back where we had started. The bicycle was hidden at the corner-shop leaning against a dustbin.

"We had to keep the old man safe," my father said nodding at the two boys when they got out of the car.

Just to be sure, the Other Boy gave a slow measured twist of his neck at the door and checked his watch. "We'll keep him safe," he muttered patting his sleeve softly.

I looked at his back for a long time. His rear swayed like a slow-moving reptile across the pavement. The ridges on the seat were still warm where he sat. His arse had fire.

"They don't look it at all," my father whistled staring with a strange light in his eyes.

Finally the Other Boy turned into the crowded market past a traffic control room, slumped on the shoulder of his friend.

"Look like what?" I stared at the market.

The boys walked close together. There was a small bulge under their vests, white with tiny threaded checks as if they carried a holster around the waist.

"Nothing."

I couldn't take my eyes off them.

"Mr. Ghosh helped me hide the old man," my father said sitting at the steering wheel. The car wasn't kept along the kerb like the other vehicles which were parked side by side. We stood on the road blinking a hazard light at irregular intervals.

The hunchback flitted through a line of confectioners in the distance. His head wobbled on the neck near a riot of clarified butter and almonds. I saw him enter an empty stall. He raised a small rug on the ground and then he put it back quickly, shuffling his feet as if he were removing the stain of a spider from his sole. A cloud of slow dust rose in the air. When he emerged from inside the stall, raisins, pistachio and saffron had joined in the fare. He put an object on his tongue and spoke to a few grown men mounted on bicycles around him. I saw the sharp glow of his made up face between mouthfuls of *halwa*.

It was Debangshu Ghosh's idea. "A good idea, if you think about it," my father said. They needed to keep an eye on the old man. He had to be held somewhere safe and sufficiently close without drawing attention.

I saw my face in the rear view mirror. "How did you manufacture his death? Didn't people go to Murshidabad and check?"

"They did. At least one of them did." He turned his back to look at me. "Your friend Shibshankar. That's why we brought the old man away."

My gaze returned to the man with the tattered sleeve. He had lawsone on his hands like a wedding girl. I caught him ogling another road stall. Through another parabola, he gently moved his head and gauged the exact dimensions of a blanket on display.

"Surely other people also enquired after him?" I said. "He was fairly well-known in Murshidabad."

"I got a dead body to replace his."

My eyes were big so they didn't fit the block of glass mounted on the windshield. My father twisted the mount slowly, adjusting its angle to suit my face and then he swung it harmlessly out of the way.

"How did you replace him?"

"A man in our neighbourhood died a few months ago. He died from natural causes as far as I know. There was no one to claim his body. So we took the corpse and placed it on a bed in Murshidabad. We covered the face of course."

"Prince of Persia!"

My father looked at me in surprise, drumming the steering wheel with his fingers. "When we heard about the man's demise, we took his body before there was a row among the neighbours. Mr. Ghosh arranged it with the local police."

For the last time, I turned to look at the two boys who stood barefoot in the crowd. They were concealed by an udder of brassieres, sagging, on sale from a drawstring on the road. The cups knocked against their foreheads but no one bought them.

My father looked at me. "Why don't you stay on guard? I don't want to leave Shushobhon in the shop." He had a piece of urgent work in Entally at the Sealdah Court. "I'll be back soon."

"Who were those boys in the backseat?"

"Never mind." He fiddled with his car keys. "You should go."

"Tell me now."

"In case there was trouble," he whispered as if policemen were hiding in the boot. "Not everyone knows we have Shushobhon."

I didn't get out of the car. "If Shelley took you to her father in Murshidabad, why did Mr. Ghosh get involved?"

My spit flew furiously in the air settling on the seat rest across a patch of brown leather.

Meanwhile my father scratched his bosom. We were back in Rajabazar market.

"Mr. Ghosh was married to Shelley," he told me quietly.

*

I went back to the shop and settled down in the foyer among reams of cloth.

The tailor had ponderous lips which moved very slowly. They were loosely attached to his jaw. He shifted his spittle left to right when he spoke.

"Shushobhon is sitting in the trial room," he told me.

Presently a woman arrived. It turned out to be the tailor's wife. She was a frail woman, easily blown by the force of the wind. But she had left her veil at home. Her naked face spoke of many things.

The tailor grew a pair of eyes in the heat of the moment. I knew he would. His wife's presence gave him unknown powers. He rushed towards her, rolling past a shutter in the black accordion entrance of the shop.

Midway he remembered he was blind so he took an expert tumble at the collapsible gate. Down broken steps he went and fell on her like a fishing net. Her bumpy chiffon jumped from her torso. Then it splayed around her lower body like the limbs on a dead horse but not enough to make her budge.

I didn't overhear their conversation. But I didn't have to. They argued until I saw her *faille taffeta* disappear around the bend. I thought I caught a mention of money, I couldn't be sure. A gambling debt gone bad, maybe.

I took the opportunity and thought about the situation in a quiet corner of the shop. Too many people had died.

My father said: "I have a copy of Shelley's marriage certificate."

"Balls," the thought came to my mind but I didn't say it. I knew about that already. I had seen the paper. Debangshu Ghosh's name was on the certificate. "I also saw a copy of the old man's will in your chamber," I told him.

It was the new testament - the cops were still looking for it to test Shushobhon's motive. The landowner had left all his money to his grandson, Shibshankar Dasgupta. Shibu.

"Yes, he did," my father agreed when I told him about the contents of the revised will. "I made him sign it." He frowned when he put the key in the ignition and then he drove away without waving at me.

Maybe Mr. Dasgupta had changed it again? Maybe my father didn't have the last will.

*

I sat in the shop for a long time to protect Shushobhon in the trial room. I watched pedestrians sally back and forth across the gully. The tailor didn't return and I didn't expect him to.

A little later a young khaki-clad man strolled down and enquired after the tailor.

"He's out of office," I replied.

"Leaving you in charge?"

He looked at me suspiciously.

"You know how it is, officer. Blind man," I winked.

Maybe I was a little nervous.

"Never mind I'll go find him," he said and turned away.

"Was it something, officer? Your uniform?"

A star flashed on his gabardine near the chest.

He stopped in the middle of the alley and looked at me.

The shiny star on his badge caught my eye. For a moment I thought it was a fake – like the one I had seen in Ghosh's toiletbox.

But I had spoken too much. Shushobhon was still inside the trial room locked in a cubicle. It wouldn't look good if the copper checked inside the shop.

His khaki rustled in a gust of wind and then he walked away without replying.

Soon I became restless. A pale blue polythene bag lay shoved inside a shelf. Its sabled contents were folded flat with a clipped thread. It looked like a court outfit in black and white.

I pulled out piles of penguin fur from the thin poly bag. There was a slip of paper with making charges scribbled in a shaky hand. It looked like a lot of money.

Still no one came. The white shirt felt crisp to the touch and fit my bust beautifully. I decided to try on the rest of the clothes, the black trousers with a wide seat and a pair of slightly tapered legs. I went to the small room in the back. Besides, Shushobhon was being very quiet. I should check on him. Maybe he wanted food and water.

The wall was pushed beyond a false ceiling, ebbing low at the back. It had a narrow slit along its face which served as a mouth to a passage. The opening led to a short corridor with little ledges tucked in the flanks. The outcroppings were barely three feet wide, covered with wooden planks. Someone had boarded the wood and hinged them to a side. Pegs, hooks and dirty pieces of glass were packed inside the flanks. There were two swing doors a foot apart, opening out to trial rooms. The floor was cold.

I went ahead and swung the first door open. It was a bad decision. But no one warned me otherwise.

I found a peacock man lying in a pool of blood and catechu on the floor. Renuka stood above him staring deep into a mobile phone.

I noticed that his neck was fat with a set of holy strings tied around it like cowbells. He had two eyes but they were closed. I remembered the heave of his chest when he breathed once upon a time. He had breathed often.

It didn't matter anymore.

I stared at Renuka. She wasn't supposed to be here. There was a small noise in the narrow passage. It may have been my jaw hitting the ground. She looked at me without any surprise.

The peacock man didn't look at me at all.

He had a fleshy corpse with lots of artificial colour. His dyed hair bounced on the scalp. The lips were slightly parted. They had belched wads of betel juice on his chest. He wore a party shirt: rusty red polka dots on a flaming yellow. His ruff-stiff collar was carefully starched and hung widely around his neck. He looked a lot like he did in Murshidabad when he came to visit me in a tight green t-shirt. He had his good sports shoes on.

A palette of red paint made merry on the floor and rolled away from his carnival clothes.

My jaw hit the ground again. I knew because I heard the small noise another time.

My eyes strayed to Renuka and her fingers. They were wound tightly around a mobile phone.

"I took it out from his pocket," Renuka explained and knocked on the device. Her nails tapped the surface in sets of three.

It was her that made the noises. My jaw was still there.

She looked concerned. "The keys don't work."

It was a light, cheap cell with a 12-key keypad. No one used it anymore. "Why don't you take a look?" She handed the phone to me.

It weighed barely an ounce and the texture felt funny. I spliced the back open. The inside was made entirely of spurious plastic. Someone had removed the circuits and put a vial inside the hollow which housed the battery. It was a dummy set.

I let Renuka know and handed her the cylinder. Crystals bounced inside the vial but they had lost colour, if they had any to begin with.

"Cyanide," she said.

Bending over, she took a strand of his hennaed hair and burnt it in the flame of a lighter. Her butt brushed my hand in the small cubicle and then she rolled his body around until his face was hidden in the floor. The arse was as big as a hippo's. A hairbrush nestled on his derriere along with a toilet of chemicals.

"Fucking Emma Rose," she whispered under her breath.

It was like a drumstick on my head. "What did you say?" That funny name.

"He sold roofies in a bottle."

She hunted through the clothes and produced an unlabelled sachet from his chest after a minute's search. The first three buttons popped off from his shirt. His chest was smooth like a girl's back.

I watched Renuka with my mouth open. She ungrooved a plastic zipper and poured the liquid into her tongue. "There now you can rape me," she said.

"Airy Fairy," I read from a sachet in his pocket, a different plastic container this time with a logo attached along the perforations in the margin. "You must have tried it before?" I handed her a swirly bottle from my pants.

Renuka smiled and took the bottle. "Rita kept some at the Black Pearl."

"Emma Rose?" I repeated.

"That's him." Renuka kicked the peacock corpse much harder this time. "Shibu washed his hair before the storm, Sabbie told me."

The drumstick hit my head again.

"Don't tell me you didn't know that."

"I met him in a small hotel a few months ago. He crowded up my bed with his one eyed crony."

"Ghosh took his diamond that's why," she said. "And now back to business."

The black trousers were still in my hand. I didn't get a chance to try them on. They flopped like a pair of giant ears the way I held them. I felt shy. Renuka was watching me. So I tossed the pair carefully on the cleft of a V-peg on the door.

Then I looked closely at the masquerade on the floor.

"Is he really dead?" I asked her.

I didn't check his pulse. His wrists were brown and gooey. Renuka didn't even look at me.

She was looking somewhere else. I followed her gaze behind me where the wood was hinged like a band-aid. Her eyes were beautiful. They bored through my head above the tiny cubicle door into the distance.

Someone else had come inside the passage. He had taken off his shirt too.

I turned around and found Debangshu Ghosh at the door. He hadn't changed much since the last time I saw him.

Mr. Ghosh was wearing a blood-splattered vest.

It had numerous perforations in it but they had clogged up with blood. In some places they had turned into big holes. He had lost his *lungi*.

The tailor's blades were wrapped around his fingers. He bared its saw-teeth out using a pair of scissor frames between his fingers. He held the edges close to each other and showed them to me.

"Meet Shibu's real father," he said, pointing at the peacock man sprawled across the floor. "He's the man. I bet Bani didn't tell you that."

Renuka laughed in the distance.

"He came to rob the tailor but he ate a giant moth-ball instead. Look at his eyebrows."

His eyebrows were bushy. His nose was straight too, like Shibu's, but it wasn't sickly blue. It had picked up many colours.

"Dogs and peacocks," he said, "it's all the bloody same."

I had nothing to say.

*

A minute passed but I wasn't counting. I couldn't tell the passage of time. We looked at each other shyly like a pair of schoolgirls caught in a flesh racket. I noticed all the cracks in the wall.

A faint draught of air came in from nowhere and made the blue plaster quiver on the wall.

"I'm afraid you'll have to kill him," Renuka told him softly. "He knows too much."

Ghosh had followed us from the hospital. "Emma Rose tailed you too. He tracked Shushobhon to your cab and we followed him. Simple."

Sometimes my mind goes blank. I think of many disjointed things. Even today, I think of the time when my father died. I'm standing on the banks of the Ganga with the weight of a bald head. The sun shines brightly throwing arrows of pain on my shoulders. The crows are getting restless. Some of them can't hold their shit so they relieve themselves. There are too many trees around but nowhere to hide.

There's a large iron chest in a cubbyhole next to the river. Someone calls it 'Female Hair'. I know that because he's painted it on the chest in large white letters. That sounds gross I think to myself. Opposite my chair sits a priest shaking his knees with a strange anxiety. His *dhoti* furls up around his toes but he doesn't trip. He has a train to catch that afternoon. He's headed north to perform the last rites of someone else. The man's son is crying.

Aluminium sheets give the bystanders a roof. It's an unpainted room. Telltale signs of a painting plan in the past are smeared across the shelves and ceiling. Empty cans of colour and a large brown paintbrush gather dust on the window ledge overlooking the river.

I think of all this but my mind stays blank. I daydream all day but it doesn't help me.

Mr. Ghosh was still there. He pointed at Renuka and said: "Meet Aparna. Or do you know her already?"

*

"My father is a lawyer," I mumbled.

It wasn't a threat. I wanted to buy time. Renuka looked at me with interest standing in the corridor.

"I'm the fucking judge," Ghosh said. "You are in my court."

I didn't have anything funny to say.

"I killed your friend one eye by the way," he said. "I'm sorry."

I didn't find that funny either.

"I could have killed Surjo as well." He closed his eyes and smiled. "Shelley brought him to the roof the night she died. But I have a heart. See?" He pointed at a red blot on his chest.

"I don't see anything."

He laughed merrily. The blood bounced on his vest. "I nicked him on the lobe and let him run bleeding. He promised to keep his mouth shut. See," he said putting a finger to his lips.

Debangshu Ghosh still had the cere of a pigeon.

"But I'll have to shut you up too. Maybe a nick won't be enough."

*

An hour passed but I was still waiting at the shop rubbing my conchas wistfully.

Hollow bowls had developed on my pinnae ever since, like nodes on the surface of old skin. My ears were precious.

We had moved the peacock body to a mammoth chest. We covered it with reams of white cloth. Soon the shroud was dotted with corpuscles of death.

194

The red cells refused to die without a show so we wrapped the body in a smelly curtain. Renuka produced stacks of strong cord and we tied the plume securely.

"I can't stand the stench," she said. "It gives me a rummy headache."

"What stench?" Ghosh asked.

"Someone will smell the dead."

The gully was deserted. The shop owners had retired early. Food stalls on the main road buzzed with feeders but no one noticed us.

We drew the sliding doors shut and fastened the collapsible gates. Ghosh asked Renuka to buy a strong bleaching agent, six pairs of gloves and some sodium bicarbonate.

"Are we blowing up the place?" I asked him.

"Just ask for a bottle of baking soda," he told her.

Renuka wriggled out of the backdoor and Ghosh locked it behind her.

"She's not really my daughter. You know that right?"

"I don't care."

*

A few minutes later there was a knock on the backdoor.

Ghosh limped to a window and opened it a crack. "There's a policeman outside," he said.

"Right up your alley."

"We should have killed the lights. Shit."

I walked to the door.

"What are you doing?" he whispered frantically. The scissors were bared ominously in his hand.

I looked out of the window. "I know this guy," I said. It was the guy in khakis who had come before looking for Sulaiman the tailor.

Ghosh raised the portcullis and opened his castle. The man in uniform quickly crossed the open door with three long steps. I hid behind a table.

"A drink?" the officer said.

I saw him from where I crouched. Ghosh took a bottle out from a steel drawer.

"There was a sourpuss sitting in the shop earlier. Who was it?" the copper asked.

Ghosh decanted some clear liquid from the drawer. They exchanged a few glances between them. The policeman's eyes darted around the room checking its dark shadows.

"It wasn't one of our boys," the policeman said. "He looked different. Not nice, but different. I remember his face."

Great. Now I was the missing guy. If the copper looked inside the shop, he would find two dead bodies and me hiding under a table.

But he wasn't looking properly. His eyes were elsewhere.

Renuka returned early wearing a dress that showed the goodness of her heart. The table stiffened in front of me.

She didn't hide her carryall. It was slung across her shoulder and chest like a messenger bag. The policeman got lost in her straps. His eyes didn't reach the end of the bag where her hands were clenched behind her lower back.

Noticing his gaze Ghosh took the policeman aside and whispered in his ear.

The ear wasn't occupied. His eyes were full with Renuka. But the words from Debangshu Ghosh worked like magic.

"I understand," the khaki man smiled rubbing his badge nervously. "I get lonely sometimes. If you need any help let me know." He looked at Renuka one last time. "This is a rough neighbourhood." He pulled up his collar and left.

Ghosh saw him off to the door and pulled his drawbridge shut.

Renuka unclenched her bosom. I came out from under the table. She rolled her eyes and put the extra lumps of washing powder that clung to her dress in a small rubber-capped bottle hidden inside her carryall.

"The police will get to you," I warned Ghosh wiping beads of perspiration from my forehead. I was breathing again.

Renuka took a snifter from the steel drawer, filled it with brandy and exhaled fully.

"Eventually they will," Ghosh said. He put the brandy in a short-legged balloon glass with a big bowl. The brandy fell through the neck in a churning wave. It was an old brown glass matching the colour of his drink. The smell stayed inside the balloon.

Ghosh let it stand between his cupped hands warming it up slowly. That tempted me. The bowl was plump around his fingers like a dancer's bottom.

I told him I was thirsty. Ghosh pointed at the red blot on his chest. "See? Big heart."

He passed me the bottle. A shot of brandy was all that I needed. I swigged from the bottle without thinking while Renuka inhaled her snifter a second time.

I didn't have time for a fresh glass. It wouldn't have helped anyway. Ghosh capped the caramel coloured liquid quickly once I was two swigs down.

I noticed Renuka hadn't swallowed her drink.

I looked at the balloon in Ghosh's hand. It looked like chocolate water though the smell of grapes was unmistakable, spoilt in casks made of old wooden staves bound by hoops of metal. Ghosh threw his brandy in the sink.

My swig tasted fine.

I missed Renuka's hand when it slipped inside the bottle. She had quick fingers. She'd never used them on me so I didn't know what they were capable of.

*

"Where's the one eyed man?"

Ghosh looked at me. "He's dead. I told you."

"I don't believe you. Where's the corpse?"

He took me to a small workshop which was adjunct to the shop. He had knocked him cold first and then strangled him.

"What with?"

"I dug his eye out. The rest was easy."

I noticed a pair of keds lying next to the dead man's head. "Those are Renuka's," Ghosh informed me.

My head swayed a little.

"Did you step on his throat?"

"I used the shoelaces," he said pointing to the left boot. Then he opened a connecting door leading back to the shop through a dark tunnel.

We walked into the tunnel. Big rats ran around on the floor. The cockroaches were oily, scurrying past puddles of dirty water. Some flew into the corners with their dark wings. A part of the wall was broken like a half-eaten carcass. Water pipes dripped incessantly and reeked of foul smells – dead decaying water bearing infected organisms of death. The flooring had given way to an open sewer. That's where the rats came from.

"I'm feeling sick," I said tottering.

"How can I help you?"

"Look I'm going to throw up. Is there a bathroom?"

"Why?"

"Just tell me where." The brandy felt funny inside me. Maybe it wasn't brandy.

Maybe it was airy fairy shit.

*

Debangshu Ghosh took me to a tiny wet room enclosed with a latch.

Inside, I retched like a lion. A soupçon of bile trickled out of my mouth. It wasn't enough. I threw up some more to get the poison out.

A long time ago I had strolled into a film set with Amit and Sabbie. The villain had forced himself on the heroine whom he loved. He was an unusually horny specimen. In the process she became pregnant with his child. That was the basic story. The papers called it a bold film.

She was made to vomit on the fake furniture in the studio floor. They had to prove she was expecting so they made her puke. We had watched her mesmerized.

A bunch of boys in short *kurtas* assembled at a corner table next to the sound recordist. Some cornflour was added to a saucepan filled with water. There were two boys who did the main running around.

"Let's call them jack and johnny," Sabbie whispered in my ear.

Jack brought a tin mug from the bathroom. Johnny purchased a packet of cheap oatmeal from a store nearby. A quart of milk made the cereal rise on its head.

Seeded mustard and flour were mixed with the oats and then poured into the mother slurry. The saucepan was big. While jack and johnny hustled the paste, an assistant with a long nose wanted green coloured puke for the camera. The DOP agreed, casually ashing a cigarette in his tea.

They got some paint from the make-up man. The actress draped in mascara vetoed the plan. It had to be *edible* green she said. Her lips were delicate.

A mad scramble ensued until a spot boy discovered wild tomatoes in a shrubbery behind the parking lot. The unripe ones were plucked, mashed and cut into little pieces. The green flesh was ready to be fed.

An unused pail of milk was added to the saucepan and then the feed was transferred to a transparent bucket. Johnny left his team and sprinkled red seeds above the surface for a surreal touch. The assistant with the long nose whined about the vivid redness.

Jack came to the rescue. He spat out a few sickly green biscuits from his mouth. The assistant was satisfied with the colour. Jack also added his biscuit pulp to the bucket.

"There's something going on between them," Sabbie said, "I can tell."

Once everything was mixed with everything, johnny decanted the mixture into another bucket. This one was smaller, clean and spotless. The second bucket was for the reaction shot once the diva had delivered her first vomit.

The long-nosed assistant reminded jack and johnny that the scene symbolized a dead meal. He checked his continuity sheet. Jack rushed to the caterer and johnny wrestled with some scavenger crows that fed on a pile of paper plates in the garbage.

At last a great heap of stale after-lunch residue was amassed. The fish bones were removed from the heap. The woman couldn't have barfed out a skeleton, johnny told jack scornfully.

Finally the diva emerged from her make-up van. The powder puff girl rushed to her side. The lights were set up already. The main monitor was ready for the shot.

The woman glanced through the script. Her lines were simple. 'Waahhhhh, wawwahhhhh, whhhhhhhh,' and then a close shot of 'wawawawawahhhhh'. That was it. She memorized the words in a flash.

The director refused to have a rehearsal before the shot. "Let's go for take," he said. The costumes man brought a packet of thin arrowroot biscuits for the diva to chew on.

But she said she wasn't hungry yet.

They explained to her very carefully the biscuits were required for her scene.

"Why?" she pouted.

"For the close shot," they said. "Wawawawawahhhhh," went johnny and jack together to give her a demonstration.

She demanded creamy biscuits instead. Johnny went back to the store and returned with diskettes of chocolate flavour and vanilla.

She was allergic to vanilla.

The vanilla fills were cast aside. Jack stole some of them and handed the rest to the director. From behind the monitor they went to the DOP and then the sound recordist. The assistant with the long nose sulked behind the lights.

"See I told you," Sabbie said in my ear.

The diva chewed on the chocolate biscuits while the whole unit watched her. Then she swallowed a bottle of *Bisleri*. Holding her mouth like a fire eater, she pretended to have a fork in her throat.

She was good to go.

The DOP okayed the frame in a jiffy. The woman puked in style when the cameras rolled. It was a good take.

The next shot was readied thereafter. The solution was poured across the dinner table and inside the kitchen sink. Noodles of everything were stuffed into her mouth. They oozed from her voluptuous button-shaped lips down the chin. At long last they said "cut!" The DOP gave a thumbs up. "Ok shot," he said.

The diva retired to her van, exhausted.

Jack, johnny and their wide-eyed brothers cleaned up the wreck. The lights men dismantled thermocol sheets and the black cutting board from their frames. Boxes of daylight disappeared quickly leaving the studio floor dark and listless.

*

I didn't have cornflour with me but I kept retching. It was lonely puking on my own at an unknown commode. I could do with some chocolate biscuits.

I stayed inside the toilet for a long time. At length I emerged outside into Sulaiman's moist corridor shaking with sweat.

"What took you so long?" Ghosh asked me immediately back in the shop.

"I took a dump."

"Didn't you want to vomit?"

"What can I say?" I raised my hands helplessly. "I changed my mind."

"Why?"

"The brandy curdled up inside. Understand?"

"One dead body and you emit every pore?"

"Don't worry, I'll get used to it."

"I heard you mumble to yourself."

"What?"

"Yes," Ghosh alleged shaking his head forcefully, "I put my face to the door."

"Great. Did you smell me?"

"You were muttering inside."

"I do that often. It clears my head."

"*And* your bowels." He looked keenly at the seat of my trousers.

"I recover fast. That's how I am."

What I did in the bathroom was my business.

★

Before making me work, Debangshu Ghosh patted me down, frisked my body and took all my things.

Both the dead bodies were placed in a room at the back of the narrow passage. It was the largest space available within the shop. We removed the furniture, cloth materials and instruments from the room. Renuka scrubbed the floors with a strong peroxide. Some candles were lit on the window sills. Ghosh sprinkled heaps of baking soda everywhere across the floor into the corridor and trial areas.

"We must suppress all odours of death," Renuka said. She found an old vacuum cleaner and aired the rooms.

We sucked up the shreds of damning hair, fibre and granules of betel quid from the floor. Ghosh went and tossed the machine in a garbage dump behind the shop. He covered the cleaner with a pile of debris and came back in five minutes.

"Shouldn't we burn the bodies?" Renuka asked me.

I didn't say anything.

"Of course it will smell for days," she said thinking about it.

Ghosh looked at her. "I want my stone back."

"There will be ashes and nothing else if we burn them. I could clean it up quickly."

Ghosh looked at her again. They had a long moment in silence but I didn't get the message.

"Let's cut up the bodies," he said finally. "No arguments."

"Maybe it is for the best."

Something in his voice changed her mind. "Into small pieces. We've done this before," she said.

"I don't want arguments," Ghosh screamed.

Renuka quickly got a hammer and a big knife from the workshop and held them close to her body.

"Start hacking then."

Debangshu Ghosh took the hammer.

"Wait."

The blood would splatter on our faces if we didn't plan the whole process. Body fluids should be drained off first, Renuka said.

"Body fluids?"

"Like you drained yours," Ghosh complained, "in my bathroom."

Obviously I didn't tell him about the call to Bobo before he frisked me clean.

*

"First we have to shrivel up the corpses. The bodies should be dry before we hack them."

My throat was parched and it itched along the breathing sacs. It happens when I smoke too many cigarettes. I asked Renuka for an explanation.

"We'll bury the corpses eventually."

"So?"

"Like blood, gases can escape too," she explained. "You call them farts."

Debangshu Ghosh crinkled his nose.

"Otherwise the burial ground will rise like a pair of pants. The spot will look suspicious."

"Okay let's get rid of hair and teeth first," Ghosh barked out. "I don't know where the stone is. We'll have to find it quickly."

Renuka ground out a set of peacock teeth from the first body. The teeth were stained and small, sharply chiselled at the ends. I couldn't bear to look at them so I left the room.

Five minutes later Ghosh came after me. He asked me if I smoked.

Yes, I said. I looked around the main tailoring space. Small vents were hiding above our heads in the wall near the ceiling. "We could fill up the morgue with strong smells."

Ghosh looked through an old sack where he stored the stuff from my pockets. They needed to burn off his fingertips. Then he kept my phone and wallet back in the burlap and kept the sack with him.

"I mutilated the faces beyond recognition. It's beautiful work," Ghosh told me proudly. "But I didn't find it yet." He took my cigarette lighter out. "Come and take a look."

Meanwhile Renuka suggested the use of acid to obliterate his fingerprints.

She quickly stripped the peacock man nude in front of me. I watched his soft white flesh crumble in her hands. He was gooey and disgusting with strips of collagen sticking out of his gelatinous body. The corpse fell on the floor with its discoloured folds and many complex layers of fat. Ugly splotches of skin infection and allergies, dark granules of blemish like cow dung with flies around it, scarred his lower half from cheek to cheek.

I made a face I made every morning before flushing the toilet.

Renuka dragged the limp body by the feet towards one of the bathrooms. She looked like a hunter with its prey. The dead drooping flesh of Emma Rose brushed against the corridor with its overlarge udders, flabby and fleshy, a giant monument to his life.

I was taken under the shower. "Hold him upside down," she ordered.

I held him by his ankles with his long pointed ears almost grazing the floor near his bald head. They had cut off his hair too.

Renuka looked at me. "You have to remove your clothes."

I blushed. "Why?"

"You have to cut his throat. If you want I'll hold up a curtain for you."

She passed the pointed knife to me. "Make a slit ear to ear. Let him drain out his blood. Be careful."

A few seconds later Ghosh came in from the other bathroom. "I can't be alone with a naked man."

"What's the problem?" Renuka held the curtain in her hand.

"He doesn't have a shred of hair on his body."

"You think I'm enjoying this?" I hissed crouching above the drainage hole.

The sound of my voice startled everyone.

Renuka peeped behind the curtain and smiled.

"See what I mean?" Ghosh pointed at my huddled form with disgust. "It's not a man's job."

"I'll go to the other bathroom," Renuka said. "Keep an eye on him."

Mr. Ghosh nodded happily.

"I'll do the one eyed man." She dropped the handheld curtain and left.

I was alone inside the bathroom with a corpse. Emma Rose hung from a pair of shower rods above my head. His heels were fastened around a pole with pieces of towel and a bedsheet.

I felt naked.

With the knife I hid my penis from Debangshu Ghosh. The blade strayed around my fingers and touched the soft lumps of my foreskin. The edges were sharp. I got scared and went back to my original position.

"That's my boy," Ghosh cheered, flashing his teeth. "You should get some exercise. Look," he pointed at a bag of extra layer around my waist. "Unfortunate."

"Stop doing that!"

"Doing what?"

"You're making me uncomfortable."

"I would better stand here and watch. In case it spills out."

"What do you want?"

"Make perforations along the body. Slash the thighs in the fatty parts. Pump his breasts." He held the curtain up again. "And collect the blood in a bucket." A few minutes later he asked me to cover the drain with bleach before I let his juices flow down the culvert.

I followed his instructions carefully. Would I ever get out of it alive? Once not long ago my limbs and organs were healthy. They needn't have been. I could shut out the mass of mammalian grime around me, the sordid familiarity with death. But bodies and sickness were now becoming a part of my memory.

Renuka came back to our bathroom. She had taken off her clothes as well. Both Ghosh and I stared at her from our respective positions.

We didn't move for a minute. We watched her nubile body with different sets of eyes, running vivid images while she dared our fancy to match hers. Renuka stood like a noble figurine dappled with human blood. Her soft hair glistened unabashedly with varying pleasures.

"Nothing inside him," she said quietly. "I looked through his parts."

She was a goddess that devoured her young; an epitome of midnight orgies, of satanic cults which pull rivers off their beds in search of celestial honey. But I had to stop staring.

"You better put some clothes on," she told me, "I know what's on your mind."

I had nothing to hide. Not a shred of clothing, no will power left to disguise the foray into nature's silent processes. My flesh rebelled with fury. Right then Ghosh removed the curtain.

He did it on purpose, the impotent bastard. Hormones flowing like cold pale water through his capillary tubes. A mass of envy but not a drop of libido remaining, not a drop to pollinate a simple thought.

"Why all this hygiene?" I asked Renuka pointing at the bleach at my feet.

"Else the sewer gratings will reek."

"You are obsessed with death smells," Ghosh said.

"I'm getting tired. Can't we hurry this up?"

"You could try CPR," Renuka told me.

"What?"

Maybe another phenyl to wash his dick with, Ghosh said happily.

"Mouth to mouth."

"No thanks. I'll keep the water running. Pass me your peroxide."

A little later we re-assembled in the back room. Our living clothes were burnt along with the punctured circus that was once Emma Rose. The tailor shop had new pants so Ghosh scattered our ashen remains in a municipal bin once we had dressed ourselves.

Renuka got some construction grade plastic from the workshop downstairs. We covered the entire room with plastic sheets.

Ghosh wanted to remove his gloves and start digging but Renuka wouldn't let him.

"You *have* to keep your gloves on."

Debangshu Ghosh went downstairs and returned with an asphalt floor-saw from the basement.

"This shop is beautifully equipped."

Ghosh spotted a cement mixer hidden in the back of the cellar. "Not bad," he said. "We could bury them in concrete later."

Renuka threw up her hands.

"Why didn't you tell me? This is very stressful. You can't keep changing your plans."

"Excuse me?"

Ghosh screwed up his forehead. The eyes looked like blocks of ivory, white hard vegetables built from an endosperm. "Maybe you think *you're* running the show?"

"No relax."

"Why don't you give me your clothes and leave?"

"We need some binding material," Renuka said softly.

"No."

"If not cement maybe a plaster of lime? We could burn the lime right here."

"No."

"There are sacks of sand in the cellar."

I couldn't follow a word of what they said.

"Water and gravel isn't enough. We have to cast the bodies in concrete."

Ghosh thought for a moment. A furrow grew on his forehead.

"Didn't we decide to *cut* them up?"

The forehead was a sign of danger. I was learning fast. One could get used to these signs.

Renuka scowled quietly.

"Isn't that right?"

I was enjoying the show. Suddenly he was full of caveman power.

Debangshu Ghosh looked at me. "Didn't I?"

I nodded.

"Then what happened? Cold feet?"

"Fine. *You* do it," Renuka said.

She turned and handed the tools to me.

Ghosh touched his shirt loosely and left the room. "Fine, let him do it. I'll get the trash bags."

It wasn't a nightmare.

My hands did not flinch. I stood above two depleted bodies on the table. They would have looked better with their faces intact or with a little hair. But they had removed everything.

Even the roots of their teeth were missing. Their gums were bare. The skin was pallid and faintly etched on their faces. Great blank easels of life.

Renuka stood next to me with her pointy knife. I was thirsty. But there was too much blood around.

Very slowly I picked up the hammer and pulverized their joints. It was hard work.

"Haven't you used a hammer before?" Mr. Ghosh returned with the trash bags. "Check for splinters."

The head of the hammer was attached firmly to the handle. I kept punching sideways but the wrapping got loose. The body of the hammer wobbled like a knob in my hand.

"You have to hit the body square. With the head of the hammer."

I slid my hand upwards to get a better grip. But Ghosh stopped me.

"The hold is at the *end* of the handle. How else will you get leverage?"

Go screw yourself, I said in my head.

"You should employ your arm and elbow. Use your instincts."

No one stood behind me. With a good backswing, I smashed their balls and sockets. Ghosh helped me take off the limbs one by one.

Renuka switched on a radio to drown the pitch of the concrete saw. We dismembered silently, not looking at each other. It took the better part of an hour. I tried not to remember the details.

Nothing rolled out of the bodies.

Ghosh wasn't happy with my work. "Make smaller pieces." He asked me to divide each torso into segments, telling me where to cut the lines. Then he went downstairs and came back with a bearded axe.

It was a massive instrument. The blade dwarfed the felling haft by a third. The handle disappeared into the throat of the axe but the grip was large and stable.

I carved out six to seven parts from each body.

Ghosh got his eyeballs to bounce on them. First ricocheting on the ribs, they fell on the tender joints, then sliding down a sphinctered canal, they hit a greasy object.

"Here it is!" he exclaimed.

He put his grubby fingers inside the segment and kneaded a parcel of tissue. It was like a sponge in his hands. I almost retched in agony.

"But I'm done with bathrooms," I reminded myself.

When his fingers emerged from the flesh, they clutched a piece of stone. The stone was blue in colour. But it was too opaque.

We couldn't see the other end. Ghosh carefully removed tiny bits of hair from the surface. There were crowds of folded villus, mucous and goblet cells on the surface, the coiled remains of Emma's insides.

"Not again!" he cried as the ghastly muck of lipids slipped through his fingers. "Not fucking *again!*"

Emma Rose softly oozed into his hand.

✱

An hour passed. We collected a mountain of cutlery from a small kitchen beyond the passageway. Breakables were smashed. Skin and shards of skeleton were packed into cardboard boxes alongside the utensils to mask the flavour of human remains. Ghosh put everything in a double layer of black trashbags and squeezed the container.

Nothing else came out.

It was just a piece of *feroza*. Not worth the trouble. It wasn't the blue diamond Ghosh was looking for.

"Then Sulaiman has it," Renuka said.

"Fucking tailor."

I let them talk.

While my father and I went for a walk in the gully, Emma Rose had come into the tailoring shop. "He found the stone but Shushobhon had slipped away."

And then Debangshu Ghosh and Renuka arrived on the scene.

"How do you know Emma Rose actually found the diamond?" I asked.

"We saw him swallow it."

"There was no other way to find out." Ghosh looked at the hacked bodies on the floor sadly.

"Like the last time," Renuka sighed.

"So it's still here in the shop?"

Debangshu Ghosh looked sharply at Renuka.

"Sulaiman handed it to Shibshankar," she said avoiding my eyes.

"*Shibu?*" I cried.

"But he returned it once his grandfather passed away. It wasn't safe with him."

"Obviously," Ghosh sneered, "If his balls fell off, he would roll a joint instead."

Renuka put the bodies in a soft carpet and rolled them up together. We placed the parts gently in the cargo compartment of a cab and drove off into the black night.

Mr. Ghosh took the wheel.

"Where are we going?" I asked.

"We need a safe place for disposal." Renuka sat next to me with a large hammer.

"Let's dump them on the road," Ghosh said. "We have to find Sulaiman before he runs across the border."

"You could stash the corpses in a morgue. No one will be able to find them."

"Don't get smart with me."

"I know of an old mill," I offered.

"Shut up," Ghosh hissed behind the wheel.

*

The day started at dawn with pebbles of kidney beans at a roadside *dhaba*. The kidneys jostled for space on the steel plate. The beans were red in colour. A thick cress of rice lay around the edge of the plate with toddy at our elbows.

Debangshu Ghosh and I were drunk at a low table in the shack. We were sitting near the truck stand. Right then Renuka walked into the *dhaba*. She was backless. The bulb rays bounced off her flesh.

Her *ghaghra* is deliciously low. She unfurls it slowly revealing a prism of sequins and belly buttons. Her hips wobble like a mare's rump. She stands above our *charpoy*, smiling mischievously through her kohl. I feel my legs tighten.

She notices the bulge in my pants and heaves her bosom towards me. That is my reward. Her hair is very straight. Her blouse is firm. She has henna on her hands. A rainbow of resin bangles rolls around her wrist. There are large hoops hanging across her ears.

Ghosh catches me staring at her. He knocks the plank down where we sit and hurls himself across a netted cot. I clench my fist and strike.

Debangshu Ghosh lies in a pool of blood. I undress Renuka on the roadside *charpoy* amidst wild cheers from truck drivers in the shack.

And then I woke up with a start.

At daybreak Ghosh went prowling in the neighbourhood and managed to pick up a flat footed scooter. The key was in the ignition.

He woke me up with a jug of cold water. I quickly ate my beans, big fat corpuscles of false meat until I burped like a truck driver. Finally he thrust me into the saddle of the scooter.

"Let him drive ahead," Renuka said. "He can give us cover."

"You try anything funny," Ghosh warned me, wagging a finger, "I'll cut you into pieces."

At noon, still burping, I swung the old Bajaj Chetak on the main road. Our yellow cab followed the scooter a few hundred metres behind me. The kidney beans screamed in anguish inside my stomach. Beans don't go well with heat and sunlight. The 150 cc purred into a fringe of betel wood near a temple on the banks of the river. A draught escaped from a wind tunnel ahead where the jute mill was. On my left I could hear the river.

The full sleeved shirt on my back in broad boring checks wasn't hiding anything. The baggy pleats on my trousers weren't hiding anything either. The only object they showed off was the craftsmanship of Md. Sulaiman through a black tag with yellow embossing on it.

But no one could have seen the tag. It was sewn into my pants.

The fresh faced officer on the bend couldn't have known. Nevertheless he flagged me waving a hand lazily at a check post.

I slowed down but I kept the engine running. Ghosh's cab was behind me though I couldn't see it when I looked back.

The policeman slid a barricade across the road and took me to a kerb. A practised index leered at the ignition until I was forced to kill the two-stroke engine. The shiny diskette on his bosom spelt out his name.

"Where the fuck are you from?" he said looking at my face as if the address was pasted across my forehead.

The beans in my belly groaned again.

When I didn't reply he tried one more time in a different language. "Yes, I'm talking to you accidental child."

He smiled at me nicely with a jerk of his chin.

"Your sister's cunt my friend," I told him.

The response came in a plain voice. Sometimes I have answers at the tip of my tongue.

He was happy that I spoke his language. The disk on his uniform gleamed across his chest. When he slapped me on the back, I almost got knocked off the chassis into the road. The broad twin checks fell from my shirt and broke into a thousand pieces.

"You've inherited your mother's tongue. Why didn't I cut it off when she flicked it abaft my glans?"

"The woes of circumcision officer," I said devoutly, "you and me both."

This time he laughed and held me by the collar. "Get off the Chetak, Rana Pratap. This is a stolen scooter." He checked the number plate and compared it with a scribble on his pad.

I stole a glance behind the police check post. "Take me with you."

The officer had another slip of paper in his hand with a name written on it. Besides, there was a photograph in his back pocket.

"That's him," I said.

"Follow me." He led me inside his grilled van.

When he fired the engine, I caught a glint of yellow in the rear view mirror. Mr. Debangshu Ghosh turned left through a half opened gate inside the jute mill.

The premises were deserted. We turned through another gate near the end of the compound. The police van swerved sharply through the gate and kept swerving.

"What are you doing?" Somehow I clutched the upholstery on my seat. He drove like a mad stallion across the mill complex. Giddy with its own torque, the van almost toppled over.

"We don't have time."

The turn lasted a lifetime. We went deeper inside the jute mill until there was a clearing between two large trees standing in a line. A bicycle was parked behind a red flag and a tricolour.

Someone took a leak on a high bluff wall next to the clearing.

It was Indrojit Sahoo. He stood facing the wall with his pants down between the cycle and the flags.

The cycle had a curved handle with a stem of burgundy. Indrojit rubbed his hands on the hard metal bar when he finished. The wall was thoroughly wet where he stood with a dark patch across its surface.

In the middle of the clearing, a *Fiat* draped in yellow and black was surrounded by three police vans. The vans had three open sides of the clearing blocked with the wall behind them. When we reached every possible exit was covered.

Debangshu Ghosh emerged from his cab.

The blind tailor came out after him with his hands behind the head. Sulaiman appeared into the clearing from the entrails of a police van. His back was stooped, coiled up like a spring looping around itself from his feet back to his white scraggly beard. He stood next to a policeman. It was the khaki clad cop who came looking for him in the shop the previous day.

At last Rathikanta's brother slid out of his special seat pulling his pants above the waist. He was dressed in plain clothes and a cap. He had four men alongside and four guns behind him. A fifth man unfastened the carriage and let Bobo out. Emerging into the mill compound, she ran across the clearing like a freed animal.

She waved at me happily with her half moons glistening in the sun. It was morning already but the sun was yet to come out in the open. "I got your message in the bathroom," she yelled across the compound, "here we are."

I had made a phone call to Bobo letting her know where I was. With a scented soap, like putty, I had scribbled the coordinates of the mill on the bathroom wall.

It was a good thing Ghosh took my advice and drove to the jute mill.

My father and Shushobhon Dasgupta sat quietly in the last van. They held their hands above the mouth like punished children. We were alive.

Next to Mr. Dasgupta, the two dark skinned boys from the backseat of my father's *Fiat* huddled together. They hadn't bathed yet, I could tell. Their faces were soiled with heaps of emulsified grease across their bodies. The grease erupted in viscous lumps in their garage hands. They were barefoot as well.

Rathi's brother told us later they were undercover cops from Bombay.

They had come to take Aparna back. Several warrants for Ms. Anjali were stuffed inside the ash grey sleeve that one of them carried. He still had the sleeve, holding it like a prized potato under his arm.

All of a sudden, a piercing scream hit the air. Pigeons flew out from ledges on the wall into the crisp river air that hugged the trees. Debangshu Ghosh looked intently at the flight – the flurry of white underwings rising with a clatter – as he held up his hands and surrendered.

There was a time in the past when Mr. Ghosh and pigeons appeared in the same frame every morning. But I let the image seep through my head because this was the last I would see them together.

Meanwhile Renuka had smashed a cyanide vial inside the yellow *Fiat* cab. Her hammer was lying in my seat beside her.

They told me later she was victim number six.

*

24

Bobo's Uncle

"It started years ago. I have the police version of course. The rest of the story I tracked myself."

We sat in a huddle at the police headquarters.

The policemen had retrieved my phone from Debangshu Ghosh's sack but the sentry at the gate took it away. He gave me a slip of paper against it.

Shibu had come with me. The guards didn't notice him when he entered.

Rathikanta held Bobo's hand into the wide quadrangle. We took the lift upstairs, walked down a sparse corridor and then we bumped into Bobo's uncle.

He was a big cop but we had an appointment with him.

Lunch was served comprising tea and biscuits. Bobo and her father listened to him carefully but I was distracted. I noticed the little details in the room. For example we sat on three chairs of three different sizes. They were uncomfortable – at least two of them. Their arms were broken. Someone had sawed them off.

Shibu sat on the floor in the corridor outside. I was surprised when he decided to come. He usually stayed away when there were other people around.

"I want to know," he told me. "I'll stay by the door."

"Once upon a time," the big cop started looking fixedly at Bobo, "Shelley Dasgupta was the daughter of a rich landowner in Murshidabad, a girl from a very powerful family, with terrible and revolutionary ideas."

Rathikanta scowled in a corner. He was in the middle of setting a fold across his shoulder cloth. He was a much smaller man than his brother, neatly organized into blocks of starched cloth and greying hair. His chair was pushed to a ledge in the wall, dimly lit, away from the sun-filled window.

"She was born into the idea of a new communist regime," Rathi's brother continued in a steady voice, "and her father, with large tracts of land, generously donated towards the party funds. His citadel was used for meetings and propaganda."

He stopped to take a sip, wiping his mouth gently with a napkin on his lap and settled into his chair. His arms, folded across the chest, were unbuttoned dangling a gold-plated wristwatch.

"Unfortunately she married a lowly comrade, a noisy man she worked with while clamouring for land reforms, a man called Debangshu Ghosh." He wiped his mouth again flicking the dry crumbs of biscuit that stuck to the outline of his lips. Ghosh was a local goon with some connections of his own.

"He was mixed up in some bad business." The big man checked a separate sheet of paper in a green box file: "But the police had an arrangement. He could do anything as long as someone covered him locally."

Rathi's brother took out an eraser from a pile on his desk wrapped in a brown paper packet. He rubbed it gently on the wooden board – slowly at first then he made vigorous lines across his table until the latex came out in strips from a vulcanized shell and shreds of tree sap lay in a heap in front of him.

For some reason I remember these things.

Shelley's father, an old world comrade, didn't approve of their alliance. Shelley was aware of that. Not only was she familiar with his ways, she knew they needed his money. Perhaps Debangshu Ghosh married Shelley for the same reason.

"So," he continued dusting the debris on his rubber, "in order to avoid her father's disapproval she came to Calcutta with a teaching job. That way she could live with Ghosh and not spoil her chances of a large inheritance." He flicked the last splinters from the table.

They lived quietly for some time while the rest of her family thrived in Murshidabad. Debangshu Ghosh worked with a set of policemen feeding them information so he made a lot of money in the process.

"Meanwhile," he continued, "senior Mr. Dasgupta's son, Shushobhon, was smuggling diamonds across the border through a small party base in Jalangi." The town of Jalangi washes up with the river a mile from Bangladesh. Shushobhon used his father's capital and his contacts at the party office to push his deals through.

Rathikanta changed the position of his legs replacing one with the other. He sat slightly cross-legged, upright and disapproving in the still room.

"They were flush with party funds," the big man said glancing briefly at his brother, "but having cut a few hard bargains abroad, Shushobhon got into a racket. He set up a base in Calcutta too – in Rajabazar with the help of a Muslim family, one that he worked with in Jalangi."

I noticed Shibu peeping into the room through the door. He kept staring at Bobo but I don't know why he did that.

When I looked at him he smiled mysteriously.

"With the help of a tailor called Sulaiman, Shushobhon Dasgupta chanced upon a blue diamond worth crores of rupees. It changed his fortunes completely," the big cop said.

However by this time Shushobhon was in serious debt. In order to stay afloat, he sold the diamond to a dealer his wife knew from her previous marriage. He hoped to get it back some day.

"Emma Rose," I whispered in Bobo's ear.

"Shhh, shut up."

Somehow Shelley found out about her brother's diamond. She leaked the news to Debangshu Ghosh and her father. Mr. Dasgupta discovered that his son was using family money to smuggle goods across the border. The landowner got pissed and threw him off his land. Separately Ghosh whored out to cops about the sale of a stolen diamond in Murshidabad. Emma Rose panicked and asked Shushobhon to get rid of the stone.

Shushobhon Dasgupta was without a home. He had little money of his own. In desperation he turned to his sister for help. Eventually Shelley found a place for him in the city.

The big cop looked at me. "*Your* building," he said. Debangshu Ghosh was waiting for him. The trap was neatly set.

When Shibu's family arrived on the mezzanine, Ghosh kept a close watch on them. He passed on information about his deals to the police. Ultimately Shushobhon became dependent on Debangshu Ghosh. Every time he was in trouble, he turned to Ghosh not knowing what caused the leak.

"Ghosh amassed considerable wealth this way."

"Our young policemen made some money too I presume?" Rathikanta asked.

"That was before my time," the big man said. "Shelley came into the picture later. She spied on her brother from *inside* the house."

Desperately Shushobhon turned to Sulaiman for help. Emma Rose had given the stone back to Shushobhon for a short time until the police trail grew cold. But the deadline was fast approaching.

"How did that help?"

"He tossed it into the throat of a dog."

"What!"

Bobo swivelled noisily.

Shibu made a face in the corridor. "Why is she so loud?"

"Sulaiman handed the dog to Shushobhon." For a moment the big man's eyes strayed to the fan on the ceiling. It had four blades. The ceiling was fifteen feet high.

"And then, one day Debangshu Ghosh cut the dog into bits."

Bobo grimaced. A long siren wailed in the distance across the sun-filled window.

"But he didn't succeed." It was a booby trap. Beer didn't have the diamond with him. Instead there was a Persian *feroza* with turquoise crystals in his gut. "Sulaiman had switched the stones."

"So it's still in Rajabazar?"

I turned and looked at the corridor outside. Shibu shook his head.

As a result I drew attention to myself. "Your father helped Debangshu Ghosh," Rathikanta said dragging an arc on the table. A mole bobbed above his lips. "Mr. Ghosh was a greedy man. He couldn't wait. He wanted his golden eggs at once."

Shelley was greedy too. They landed at the old man's door in Murshidabad willing him to sign a testament. For good measure they took Renuka along as a witness. They had a will made by my father – where Shibu got everything that the landowner possessed. Ghosh made sure no one suspected their motives.

But later they went back and tinkered with the will. This time they left my father behind. They wore police clothes and got the old man to thumb on blank sheets of paper. Then they added a few more pages having ripped the old ones off.

I asked him about Renuka. "Who was she?"

She was an old partner of Debangshu Ghosh. A small time crook, he explained, before Ghosh picked her up from the streets. She used to grind against trousers, lifting wallets or sidling through a crowded minibus, things like that.

Renuka was useful. She picked up stories from the street and passed them to Mr. Ghosh. With a tiny slip of her blouse she could make men talk.

"The cops loved her," the big man said wryly returning to his green box file. "The records show they let her go a few times." But one day she went too far. She broke into a house, a target earmarked for a tax raid, and made off with stacks of black money before the police arrived.

Shibu was smiling now. I wondered if he was sniffing glue in the corridor.

Ghosh sent her away from Calcutta. As an added measure he forced Ganesh to pawn his son out. Indrojit Sahoo was assigned to follow Renuka wherever she went. He kept an eye on her through the journey.

"Where did they go?"

"She was a big hit in Bombay," he replied and took out his main file. "She's a con artist. There was a local gang but she worked alone. In the suburbs she staged robberies, pilfered accounts, etc. passing herself off as someone else."

"And Ganesh Sahoo? What was his role?"

The big man shrugged. "He was a friend with benefits." Ghosh paid him well. Over the years he learnt to keep his mouth shut.

"Then why did Aparna return?"

"Debangshu Ghosh needed her. She came back to Calcutta as Renuka."

Shibu was the main target. She obtained information about his father's dealings directly. "Shelley had become useless over the years," the cop murmured unclamping another sheet from the box. "Shushobhon Dasgupta doesn't have a single reported case in the last five years."

"Anyway," Rathikanta said coughing, "let's come back to Murshidabad and the will."

Just then, I noticed Shibu's shoulders on the railing outside. He was trying to climb over the handrail.

I got off my chair in alarm.

"I'll take my chances," he said and swung back into the passageway.

"Didn't he leave everything to Shibu?" I asked sitting down with a capillary tube. That way I looked normal. The tea was stuck to my tongue.

"In that case Bani Dasgupta would inherit the estate at Shibu's death," Rathikanta said turning towards his brother, "right?"

His lips were moist with excitement.

"By Hindu law, yes."

Shibu made a spit ball in his mouth and hurled it at nobody.

"What do you mean?" Bobo said. "The old man was alive when Shibu died. So he didn't inherit anything."

"Yes," Shibu hissed from the door. "That's right."

"I have a copy of the will." Rathikanta's brother leaned heavily over his cushion. "Mr. Sen drew it up." Mr. Sen was my father. "Would you like to hear it?"

The big man extracted a pair of reading glasses. It was a thin curvaceous pair resembling a violin case. He skimmed through a page silently. The glasses sat like a charioteer on the edge of his nose. He read the recitals by himself. They were arranged in well-spaced paragraphs along the sheets.

"Shibu was the sole beneficiary of the estate." He took another sip of his tea. The double layered cushion disappeared behind him.

"Dumbfucks," Shibu said.

The big cop's face was hidden by the will. There was a mass of typewritten words spaciously strewn across the jumbo-sized sheets. "However," he said, "in the unlikely event of Shibshankar predeceasing the testator, the estate would automatically devolve upon his daughter Shelley."

Rathikanta smiled happily. "And what if Shelley died before her father?"

"Then it would go to her husband." The big man peered at a clause, mapping the words carefully with a finger. "It says so in the will."

Rathikanta let go of Bobo's chair and slammed the wooden table.

"So Mr. Ghosh killed Shibu?"

The cop rolled the tea in his tongue. When it grew insipid, he swung his uvula out and let the blubber breathe.

"He didn't." He licked the sediment in his teacup.

Shibu was looking at him too.

"Someone else did."

"Who?"

"Was it someone in the family?" Bobo asked him.

"Yes."

"Surjosekhar," I muttered under my breath. "*Surjo!*" It had to be him.

"I don't believe it."

For the first time that afternoon, Shibu looked worried in his corner.

Shushobhon Dasgupta was in police custody. They were asking him questions. Bani Dasgupta was locked up at home. With Surjo.

Bobo shook her caramel frame clutching her head. I held my breath.

"It wasn't the Dasguptas," the big man said.

He yawned, thrusting a finger in his mouth. The protruding papillae on his tongue stuck out like nipples.

Bobo held my hand tightly. Shibu turned his face although his ears were visible behind the frame of the door.

"It *was* Ghosh," the cop said flatly closing his mouth.

I stared at Bobo. Rathikanta was poised on a slab of wood, legs stepped on each other crossing at the junction of his knees. The end of his walking stick clung to an elbow like an umbrella.

Bobo sat crumpled on her seat.

The big man was fucking around. "You just said it *wasn't* Mr. Ghosh."

"Yes I did."

He turned his head slowly, resting on our faces. He stopped twice.

"It was *Mrs.* Ghosh," he said. "Shelley killed Shibu that night."

The cop took Bobo's recorder out of a bubble wrap and pressed play. It was a statement made by a little girl when we went to meet the prince of Persia. I heard the statement once again:

"*A plumber came, but that was later; in the dark.*" (a girl's voice)

"*And before?*" (my voice)

"*Not much. A lady came and looked around. She knelt near the sick boy, and then the storm hit the roof.*"

He stopped the recorder and sat back on the cushion.

Shibu smiled at me. I saw that he was pointing at Bobo.

"That's when Shelley slit his wrist," the cop said putting the tape recorder back inside the bubble. "Shibshankar Dasgupta bled to death."

"I can't believe it," Rathikanta said. He clutched his forehead.

"Where's her voice *now*?" Shibu whispered into my ear.

"We found traces of barbiturates in his blood," the big man said glancing through a forensic report. "She was a quick lady."

★

"Shelley had a lot to gain. When Shibshankar died, she inherited her father's land and all his money."

The cop pointed at me. "Only *your* father and Shushobhon Dasgupta were aware that the old man was alive." His fingers paused between their tips like restless insects. "And of course Debangshu Ghosh knew as well." He juggled his eraser.

There's a drawing of the eraser in my diary. I drew it later that afternoon when I was alone.

Ghosh kept the truth from Shelley. "Deliberately," he said.

It was part of the plan. When Ghosh asked Shelley to remove Shibu, she agreed. "Like everyone else she thought her father was dead."

"Ghosh kept her away from Murshidabad once the news came out," Rathikanta said softly.

"But in the meanwhile, Ghosh meant to kill her once Shibu was dead."

"How did Shelley die?"

"Later in the night." The cop read a statement carefully. The nares on his nose were clenched while the glasses bounced along his cartilage. "We beat up Ghosh in custody." He scratched his nose.

Rathikanta blew into a large handkerchief in the corner.

Ghosh met his wife on the terrace when it was dark. Shelley had managed to kill Shibu. Everything went according to plan.

"So that's when Debangshu Ghosh..."

"Not so fast." The cop held up his hand. "Renuka Sharma was assigned to do the job."

"Renuka!"

It was Bobo who screeched.

Rathikanta's brother looked at his niece. "Mr. Ghosh paid Renuka for the job. That's what he told us."

Bobo held the table in front of her.

"That way Ghosh didn't get his hands dirty," Rathikanta said approvingly.

"See," Shibu said. "He's a glutton, Debangshu Ghosh."

"No, Renuka didn't kill Shelley." The big man shook his head. He swivelled and took out another file stacked with transcripts. "Indrojit Sahoo clarified he saw a running figure *before* Shelley fell from the roof."

"So it has to be Ghosh. He was the only one on the roof."

"Fuckers," Shibu said.

The big man looked at me. "Yes, it couldn't have been anyone else." He put the file back on a shelf behind him. "He hasn't confessed. I daresay we'll get it out of him."

"Nice." Rathikanta folded his white handkerchief into a bundle.

Bobo said: "Mr. Ghosh may have seen Surjosekhar on the roof as well."

She looked at me.

"Surjo followed Shelley upstairs that night," I told the cop.

He put his fingers together and considered me carefully.

"There, there," Shibu grinned from the corridor.

Bobo stared at the table. But my face was blank.

"Anyway, when the hoarding crashed, Debangshu Ghosh pushed Shelley off the terrace. She fell with the debris from the parapet."

"But how do you know that?" Rathikanta asked.

"Indrojit is ready to declare that in court. We will make him say it."

"As simple as that?"

When the hoarding fell, Debangshu Ghosh had a new idea. "Quickly getting rid of Shelley's razor, he created the impression of an accident," he said.

"So Shelley fell off the roof?"

"And what about Shibu?"

Debangshu Ghosh dragged Shibu across the roof and put his body near the fallen hoarding. The corpse was carefully placed under the heavier iron fragments. He covered his arms and chest with the colossal body of the web.

"Why?"

A fly was wrapped around a leaf in Rathikanta's cup. He spat out the fly distastefully. "If Shelley killed Shibu, why did Mr. Ghosh take the trouble with his corpse?"

There was a fan near Rathikanta's elbow. The tea danced in the air and settled on its blades near the table.

Strangely none of the tea leaves fell on Bobo. Shibu smiled in the distance.

"Mr. Ghosh wanted to hide his link with Shelley," the policeman said. "Shibu's death could be a problem once the new will was discovered. It was best that Shibu died under the hoarding."

With Shibu and Shelley out of the way, Debangshu Ghosh inherited everything.

"He was a clever man," Rathikanta said.

"Why did you arrest Indrojit Sahoo in the middle?"

The big cop didn't say anything.

Rathikanta laughed. "That was a bluff. Indrojit's confession was a bluff."

We looked at the big cop.

"We were waiting for Debangshu Ghosh to come in the open."

"Who sapped Shushobhon on the head?"

"I don't know," the cop frowned. It may have been Mr. Ghosh or Emma Rose. "Finally we asked Mr. Sen to track him down."

"And how was Mr. Dasgupta killed at the shop?"

"Ghosh mixed poison with his sleeping pills. We found stacks of shampoo at the Black Pearl."

Bobo looked at me again.

Shibu ran out of the corridor laughing.

*

The cops wouldn't tell me a few things. I had to find out for myself.

My father's card was in my pocket. I took it from Bobo's *durrie* bag. She had pilfered it from a drawer in my father's chamber.

I went in a shared auto through a narrow partitioned road. The slow traffic flowed in and out of Salt Lake. I left the first two islands and jumped down at a water tank. It was Tank Number three.

My bag was heavy with pink files. The sun was warm when I took off my slippers and bathed the toes in a pit of balsamic sand. A thin man, sitting with his feet up at a rickshaw stand, directed me to a half-eaten rung on the water tank.

It was an empty afternoon. A pretty girl served me tea on a chipped ceramic saucer with a few biscuits. The cup was shaped into a vessel, wide around the hips, and coloured in yellow ochre. Opposite us, a cream building stood resolutely in the heat with a few red tiles on its head. The walls had carefully exacted cracks looking like rows of silhouette.

I hung my father's cloak on a piece of nylon string next to the tea shop.

I quickly finished two pots of tea and buttered biscuits. Then I bought some cheap milk and a wheat slab from the shack. With the purchase, I fed a family of street dogs at a drain along the pavement. I washed my hands thoroughly once they were fed, wiped them dry with my handkerchief and lit a small cigarette.

Finally a man came down from the water tank.

"You're not Mr. Sen." He waved a stick of cannabis at my face. "Who are you?"

Disengaging his feet from a stone ladder, he landed on the pavement. His voice was like a poet's, soft and organic.

I looked at my watch. It was a minute from the appointed time. The meeting was scribbled on the back of the card. It had an oilcloth finish to the rear with my father's smell.

A cyclist came quacking down the island. He had a loom clenched expertly between his legs. Stray wisps of cotton fell from his saddle when the cycle moved. He stopped when he saw the billowy cloak, and parking his cycle in a corner, he took off his turban.

The man from the water tank untied the cloak from the nylon string. "Take it away," he said. "You've come to the wrong place."

I folded the cloak vertically with the arms pressed together. A trail of liquid cape spilled out from the mass of padded shoulders.

"He has some money you can talk to," the cyclist said wiping his sweat. "The gent gave me some of it."

I stood with my father's card and the cloak in my hand.

The cyclist put on his turban. He looked like a seller of coconut sweets when he wore the turban in layers.

A few days ago I tasted his sweets for the first time. They were white and sticky around the body with flowers and genuflecting elephants engraved on them. Sinking his teeth into a big fleshy chunk, he had given me the address in Salt Lake.

The poet put down the cannabis from his mouth. We stood at the foot of the water tank. I passed him a bundle of notes arranged serially and numbered – one of the few from Ganesh Sahoo's vault.

He counted out the money licking his fingers.

Then I handed him the files. Three sets of news insertions were marked in red. Bobo had given them to me, having pasted the articles on scraps of chart paper.

"He was working on it," the poet said glancing through the newsprint.

"This is his son," the sweet seller explained.

"Didn't he tell you?"

Taking back the file, I inserted it carefully between the black leathery folds of the cape. "Who put him to it?"

"The old man in Murshidabad." The cannabis burned a patch on his skin. He wiggled his fingers and lit the stick again. Taking a puff between two clenched fists, he exhaled like a steam engine.

"The old man thought his son was cheating him so he hired Mr. Sen to keep an eye on Shushobhon."

"When was this?"

"I don't know. A few years ago? When the Hooghly swelled up and flooded her banks. Many people died that season."

"What is the connection?"

"No connection," he murmured. "The old man was visiting his native village near the border. Incidentally that's where Debangshu Ghosh comes from."

"Where is this place?"

"In a small submerged town," the poet puffed on his chalice, "on an embankment. Forty kilometres east of Behrampore, the river diverts. I've been there." He sprinkled flakes of ash on my face. "That's where the old man was, distributing food and building shelter. Ghosh was doing the same thing. They were good people."

"Did they know each other?"

"No, they came from warring families. Debangshu Ghosh hailed from a clan of gunrunners."

The coconut man fingered his money impatiently. "Get to the point, brother. We haven't got all day."

"That's all."

He picked up the brown loom and put it between his legs. The poet slowly climbed up the stone ladder and returned to his water tank.

*

Bani Dasgupta didn't want to meet me at the redbrick. "It gives me the creeps," she said.

The building overlooked a small triangular park across the tram lines. The park was covered in banners from the past season. We stood at the railing.

"Was there anything between Shibu and Surjo?" I asked her.

She pushed a small purse near her hips. "It was an accident."

A few strands of hair came loose in my hand and flew away.

"Shibu made the dog jump on him when he was a child. One day Surjo fell off the stairs and hurt his head."

I kicked a tuft of grass on the ground. It was a dead piece of grass.

Bani Dasgupta stared across the street above the tram lines.

"That night I came out of my room when the power failed. I went to check on Surjo. But he wasn't in his room. Suddenly there was a huge noise outside. I went to the kitchen and found the back door open."

Bani looked around the triangular park. A few boys played football in the corner. It was a small *cambis* ball made of hard canvas. Each time someone scored a goal, she shuddered when the ball hit the railing.

"I thought he went downstairs so I crept to the lobby. The collapsible gate wasn't shut. Just when I was about to step out on the porch, I saw someone. It was a big man with a moustache staring at the terrace. He looked as if he had seen a ghost."

"Indrojit Sahoo."

Bani Dasgupta closed her eyes. "I remember the look on his face. That moment I knew Surjo was on the roof."

"Didn't you go and look?"

"I heard Shelley's voice outside. The storm was loud but I heard her body clearly when it hit the concrete floor. It sounded as if she cracked herself to pieces. In a fright, I ran upstairs."

"Did you meet Mr. Ghosh on the way?"

"When I reached the mezzanine, Surjo ran into my arms. He was bleeding and wet. I was quite certain that he pushed her."

226

Bani pulled out a pair of sunglasses from her purse. The flared edges had emerald green spots on the surface. They were big for her eyes.

"I put Surjo under a shower. There were dry red stains on his clothes. The stairs were streaked with blood. I didn't want Shushobhon to know."

"Why did you think it was Surjo?"

"In my place, you would have." Bani Dasgupta walked away across the tram lines.

*

25

Sulaiman the Tailor

*B*y dint of habit, some men start resembling their tools. They absorb their features until you can't tell one from the other. So it was with Sulaiman the tailor.

I went back to the tailor shop and asked him about the diamond.

Sulaiman shook a grey tangle on his beard. "I was travelling with Shushobhon to a small village called Jalangi. The river *Padma* flooded its banks. Then we chanced upon a ghost *mauza* in a neighbouring village called Ghoshpara. That's where I met Debangshu Ghosh for the first time."

Sulaiman put his scissors down and picked up a fresh spool.

"We became friends with a swineherd across the border. Someone sent the stone to Ghosh from Bangladesh. Shushobhon picked it up. It hung from the snout of a pig, a massive animal with a beard and belly. The swineherd marked the pig with distinguishing lines on its toes between the hoofs."

Sulaiman caressed his beard slowly. The hair was matted with wool, flax and hemp. Once, a moth entered his beard by mistake. "Never seen again," he told me happily.

I asked him about Emma Rose.

"He came to Rajabazar in search of the stone. The eunuch thought the diamond was with me."

"Did Shibu know about his father?"

I heard the wood-pecking on his treadle. It was an old *Singer* machine made with wrought iron. Sulaiman had morphed into a creature of his own produce. He made god in his own image. He made pants in his own image.

"If Shibu knew about Emma Rose, he would have died years ago. I wouldn't have waited."

"What do you mean?"

"I killed Emma Rose," he said proudly.

I stared at him. "Where was Debangshu Ghosh?"

"He followed Emma to my shop."

An underground passage led to a small sweet shop in the Rajabazar market. The plainclothes policemen from Bombay discovered the tunnel under the pipes of the tailor shop. It led to a smelly corridor, an open drainage system amidst rats and flying cockroaches along the half-eaten wall into the fringes of the market.

Bobo's uncle had sealed it up.

"Obviously I sent him away," Sulaiman said. "If Shushobhon left it to me, I could have saved his father."

My mind worked slowly in the decaying light. "Why did Ghosh kill the one eyed man?"

"He didn't. I strangled him with my belt."

★

Sulaiman's shop was new in Rajabazar. In many ways he didn't belong there.

He came from a corner shop in Chandni. Chandni Chowk was spread-eagled over a giant rhombus in the central business district of the city.

Sulaiman had worked on its pavements selling paint, metal and drugs, easy blue pills of happiness. His friends were shady men and *firang* hippies from dirty hotels in Sudder Street.

Some months ago, he slipped a blue diamond to Shibu at a rear stall of a cinema. "I put it in a packet along with the rest of his stuff."

"Where did you get the stone?"

"A long time ago, my forefathers came to Bengal in the footsteps of Wajid Ali."

"Who?"

"Wajid Ali *Shah*." He clenched his fists proudly. "The Nawab of Oudh. He stayed in Calcutta in his last years."

"That was a long time ago."

"I wasn't born at the time but I came in spirit." The rebels in the imperial army were fighting back but the British had annexed Awadh already. The great mutiny was squashed. There were scores of disbanded men in villages around the barracks. Some of them had stolen guns.

Sulaiman took out an antique map from under his treadle. It was made with gilt-edged cloth and the outlines were engraved in copper.

"Look," he said, tracing the fall of the Ganga with his thimble across the cow belt of northern India. "They came through Bijnor and Kanpur with herds of Sahiwal cattle."

Sulaiman rooted his thimble on the gilded cloth. The brass dimples on his thumb glistened under the bulb.

The men came out of his thimble through Awadh, with the soft cling-clang of Sahiwal bells. A hundred miles away, the village drums marched through the streets of Lucknow. Fingering the placental lobe around Allahabad, "I'm sticking to the right bank," he said while the thimble missed Mughal Sarai by a whisker. "Varanasi is across the embankment."

"I'll go north now," he continued tiptoeing across the tomb of Cornwallis in the fringes of Ghazipur city. Athwart manicured greens in an old cantonment, his fingertips flew into a north westerly climb. "Here are the opium workers," he said, "and here are the alkaloids." Sulaiman smoothed out a crease in the map and put down his instrument box for support.

I peered over his shoulder and spread my palm across Azamgarh. The gilt cloth creaked across a fold.

Sulaiman watched my hand with disapproval. "That's a mistake. A native regiment is waiting in the bushes. They killed the *goras* and looted Company stores across the district. There aren't any women or children left. They are on a rampage. It's an ambush. Move!" He pushed my hand away.

I looked at him surprised.

"Those are the indigo plantations of Gorakhpur." Sulaiman pointed at my little finger. "Their livestock is waiting here." Softly, he scratched the hem of the Ghaghara. Long glacial pleats of the river unfurled themselves across the copper sheets. Sulaiman took off the thimble and his naked finger went skinny-dipping into the folds of the Ganga. An alluvial megafan lay slightly ahead.

"One night, we slept in a village in Patna. There was a violent police raid. Our men were beaten up. Guns were dug out from under the beds." He swung his thumb and plunged it into the throat of Bengal.

"That's when it came to us," he said, "the blue diamond."

*

Murshidabad was reeling under an unhappy *nizamat*. The laterite soil was old and red, blowing clouds of dust in the sky.

We were huddled around the map under the bulb in the tailor shop.

"There's something about Murshidabad that makes you lonely," he said following my gaze in the darkness. I smelled gases in the air that bred the past. Sulaiman passed me some magic grains while he rolled a ball in his palms. It was a still night.

"On such a night a cunning Brahmin went into the forest," Sulaiman said sniffing deeply on his glue. "Enfield muskets were delivered to men of god, enraged priests and villagers."

"Because of the blue diamond?"

The royal debts were heavy when they entered Bengal. "They killed a Colonel on such a night." He sniffed from his withered hands. "The stone kills everyone. Look at Shibu. Look at Beer's slashed gullet, look at Emma Rose. And all for nothing. They didn't have the stone."

I kept looking outside through the half-open collapsible gate. The night flashed visions of itself.

"A lot of blood," he sighed gently stroking his beard. I heard the lament of a distant *marsiya* in his voice from days gone by. He looked at the discoloured lines of the chart and then he folded it carefully on the table. Doubling the map over, he put it back under the treadle.

"No matter," he said, "let's have some sweets."

*

Sulaiman asked me to get a box from the next room.

I went inside and looked around the shelves. There were many cartons stacked in neat rows with a golden foil separating them.

"You don't talk much, do you," he said when I came back.

231

"That was a good story."

I flipped the box over and looked at him uncertainly. The sweets rolled like lumps of stone in my hands.

"It's your turn now. Talk."

I didn't have much to say.

Sulaiman nodded. "It's either you or me. I like a good gamble." He poured out the sweets into two clean plates. Passing a crested saucer to me, he kept one for himself.

I waited for further instructions.

He tossed a couple of glazed *Balushahis* on the table. They landed on my plate barely catching the edge of the steel rim, but they stayed inside.

"I dunked them in syrup. Gobble gobble or it won't be fun anymore."

We took a bite and kept looking at each other.

It wasn't too sweet. A tang of baking soda reined in the syrup. I heard Sulaiman munch vigorously breaking down the hand-pressed lump of dough. The sugar mixed with flakes of oil and ghee in his mouth.

I bit into the deep-fried flour of the *Bulashahi* with my eyes open.

The third bite tasted funny. Sulaiman stared at me but his lips were moving.

I feigned a bout of coughing. Nothing happened. I spat out the half-formed bolus on the floor.

A small heap of clarified butter, heavy and green, lay at my feet. The butter had been boiled and stripped of residue. Without the residue, it was harmless.

A minute passed while Sulaiman kept chewing and still nothing happened.

"False alarm," I said putting my saucer down. "Excuse me."

I went back to the room behind the corridor. Stacks of polymer and plastic were bundled over a high counter. I searched the shelf thoroughly. It was dry and clean, piled with jars of fried spices carefully lidded with different shades of green.

Someone had cleaned them recently.

My hands lashed around the shelf. Frail little wrists clawed the plastic away, opening the colourful jars one by one neatly arranged in a row. Fumbling and flaying, I caught a glimpse of bogus canister flashing in the tubelight near a slab in the rear. The canister was pressed to the wall. A sheet of dark spices lay scattered on the floor.

Then I heard a soft rhythm in the other room. A series of swallows in quick succession, self assured, hungry, precise. Sulaiman was chewing but he seemed calmer than before.

Suddenly my phone rang with a tremor. I quickly turned the lit screen to silence.

Bobo was calling. "Where are you?"

My knuckles rapped the styrene on the phone. The thumb rubbed against the back of my earlobe when I did that. With my other hand, I cracked the canister open. Along a line across its body, it opened on the shelf with a click.

"Nowhere special," I said.

There was a dull knock of styrene, this time on the shelf beneath the canister. I heard it over a buzz through a window above the gas stove. Outside, a kitchen hissed on the road.

"Where the *fuck* are you? I'm worried."

"Eating out," I said. "What's the matter?"

"My uncle called." Debangshu Ghosh was still in prison. "Soon he will confess to Shelley's murder," she murmured under her breath.

I twirled the rigid matrix in my hand.

"If all goes well, he will sign a statement. They've crushed him like a biscuit." Her voice was disturbed.

"That is good news."

"Mr. Ghosh didn't kill the old man. Nor did Indrojit Sahoo."

"Go on," I said looking over my shoulder.

"Emma Rose had a big parcel when he arrived in Calcutta. The blue pills in the incense shop. The vial of cyanide. Remember?"

In Rajabazar, a few bottles had been tracked down by the police. There was a package in the rear of the tailor shop, Sulaiman told me. The pills had seeped into the floor of the trial room. I was looking at some of them.

"Emma Rose came to the city with a tightly packed suitcase. But the whole thing went missing after his death. "You be careful," she said.

I promised to call her back.

Crossing the rows of shelves and the main cabinet, I looked at my watch. It was time. Sulaiman was done with his munching.

"You should have fetched the sweets yourself," I said when I returned to the other room.

He smiled. "I know which ones to eat."

His spittle gathered thickly in the throat, muffling his voice, pulling knots over his tongue.

"I saw the plastic," I told him.

Sulaiman raised a hand to his neck.

"I have hands as well."

Sulaiman gripped his throat. The naked pair of scissors fell off the table.

"I fiddled with your box. You want the diamond back, don't you?"

He sat on his chair quietly, not moving, not saying anything.

"Mr. Dasgupta doesn't have it," I told him. "His father didn't have it either."

He winced and showed me his tongue.

"You killed the old man for no reason."

Sulaiman was exhausted, bent, too weary to show remorse or shame. He just looked at me.

"I don't have it." I rolled out both my pockets and flashed the loose ends at his face.

"No reason," he said at last, "no reason." His voice was a pale echo, bouncing on the hollow cadaver of his lungs and chest.

His blind eyes peered at the ceiling, as high as he could manage without exerting himself, but it wasn't a big movement.

Soon he stopped moving altogether.

Later that night, I called up Bobo.

"I went to Sulaiman's shop. They can stop torturing Debangshu Ghosh."

"Why?"

"Ask your uncle to send his men to the tailor shop."

"Has he fled?" Bobo squealed on the phone.

"I found him dead."

"How?"

"It was Sulaiman that poisoned the old man."

234

26

The Diamond

A few days later, I was back at the redbrick building.

The lobby was quiet. I went across the Bombay blackwood avoiding the pungent smell of leather across the giant mirror. There was a sharp rush of linseed oil at the foot of the staircase. Funnily, the float glass didn't reflect my image in its frame.

I went to the end of the staircase and peered under the storage room. The door was ajar as usual. I looked into the room and whistled. Two heads bobbed from a shelf.

"Let's go, girls."

The armadillo was in my hand. It was a knife that could cut through anything. I dropped it into the frame of the door and scratched the edges. The latch flopped open like a child.

"In here," I said leading the way. A solid cone of yellow light shone ahead of us.

A wide desk with a leg stand was lying in the centre of the room. Its edges were firm, helping a piece of canvas fall squarely on the floor. The brackets on the wall were empty and everything else was missing.

Debangshu Ghosh's flat was the same as I'd seen it last.

235

We went straight to the bathroom. The patch of water had dried up on the floor. I picked up the flush above the commode.

The torchlight flashed on a few pieces of marble inside the box. Sheets of wax were wrapped along the walls near the flapper.

I unwrapped the paraffin carefully.

"There it is!" Sebastian cried.

He was standing next to me. His eyes gleamed with the flat-pressed diamond in my hand. "We'll split it."

Amit scooped it up in his wide fingers, twitching with excitement. "What happened exactly?"

Sebastian laughed. "Shibu wrapped up the stone in his underpants and heaps of ammonia. That's why it smelled funny."

"How come?"

"He stole a box of Shelley's, put the diamond inside and hid the box."

Shelley had saved her letters in a secret compartment within the box. Shibu didn't know that. He buried the whole thing underground.

"But Ghosh spotted Shibu at the park. So he knew where the diamond was hidden."

"Shelley had a secret key in the box," Sabbie said.

"It opens the store room where Debangshu Ghosh hid the stone. But that was later."

"Go slow," Amit said.

Sabbie looked at me.

"One afternoon, after Shibu buried the diamond that Sulaiman gave him, Mr. Ghosh dug out the box," I explained. "We were in the park together. I followed him from the Black Pearl."

"That was Beer's skeleton," Sabbie said wagging a finger.

"Mr. Ghosh took the diamond and left the box behind."

Amit looked at me.

"He hid the diamond inside the store-room. Ganesh sealed it up – windows, doors, everything. Then Ghosh took the key and kept it with himself."

"He was under the impression there was only *one* key."

"Which store-room are you talking about?" Amit asked.

"Shelley's secret key was hidden inside that box," Sabbie said.

"But Ghosh didn't know about the key. Shelley was supposed to destroy the letters. In turn, Mr. Ghosh wanted to keep the diamond for himself."

"Shibu didn't know about the key either."

"Finally Shibu found the barrel in a small compartment," I continued. "But the diamond wasn't there. The box was empty."

Amit shrugged. "Then how did Shibu get it back?"

"When we searched the store-room with Shelley's key, he pocketed the diamond."

"*In front* of your eyes," Sabbie said.

"I think Shibu caught a whiff of ammonia inside the cabinet. It was very dark inside."

"Sandy was busy with Renuka." Sabbie laughed and rummaged through a bag at his feet. "Here," he passed a stone across the bathroom.

Amit handed me the *shilnora*. "Get rid of it." He had broken into Renuka's apartment a week ago.

But there were better things to look at.

The glassy ellipse of the diamond looked exquisite in my hand. Ironed with precision, dazzling hydras grew out of its blue edges. The cuts were beautiful. Shibu had wrapped them in rugs having doused the cloth in alcohol.

"Shibu's ripped underwear," I laughed wiping the stone.

On the evening that Shibu died, Renuka and Amit had come to the mezzanine. They walked with me to the staircase on the porch next to the storage room.

Amit hugged the main frame next to the generator. Then he thrust a blade on the lock between the door and the wall.

"Give me a hand," he said. Very quickly he slipped the blue-eyed diamond into my palm yanking the tongue from the door-lock.

"But who smashed Shibu's head?" Amit asked me in the bathroom.

"Didn't you? When you smashed the poles around him on the terrace?"

Amit shook his head. "Did *you?*"

They both looked at me.

Sabbie winked in the low light and nudged my shoulder.

The flapper lay above the flush box. Through a silver beam from a lamp outside, shadows danced on the stained glass that served as a vent above the back door. A pair of naked brooms was huddled over a paint bucket.

I dropped a few shiny pieces in the toilet. "It was a dark, stormy night," I said, "anything could have happened." The rest I put back inside the flapper.

"Cut the crap, Sandipan Sen."

Suddenly a splinter pricked Amit's middle finger. He picked up a paraffin tablet from the commode and licked his fingers.

Surprised, Sabbie looked into the toilet box. "What are those things? Did you slip them inside?"

He inserted his hand and picked up the sharp pieces. Amit was sucking his thumb to clot the blood.

"What is it?" Sabbie tasted the paraffin on his fingers.

Eventually, they settled down on the floor. The toilet was dry when they dropped so I sprinkled some water above their bodies.

Finally I walked out with the diamond and the torch.

*

27

Flashback

*T*he day Shibshankar died, I went to Sabbie's apartment. It was late afternoon. Amit had given me his knife.

Shibu was drunk already. He lay like a bear on a soft black beanbag across the floor.

We acted quickly. "Give it up," Sabbie growled. I flashed the armadillo from a corner.

Somehow Shibu stood up and hid among the beads on the wall.

"The diamond, please."

"Help!" he cried running towards the door through the whitewashed corridor. "Help!" He knocked Sabbie to the ground clutching his pockets. "Someone help me!"

"What are you waiting for?" Sabbie yelled. "Get him!"

I pressed the armadillo to his neck. "Back off, Shibu. I'll slit your throat."

Shibu ran towards the foam mattress on the floor. Sabbie took the knife from my hand and slashed his belly. In a few moments Shibu was dripping with blood.

"Finish him," I wailed from behind the jade lamps. "It's either him or us."

In a minute Shibu lay sprawled on the foam.

"I know how this is done," Sabbie said panting like a madman. He took the knife and split his wrists with one stroke.

"Shibu is dead."

We quickly cleaned up and changed his clothes. I wore Shibu's bodysuit, propping the buttons near the neck. It fitted me perfectly. I had tried on the bodysuit before.

We transferred Shibu's body into my clothes. Then we wrapped him with pillow covers and put the corpse inside Amit's black bag. His body was cramped within the edges of the canvas cloth. We pushed his knees to the chest, changing the contours of his bulk into something a bag could hold.

Sabbie called Amit to his flat and handed him the diamond. "Take it with you."

"What about Renuka?" Amit asked.

"Keep her busy. I'll handle her. If required we'll set her up."

When we reached the redbrick building, Ganesh was at the garage sheds watering the plants. I wore a wide-rimmed cap. "You carry the bag," I said to Sabbie. "Come, run!"

We had traipsed inside the porch through the main gate. Then we ran up to my flat.

Quickly changing back into my clothes, I made Shibu wear his bodysuit. Then we kept the underwear in his pocket.

All of a sudden, Shibu stirred.

We were sitting on the floor of my father's chamber inside the flat. I saw him move. Sabbie swore that he saw him move as well.

In a nervous panic, I picked up the *shilnora* lying at my feet. Once, twice, I rammed it on his forehead, and then Sabbie showed me the back of Shibu's skull. I smashed it over a bald patch. A ring, a seashell of receding hair. Crazy circles exposing a tiny crumb of his scalp. The *shilnora* hit the surface bluntly with brute force.

Before he put his head down, Sabbie smeared the grindstone across Shibu's sticky fingertips. "That will do," he said, "let's go."

Sabbie washed his torso and took him to the roof, propping his lifeless form across his shoulders. Putting the *shilnora* under a covered awning on the terrace, he laid Shibu out near the parapet wall.

On my way down, I rang the bell on the mezzanine. Shelley opened the door for me. "Shibu's on the roof," I told her flicking a clump of cobweb on the floor. "I think he's sleeping. He's a little stoned."

She took the bait. Shelley went up to the terrace five minutes later with a long needle. There were Surjo's barbiturates hidden under her arm, some more wrapped in her stiff sari. She thrust the syringe into his hand while he slept.

I returned an hour later. Amit had brought Renuka with him as planned.

"See if you can get Renuka on the roof," Sabbie said, "while Shibu's wounds are fresh."

And then the storm came.

*

Months later, even today, people ask me about Shibu. "Did he kill himself? Why?"

I try to give them suitable answers but I don't have much to say.

While I hid the diamond of Emma Rose, first in my den, then inside the uterine ceramic bowl in the mezzanine (among the wax fruits next to the empty casserole) disguised as a giant blue grape, and lastly inside a toilet box in a vestibule that belonged to Mr. Debangshu Ghosh, I'd spent a lot of time trying to eke out a back story.

The story emerged from a jumble of intersecting hatreds. I console myself with the truth: Shibu was a dead man long before we met him.

"Perhaps there is some truth in the alignment of stars," I tell them. "Astronomical wrath."

It was a night of three thousand deaths, bearing the sorry syllables of Shibshankar Dasgupta, among many others. Very few people in his place would have escaped. If everything is a result of cosmic coincidence, what is the point of living?

Sometimes I walk towards a river-facing balcony in my new house. "It was a dark and stormy night," I repeat, "anything could have happened."

*

I think Shibu finally understands.

A few days ago when he came to speak to me, rising above the river in my balcony, he nodded his head. It's not smashed anymore.

Good, now I can go.

He died because of a piece of stone. There is nothing more to it.

Everyone wants the diamond, even now. They're searching frantically, and they will continue searching until the end. But it's not there. I've sold it off.

Sometimes I feel bad. The diamond was all we had. And now that it's gone, there's nothing to look for.

However Shibu told me an amazing thing the other day.

"You think you're running away," he said looking at my long beard while it swayed in the Hooghly, "but you can't."

"Why not?"

"I'll always stay with you."

There was a pause while he collected his thoughts. "Unless you kill me again," he said. "But you can't."

I laughed out into the wind, admiring his form above the breath of the river.

Shibu laughed too. "Thank you."

"It wasn't me, it was Bobo."

Shibu smiled, staring at my face through the shadows of another life. He had the hard, cruel smile of a dead man.

He was looking at Bobo's walkman hidden in my pockets.

Suddenly I was wide awake. I sat up from my chair.

"What are you telling me?" My heart was cold with fear.

He didn't say anything.

"Is Bobo dead?"

Shibu shook his head. "Not so easy."

"Why? Because she's dead already?" I clutched the bulge of the recorder in my pocket.

Shibu drifted inside the river, back to the soft tide where he slept at night. "Because," he said, "she never lived." He pointed at my head. "That's where she is."

★

28

First Person

I have two iron trunks packed to the brim. I've tied them securely with a rope I found near the river.

I pulled the rope until it was taut in my hands and then I cut off the pieces with a carving knife.

The trunks are kept near the door. In a few minutes, a couple of men will emerge from the dockyard. They will stash my luggage within the hold of a cargo ship.

I'm wearing a long beard. My neck is dark and callused from burning too long in the jetty sun. The window in my flat is always open.

I sent my parents to Murshidabad. They have enough money. But in the end my father spoiled everything.

He held the sparkling diamond in his hand. That was it. His life ebbed away, slowly, strangled by a curse.

I went to Murshidabad with my father. We inspected a huge mansion on a ferry across the river. It was expensive but we bought it anyway. There weren't any other buyers.

My father didn't like it. "This house has been bought with blood," he said when I told him about my problem. And then he started telling everyone else.

Eventually he passed away muttering in his sleep. No one blamed me.

I shaved off my head on the banks of the river. I haven't shaved ever since. My beard grew with my hair. I ate well for many months. Now I am a fat man. My cheeks are prosperous, but you can't see them through my beard.

My room is bare. My walls are dusted. You can look around but you won't find anything.

The bed isn't mine. It belongs to Sulaiman the tailor. He slept on it only once. "But I didn't really sleep," he told me. "I had to marry her a few months later." Those were his words.

I think I'm going mad. "Yes, you are," my mother said when I went to bid her goodbye. She said it lovingly, the way a good mother should. But she didn't ruffle my hair. She's scared of me.

I talk to myself when no one's looking. I speak to Shibu several times through the day. Sometimes I imagine a few things.

No one has found out. No one will. Although my cousin Bobo gave me a scare a few times. Bobo is alive.

It started a long time ago when I was young. But I wasn't always like this.

One crazy moment doesn't define me. Several moments staggered over time don't define me either. Mistakes happen. It comes and goes and takes me with it. And once the moment passes, what can I do?

Many others were involved. I found out the other day that Sebastian's father was offered a huge sum to hide Shibu's body in his garage.

They are here, the men from the ship. It's time for me to go.

- The Kidderpore Docks, Kolkata Port Trust area

Acknowledgements

A big thank you to all my friends who supported the writing process and provided me with feedback, comments and more: Rashmi Raman, that famous academic with AOs who printed and read the entire manuscript in far-off Sonepat despite being young and busy; Satyajit Sarna (author of the bestselling *The Angel's Share*) for his wise words and reality checks, rare qualities in a writer (or lawyer); Amoolya Narayan, who reviewed the draft when it was nasty, brutish, etc. in Mumbai; Gantavya Chandra, the man who spent time drawing Venn diagrams in my Lajpat Nagar flat to separate right from wrong, and later, described the quaint excesses of Uttar Pradesh; Shruti Anand Shrivastava (*née* Kanodia) for telling me when the story meandered to sillydom; Rahul Dwivedi and Kartikeya Batra for battling the cold in Medford and keeping us warm; Fei Gao and Stratos Kamenis, two excellent roomies, and Aditya Ashok Kumar for keeping Tower B alive; Sanjukta Deb, who read the thing many times over coffee and what-not; Anuradha Mukherjee, Publicity Executive at Oxford University Press, for having passed me her critical comments; Ramona Sen of Harper Collins for her precious advice, and actor Shadab Kamal for connecting me to her; Arnob Guha, Saurabh Singh, Dhrupad Siddhanta, Shreepriya Das, Arindam Mahato, for being there; TC, Dhruv Mookerji and my other friends at Theatrecian for the good things in life; thank you James Kanjamala, Editor at Orient BlackSwan, for taking me through the publishing process; Baisali Chatterjee Dutt, *inter alia* Freelance Editor at Westland Publishers, Surjya Kar, singer Kamalini Mukherji, Arya Gupta, all of whom inspired me to continue; and Sanjanaa Chindalia, the one who saw me through the last mile, seven years too late.

Fresh love, respect and gratitude to my parents (and the rest of my family, especially Mishtu and Niloo) for tolerating my rubbish – my mother who believed and loved me (and still does), and my father, for standing by my dream; and above all, that man who fled with my money across the Yamuna and made me write. I'll find you one day.